Also by Bernice L. McFadden

Gathering of Waters
Glorious
The Warmest December
Camilla's Roses
Loving Donovan
This Bitter Earth
Sugar

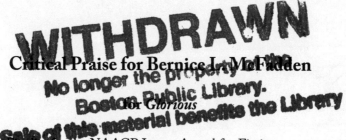

Critical Praise for Bernice L. McFadden

for *Glorious*

- Finalist for the NAACP Image Award for Fiction
- Winner of the BCALA Literary Award for Fiction
- Debut selection of the One Book, One Harlem program

"McFadden's lively and loving rendering of New York hews closely to the jazz-inflected city of myth ... McFadden has a wonderful ear for dialogue, and her entertaining prose equally accommodates humor and pathos." —*New York Times Book Review*

"[McFadden] brings Harlem to astounding life ... Easter's hope for love to overthrow hate ... cogently stands for America's potential, and McFadden's novel is a triumphant portrayal of the ongoing quest." —*Publishers Weekly*

"Bernice L. McFadden's novel *Glorious*, which starts with a bang-up prologue, has a strong main character (based in part on Zora Neale Hurston), hard-driving prose, and historic sweep of several decades, including the years of the Harlem Renaissance." —Jane Ciabattari, National Book Critics Circle President

"The book is sweeping in scope and brings to life the tenuous existence of an African American artist in the early twentieth century." —*Vogue*

"I hadn't read a word of hers before [*Glorious*], but I will follow her from now on." —Alan Cheuse, NPR

"The novel is so intense and sweeping at the same time. Some of the scenes were terrifying, and some were very comic in the irony of what the narrator was experiencing and what she was actually thinking.

The word for a journey like this is picaresque, but the ever-impending tragedy makes that word not quite right for this book."

—Susan Straight, author of *A Million Nightingales*

"A wonderful, rich read full of passion, history, wonder, and women you will recognize: *Glorious* is just that."

—Jill Nelson, author of *Volunteer Slavery*

"The seeming inevitability of cruel fate juxtaposes the triumph of the spirit in this remarkably rich and powerful novel. Bernice L. McFadden's fully realized characters are complicated, imperfect beings, but if ever a character were worthy of love and honor, it is her Easter Bartlett. This very American story is fascinating; it is also heartbreaking, thought-provoking, and beautifully written."

—Binnie Kirshenbaum, author of *The Scenic Route*

"McFadden's descriptions are sometimes wrenching, sometimes heartwarming, sometimes gritty, but always evoke emotion."

—*Books, Personally*

"This is a book that is difficult to put down. Easter Bartlett is a character who reaches out to you from the first page and who you never want to let go of."—*Curled Up With a Good Book and a Cup of Tea*

"Bernice L. McFadden broke and healed my heart in 235 pages."

—*BrownGirl Speaks*

for *Gathering of Waters*

"McFadden works a kind of miracle—not only do [her characters] retain their appealing humanity; their story eclipses the bonds of history to offer continuous surprises . . . Beautiful and evocative, *Gathering of Waters* brings three generations urgently to life . . . The real power of the narrative lies in the richness and complexity of the characters. While they inhabit these pages they live, and they do so gloriously and messily and magically, so that we are at last sorry to see them go, and we sit with those small moments we had with them and worry over them, enchanted, until they become something like our own memories, dimmed by time, but alive with the ghosts of the past, and burning with spirits."

—Jesmyn Ward, *New York Times Book Review* (Editors' Choice)

"Read it aloud. Hire a chorus to chant it to you and anyone else interested in hearing about civil rights and uncivil desires, about the dark heat of hate, about the force of forgiveness."

—Alan Cheuse, *All Things Considered*, NPR

"As strange as this may sound, Bernice L. McFadden has created a magical, fantastic novel centered around the notorious tragedy of Emmett Till's murder. This is a startling, beautifully written piece of work." —Dennis Lehane, author of *Mystic River*

"McFadden combines events of Biblical proportions—from flooding to resurrection—with history to create a cautionary, redemptive tale that spans the early twentieth century to the start of Hurricane Katrina. She compellingly invites readers to consider the distinctions between 'truth or fantasy' . . . In McFadden's boldly spun yarn, consequences extend across time and place. This is an arresting historical portrait of Southern life with reimagined outcomes, suggesting that hope in the enduring power of memory can offer healing where justice does not suffice." —*Publishers Weekly*

"The rich text is shaped by the African American storytelling tradition and layered with significant American histories. Recalling the woven spirituality of Toni Morrison's *Beloved*, this work will appeal to readers of African American and mystic literature." —*Library Journal*

"McFadden makes powerful use of imagery in this fantastical novel of ever-flowing waters and troubled spirits." —*Booklist*

"In her new novel, *Gathering of Waters*, Bernice L. McFadden brings her own special vision to the unfortunate story of Emmett Till and his murder in Money, Mississippi. This moving and magical novel, which traces the generations leading up to and away from that horrible night in 1955, drew me in immediately and swept me along through its richly imagined world. I couldn't stop reading, caught up as I was in that enticing place between truth and fantasy, the here-and-now and the what-was, the living and the dead, the ugliness and the beauty, the hatred and the love. What a rich chorus of voices McFadden has fashioned from this place called Money."

—Lee Martin, author of *Break the Skin* and *The Bright Forever*

Nowhere Is a Place

by **Bernice L. McFadden**

AKASHIC
BOOKS

Published by Akashic Books
Originally published in hardcover by Dutton in 2006
©2006, 2013 Bernice L. McFadden

ISBN-13: 978-1-61775-131-8
Library of Congress Control Number: 2012939272

First Akashic Books printing

Akashic Books
PO Box 1456
New York, NY 10009
info@akashicbooks.com
www.akashicbooks.com

For my daddy
Robert Lewis McFadden
July 22, 1942–January 14, 2005
I miss you

Acknowledgments

Gratitude . . .
My family
My friends
My readers
My spirits
My Creator

The present contains nothing more than the past,
and what is found in the effect was already in the cause.
—Henri Louis Bergson

i was torn from my somewhere and brought to this nowhere place
i felt alone in this land that was nowhere from my everywhere.
i didn't understand the tongue
i didn't understand the tongue
i didn't understand the tongue and why it was the trees here bore
strange fruit that watched me with dead eyes
cruel hands
cruel hands
cruel hands, tied me down, strung me up, dug into me, and sold off
what came out of me
time flowed on like the river
like the river, time flowed on, but i held tight to the memories of my
someplace, refusing to believe that my everywhere had always been
here in this nowhere place.

Smooth Heels

Santa Rey Obius, Mexico

Sherry

Edison Powell, all confidence with a smile that revealed glittering white teeth. Mahogany eyes that sparkled and long piano-playing fingers.

Jazz standards were his favorite

They'd first met over the music, Count Basie's "Going to Chicago Blues" spilling out from beneath his fingers, her eyes dead set on his jaw, not blinking, not wanting to miss the clench and unclench of it or the sudden toss of his head.

"Curiosity killed the cat," she murmured into her third glass of chardonnay, after her girlfriends caught her staring at his clenching and unclenching jaw, and the way she trembled when he tossed his head was a dead giveaway that she was more than interested.

Her friend whispered to her from behind cupped palms, egged her on, dared her, prodded her forward with their goading until she found herself almost at his elbow, sandwiched between two women who smelled of vodka and Chanel.

He was on to "Kansas City Keys," and Sherry was bobbing her head to the music and wondering what it would be like to have those piano-playing fingers dancing across her rib cage and down her spine and then wondering why it was she was wondering such a thing.

The crowd hollered for more, but brunet eyes shook his head no and then turned toward his audience and graciously bowed his head into praying hands before smiling and turning to where Sherry swayed between the vodka- and Chanel-smelling women.

They rushed him, the women with their Colgate-white teeth ruined by tracks of red lipstick, thrusting cosmetically altered breasts in his face while simultaneously presenting him with delicate hands, perfectly manicured fingernails, and diamond-laced wrists. He nodded at them, but kept his own hands folded behind his back.

He nodded and smiled at their compliments, favored them with his smooth talk, electric smile, and brunet-colored eyes, but would not let them touch his piano-playing fingers; those he kept hidden behind his back, stuffed into the wells of his pants pockets, or laced together and swaying in front of his crotch.

"Do you know 'Cherry Point'?" was all Sherry said to him when he was finally able to break away from the women and was sliding past her.

"'Cherry Point,'" she said again when all he did was stare.

"Yes," smooth as silk sailed out of his mouth and then a smile and a nod of his head. He watched her for a while, before he said yes to something else and then turned and started back toward the piano, brushing past the women and their frozen smiles and settling himself down onto his bench.

He positioned his piano-playing fingers over the black-and-white keys, spoke to them with his mind, wiggled them, and then dropped them down and began to play "Cherry Point," twice.

Later, after his piano-playing fingers played "Avenue C" and "Blue Room Jump" and "April in Paris" down her spine and across her rib cage; after he treated her nipples like the lip of a trumpet, played her ass like a djembe drum, and stroked the inner parts of her thighs like a sitar until the muscles went soft like cream and gave way, her legs parted until they were flung wide, revealing her very own Cherry Point.

And it wasn't until he lay sleeping beside her, his arm thrown across her breasts, that she realized that his eyes were the same color as her nipples. She realized as the sun broke through the slats of the miniblinds that he had used Count Basie to seduce her and that the clenching and unclenching jaw had reminded her of the pro ball players that mesmerized her and that the toss of his head made her think of easier times and that all of that and the chardonnay had somehow blinded her to the fact that he wasn't just a man, but a white man.

It was as easy as pie to get on a plane and fly from St. Louis to Paradise, Nevada, to tell her mother, Dumpling, that she was moving to Chicago—moving into a one-bedroom overlooking the river with her friend, her boyfriend, Edison Powell, *the musician with mahogany-colored eyes and piano-playing fingers.*

Dumpling had nodded and grunted before finally looking real hard at the picture of the boyfriend who couldn't find the time to get on the plane with her daughter and meet her face-to-face.

Blond hair, brown eyes. White boy. Sherry hadn't said a word about that part of him.

"He knows all of Count Basie and can play most anything," Sherry had gushed.

"You too, it seems," Dumpling huffed, and handed the picture back to Sherry. "If your daddy were alive, you know he'd disapprove," she added, hard toned.

Sherry ignored the words. How could Dumpling know what those fingers did to her?

And if her father were alive, he wouldn't have understood it either; he was a diehard Howling Wolf and Muddy Waters man. But he was dead and buried, ten years by then, that's why it was easy as pie to hop on that plane from St. Louis to Paradise, Nevada, and announce the plans for the rest of her life in Chicago, with a white man.

"He's the blackest white boy I've ever met," Sherry said brightly. "Not like those white folks you thinking about at all, Dumpling."

"Uh-huh."

"Cool and laid back. He understands the struggle—"

"Whose struggle?"

"Oh, Dumpling, I can't help who I love."

"You never have been able to."

"What does that mean?"

"You always choose wrong; that boy with the lisp from where was it now?"

"Manuel from South America."

"Yeah, and the other one with the slanted eyes."

"Mahain."

"And the one with the turban."

"Mohammed."

"I told you none of them would last, didn't I?"

"You taught me to see people for who they are on the inside."

"Yes, I did."

"Well, that's what I'm doing."

"So you been seeing this man for how long?"

"Three months."

"And you think you know his heart?"

"You and Daddy got married in less than two months. Why is this different?"

"Your daddy was black."

"And?"

"I know'd his heart from before I even know'd him."

"How is that possible?"

"All us black people here in America got the same heart. We come from the same place."

"Africa?"

"After that."

"What are you talking about, Dumpling? Do you mean the South?"

"I'm talking 'bout a place called survival."

"I'm well aware of our history, Dumpling. It's not like I went out looking for a white man—"

"Nah, he came looking for you. That's what they do."

"White people marched alongside blacks for civil rights."

"Uh-huh."

"Okay, Dumpling, whatever you say. I was hoping that you would be happy for me and—"

"Okay, let me ask you this: did you choose him or did he pick you?"

"What?"

"Did you choose or did he pick?"

"I don't know what—"

"White folks been picking niggers for years. Picking them off, picking them clean—"

"Stop it!"

Almost eight years and few words passed between Sherry and Dumpling. They had two strikes between them, so Sherry kept her distance to ward off the third strike that she knew would disconnect them forever.

Almost eight years passed before Sherry realized that she preferred the down-home blues—the hip-swaying, countrified blues—to the complex jazz standards.

Almost eight years, and Edison had only slipped and called her a nigger once.

She'd been in no hurry to forgive him for it, but he'd apologized profusely—and had cried and played Billie Holiday's "Strange Fruit" over and over again on his piano before she let him back into their bedroom.

A year after that, his piano-playing fingers came down across her face and sent her reeling. Not as far as the slap her mother had levied across her face thirty-two years earlier; though she would realize later on that both slaps had centuries behind them.

Sherry was just six years old on that day when she sat curled up in her Uncle Beanie Moe's lap, one arm slung across his neck, the other fingering the string of blue beads he'd brought her back from New Orleans.

Her mother, Dumpling, had walked into the room smiling, then stopped and stared as the smile froze and cracked on her face. Sherry couldn't have known that her sitting innocently on her uncle's knee would hurtle her mother back in time—back to a warm Easter afternoon when a misplaced hand had suddenly turned ugly.

Dumpling's eyes went glassy as she marched over to them, lifted her hand into the air, and brought it down across Sherry's six-year-old face so hard, the girl had ended up kissing the floor and seeing stars.

Dumpling had never said why she slapped Sherry, and Beanie Moe hadn't asked. He just helped Sherry up and carried her over to the couch and sat her down. He comforted her with words, but didn't dare touch her.

Dumpling, she just stormed out of the room, leaving the slight scent of Ivory soap swirling in the air.

Years later, Edison hadn't even missed a beat. His hand back at his side and shaking as he continued to holler and hurl cuss words at her.

She, Sherry, was sprawled across the floor, stunned, her hand cradling the place on her cheek that was stinging and throbbing. And then his hands were up in the air, flailing as he stormed like a madman between the bedroom and the living room, calling her every kind of bitch she could ever imagine, and then the toe of his shoe made contact with her thigh, giving her hand purpose and hurtling her mind further toward amazement—its brilliance so dazzling, she was forced to squint.

And then the tears came, and something with her mouth—not words but gurgling sounds that didn't even move him.

"Leave, just leave."

That's what it came down to. Him throwing her out like he had been the one to walk in on her, down on her knees, face dug in deep between another woman's—a white woman's—thighs, accommodating her in a way he had always vehemently denied Sherry.

And right then Sherry knew that she herself had been picked, while the white woman he was cheating on her with had been chosen.

The woman was wrapped up tight in Sherry's bedsheets, in her bed, her face serene, a sly silence settling around her as she looked down on Sherry with quiet amusement and outright contempt.

Edison had caught Sherry staring and kicked her again while he screamed, "Didn't you hear me? Get the hell out!"

Sherry lifted herself up; Edison's piano-playing fingers imprinted on her cheek and gathered esteem so ruined, it pained her more than the slap and the shoe toe.

Right there, in front of the woman and beneath the bad names he stoned her with, she packed and then left.

Just a slamming door and a neighbor watching from her window as Sherry struggled with the black plastic Hefty bags that were bursting at the seams, boxes of shoes, a duffel bag, and the one suitcase she'd owned since she was twenty-three.

Sherry piled it all into her rusting Mazda RX7, all that could fit, anyway, leaving some things behind, including that bit of herself that had ignored her mother's warnings and concerns. Sherry had chosen instead to care, love, and believe in a perfect world.

She drove southwest for two days, stopping only to relieve herself and fill her gas tank; food not even a thought, just getting as far away from Chicago and Edison as she could.

Pushing the Mazda's rebuilt engine harder than she should have and ignoring the coughing fits it fell into when she shifted into third to scale an incline, Sherry pushed until it spewed black smoke. But by then she was passing the familiar, weathered white sign with the black letters off to the right of the road that declared:

WELCOME TO SANTA REY OBIUS

A small fishing village just across the Mexican border, the place Sherry had spent two weeks every July since she was twenty-three years old. Two weeks of watching the ocean, listening to the seagulls sing, and musing on life so far and the tomorrows that were to come and always trying hard to figure out what had gone wrong.

It was the summer of 1993, and the green monkeys had somehow freed themselves from the village zoo and spent three days chattering and swinging from the branches of the emerald canopy the palm trees made, leaping and bouncing from branch to branch, tails curled at the tip, plucking the red mangoes that jutted from between shining broad leaves.

That summer, Nature was as vain as all get out and feeling every bit of herself; lusty even, spreading her legs and pushing forth the sea.

Summer's smile released a breeze as gentle as a mother's touch, setting the great palms to swaying. An outright laugh sent the clouds streaking across the sky. A thrust of her hip, and birds took flight.

In the heat of that summer Nature did not walk; she swaggered. And the earth writhed and rolled beneath her feet, volcanoes spat, cliffs broke away as the heavens wept with joy, and Sherry realized with horror that it had been two months since she'd last seen her period.

Two days later, the sky a mass of gray clouds and the sea as angry as Sherry was with herself with her stupidity, with her lack of cautiousness, she looked out the window of her tiny bungalow and watched as the tide reached in and snatched at sand and shells and tossed ragged bits of seaweed at the feet of flapping gulls that screamed and took flight.

The memory of the piano-playing fingers playing "Dixie" on her body, the clenching and unclenching jaw, the toss of the head, and his mouth that curled and flung "nigger" at her and had closed over that white woman's cunt—all that danced in her mind even as she walked the three miles beneath a threatening sky to the killing place on Santa Clara Avenue and wept over the green-and-white forms as she scrawled her mother's name and telephone number in the space that said, CONTACT IN CASE OF AN EMERGENCY.

On the table, on her back, she spread her legs like Nature, but no laughter followed and the walk she walked afterward was far from a swagger, and no cliffs broke away that day, but the heavens did weep and she had to hail a cab in the downpour.

Days later, nothing left to cry about and at the beginning of that summer, Sherry was counting on at least three weeks of alone time, but got so much more.

Summer became a magician, extending herself—stretching from June to June and beyond, lifting her skirt and kicking up her heels even when the calendar said autumn and the sunsets turned orange, winter and the days grew shorter, spring and the rains came down . . . Through all those seasons Sherry would look back and swear she could always smell begonias.

Twenty pounds overweight and unable to fit into anything that did not have a tag that stated some percentage of Spandex, her heart broken and self-esteem running on empty, the memory of his slap and the other like it dug in like a malignancy beneath the skin of her cheek, pulsating on rainy days and burning on sunny ones. Sherry wondered how in the hell she could be feeling nothing but sad and still be able to offer her hand to the young man with the green eyes who would guide her gently past the chill of the surf and into the perfect blue sea beyond and the future beyond that.

Taken aback when he approached her, he'd looked down into her troubled face and greeted her by name.

The Mazda was up on a lift in the backyard of Miguel's Fix-it Place even though she knew she would never reclaim it. The small efficiency cottage she rented every year from Annie Perau, the French expatriate who had started visiting Santa Rey back in the '60s before the paved roads were laid and the pot-smoking, backpacking hippies had to navigate the rocky terrain by foot or hired mule.

Annie had come to Santa Rey Obius for the same reason Sherry had started to come: to forge and renew.

Now in her mid-sixties, Annie had a thriving business, toasted almond–colored skin, white wavy hair, and a clear mind.

It was a clear mind Sherry was meditating on when the young man approached.

She'd held her hand up, shielding her eyes from the sun, and was only able to make out the dark shades he wore, the duckbill of an orange cap, and a glint of gold about his neck.

"Please don't tell me you've forgotten about me after knowing me for all these years." A smile, broad and sunny backed by blindingly white teeth.

She'd asked him to take a step to the side. "The sun is blinding me; move a little to your left."

"Aw, man. You'll break my heart if you tell me you don't know who I am," he'd said as he moved left and blocked out the sun.

She looked up and into his face. Yes, yes, it was familiar, but—

She smiled then and he removed his shades. It was the eyes that caught her: catlike, green in color and flecked with gold.

His name had always escaped her. It was an odd one—Raven? Hawk? Something birdlike.

"Uhm?" She smiled and pointed a finger at him. He smiled back and waited for her to say his name.

Handsome was what came to mind first and then a slight thought to his age. High yellow in color, a bit of blond in his mustache.

He folded his hands across his chest. "Sherry, Sherry . . ." he muttered, shaking his head and trying to sound wounded.

His father's name she could remember: Sam.

Sam, Sam the umbrella man. Everybody knew Sam. You needed to know Sam if you wanted shade from the sun and weren't resourceful enough to have brought your own umbrella.

But the son—his name?

He was squatting now, kneecaps broad and flat. He was looking at her. She could see the tendons in his arms, in his neck. Straining, pulsating.

"I'm sorry," she said, shrugging her shoulders in surrender.

Sam had children. Small ones: two boys, a girl sometimes—only when the mother was there, which was rare.

Sherry chewed her bottom lip . . .

Another boy, a teenager. Wiry, quiet, always polite.

Sparrow? Pigeon?

A reader, if she was remembering right: The Catcher in the Rye, Native Son.

He was what? Sixteen, maybe seventeen years old when she first started coming down.

"Falcon," he finally said, and Sherry felt something in her decompress.

"Yes, yes, that's it," she said, and found her hand gently swiping the back of his. "So how have you been?"

It had started that way and had evolved to him pulling her into the water, his hands brushing away wandering strands of seaweed from her shoulder and then finding her waist and settling there.

She had felt the sun on her teeth and was surprised at the sound of her own laughter ringing in her ears.

Her foot brushed the top of his, and even in the velvety wrap of the water he felt the roughness of her heel and commented on it. She'd blushed, ashamed that she'd forgotten about herself in some ways.

She'd managed to keep her nails clipped and square, but hadn't paid much attention to her toes or the heels of her feet. Her hair was decent though, and she'd continued to floss after every meal, but her feet . . .

"Oh," Sherry had muttered, turning her face toward the shore and feeling that block of blue ice that Edison had left inside of her rattle as Falcon, too young for her, forbidden even, bent and plucked a sea stone from the ocean bottom. He caught her by her arm, pulling her close to him, and then hoisted that big old leg of hers up and out of the water like it was feather light and brought her foot to rest on his shoulder. He began to work the stone against her heel as he hummed an old Bessie Smith tune that he couldn't remember the name of.

Anyone watching saw dead flakes of skin drop off and into the water, but Sherry saw ice shavings.

By September she had smooth heels and a compilation CD of Bessie Smith and knew all the words to "Gulf Coast Blues," but Falcon still preferred to hum the tune whenever he was in her small one-bedroom cottage that over-looked the Pacific, which was most times.

In the evening his sandals sat alongside her flip-flops at the door while they prepared meals together. She forgot the years that lay between them and began thinking of him as hers when they took turns reciting Rita Dove's po-etry to each other at night before making love.

In February, on his birthday, she tells him that she believes she knows his heart. Asks if he understands what that means, and he pulls her in to him, kisses her cheek where the piano-playing fingers once stroked then struck, and says, "Yes, I know yours too."

Falcon, loving her, warming her insides along with the first bright sun of a new June, melting the ice block into candle wax and then water, making it easy for another baby to float there.

After Sherry had put the phone back down in its cradle and crawled into bed, she announced her plans to Falcon. All he could say was, "The family reunion is where?" Falcon's tone carried more fear than surprise.

"Georgia," Sherry had whispered into his neck, and then threw one leg over his waist in a half straddle.

The bed creaked and Falcon tried to turn himself over, but she had him pinned and so he just breathed and asked, "What for?"

She didn't want to see his face. There would be pain in his eyes to match the fear in his voice. He didn't want her anywhere too far from him. He'd told her that a hundred times, and now that she was pregnant . . . well, he practi-cally didn't want her out of his eyesight.

"I've got to clear up some things. Learn some things," she responded, and then moved herself closer in to him.

He knew about some of the things but, he suspected, not all of the things. The slap had come up in conversation a number of times. Sometimes accom-panied by tears, other times a sheet of silence like black ice followed the ut-terance of it. "No way around it," Sherry murmured.

"Got to go through it to get over it," Falcon said, then sighed and reached his hand back, resting it on her thigh.

He wasn't a selfish man, so he wouldn't complain about her going to be with her people to handle her business, but he did say, "What about the baby?"

"Well, I'm going to take the baby with me, of course!" The humor of the statement wasn't lost on him, and Falcon uttered a small laugh.

Paradise, Nevada

July 1995

Dumpling

Sherry call the first of the month. No other time. Always the first. So imagine my surprise when on the sixteenth, I picked up the phone and heard her "hello" coming from the other end.

What's wrong?

She said, Nothing, Dumpling. Can't a daughter call and say hello to her mama?

I look at the phone and then tap the receiver on the nightstand a few times before I put it back to my ear. What? I say.

Sherry just sighs and says, What you banging the phone around like that for?

Static, I say. And then, So how you?

Okay, she say, and then ask about the weather, but I know something wrong or really right, you just never know with Sherry 'cause she always been odd.

She the strangest one of my three children. She also the middle of the three, so I guess that explains it. I don't read much, but I listen to the radio, watch plenty of television, and the people say that the middle children got a hard road to walk, not the first, not the last, falling between—not the eldest and not the baby—second in line. Always floundering, one talk-show host say. Always searching, another say.

Always asking, I say.

Why this and why that?

I answer as many questions as I can. Sometimes I say, I just don't know. Other times, I wave my hand and tell her to hush up her mouth. My ears hurting from you asking so many questions and my throat parched from trying to answer them all. So hush!

She ask a lot of questions, but don't answer too many.

I still don't know all of what happened to her in Chicago. Edison tell me some, say he messed up big-time, say he want her back, ask, Is she there?

I told him no, ain't heard a peep since the beginning of the month. You know how it is with us, I tell him, Sherry's calls come on the first, right along with my pension check and Kmart credit card bill. What you do to her anyway?

He never did say, and then the first of the month rolled around and Sherry called and said, Here's my new telephone number.

I wrote it down and said, Sure is a lot of numbers. Where you at?

She say, Mexico, now take down my new address, you gonna need an airmail stamp if you want to write me.

I hadn't been writing her, but I take it down so's I have it when I want to send her birthday and Christmas cards.

Mexico?

She says, Yes, for a while.

I say, Edison calls, he say he messed up, want you back, still love you. He sounds sorry to me, what he do?

Sherry say, He dead to me, next subject please.

I didn't ask no more.

Madeline my eldest girl. She married with three of her own children. She tall, brown, smart, marry a man half her height and twice her weight. Kids are squat and yellow like their daddy, look to me like I got three butternut squashes for grandchildren. But they okay. I love 'em. They part of me.

My boy, Ethan, we call him Sonny Boy 'cause he named after his daddy, my husband. He in and out of the house. Sometime in school, sometime working, sometime in love, sometime not, all the time wanna be onstage, he think he gonna be a star—he got another name we call him, "Mr. Hollywood"—he ain't got but a lick of talent and think his good looks gonna carry him far.

Maybe they will. I see loads of pretty people on television ain't got no talent.

Now my Sherry, she looks the most like me. We 'bout the same height, wide in the hips, big legs, big breasts, long hair, peanut-skin brown. She all of what I was when I was her age, 'cept she single, childless, and still trying to find her place in the world.

She been to Africa six or seven times, spent a month in India, been to all of the islands, South America, Central America, Greenland, and a bunch of other places that I can't recall the names of—and she still feel "displaced" is word she use.

I say, Don't the home you were born in feel like home?

No.

Her answer is short, sharp. I wince and turn my head away. My feelings don't usually get hurt so easily, but I feel a knife in my heart.

I wait for her to change her answer, to 'splain herself. Five years pass, and I'm still waiting.

Whatever, I think—it's her fault she feels displaced, don't you know. She done lived in twenty different cities since she was nineteen.

Now she living in Mexico of all places. Cleaning toilets and making beds in some dive she stumbled on some years ago.

What you go to all the universities for if all you wanted to do was be a chambermaid?

She say, It's honest work.

I say, It don't make no kind of sense!

I'm still searching.

What you looking for? I ask.

She say, Myself.

I say, Yourself? There you is right there, I say, and poke her with my finger. I see you; feel you too, don't you?

She say, Not like that. She say, I'm looking for my purpose. Why it is God put me here. You know?

No, I don't.

Sherry got respect for me, but not much love. Been like that for years now. Can't quite remember when the hugs stopped, when the Saturday-morning snuggle sessions ended, or whose birthday cake I was making when I offered her the bowl to lick and she turned the offer down flat.

Can't remember the year, but I know she was young, scrawny, and loved hamburgers and hot dogs and fried pork rinds more than it seemed she loved me.

She ain't never come right out and said she hated me or disliked me, but I saw it in her eyes, heard it in her voice, felt it all over the house after she moved out and only came back to visit.

I ain't done nothing to her I ain't done to the other two. But you would think I was the worst mother in the world, when all I did was try to be the best mother I knew how.

So imagine my surprise when she called me up from Mexico and asked, The Lessing family reunion going on this year, right?

Yeah.

Where?

Sandersville, Georgia.

You going?

Wasn't planning to, why?

I wanna go.

Really? That's a surprise.

I wanna drive.

To Georgia? Long trip.

I want you to ride with me.

Really, me and you? Like I said, long trip.

Will you?

She my child, and even though she hate me, I love her and so I say, Sure, sounds like fun, why not.

Sherry say she coming in four days and then arrive in three.

She pull up in her shiny brand-new car. I mean, SUV—she been correcting me all the time about that. It's nice. Classy is what come to mind. Sonny Boy beg and plead to drive it, Madeline can't understand how Sherry can afford it.

Sherry ain't held down a job for more than six months her entire life, she say. Always in school, taking a class for this, taking a course in that. How cleaning toilets and making beds pay for something like that?

Madeline pouts and then folds her thick arms across her big tits and sticks her lip out like she four years old again.

I say, What you care for? You paying the note? You got two cars, a house, three kids, a dog, a cat, and a parakeet. More than Sherry got.

Parakeet died last year, she say.

Whatever, I say, and wave her away. Next day, Madeline pulls into my driveway in her brand-new SUV.

It's bigger than Sherry's, got a third row and got a sunroof. Sits so high up on its wheels, Madeline's husband Aaron got to help me in.

Now we can all ride together, Madeline say, and my eyes roll over to Sherry who smile and say real calm-like, No we can't.

Madeline's face go red and she look at me and then back at Sherry and say, Why not?

Sherry cock her head and look Madeline dead in the eye and say, You can take your truck if you want to, but I ain't riding with you and neither is Dumpling.

Madeline ain't never been a fighter and so she just fix her mouth the way she do when things don't go her way and grab hold of the flabby skin of her husband's arm.

Aaron say it would be better to fly, the kids would get too restless on a long ride like that, and Madeline agree. Like that something new.

Sonny Boy don't look like he gonna make it. Something about auditions— but I think it sound more like "money." Madeline warn me not to pay for his ticket, he already owe everybody too much money as it is, she say. I nod and pretend to agree like I'm my own daughter's child, and call the airline soon as she back that SUV out of the driveway.

I would do the same for her.

We head out Monday morning. Six a.m. I can't tell if Sherry excited or not, her face always wear the same expression.

Me, I'm bubbling inside about seeing family. I ain't been back to Sandersville since I left it. Not even when my sister Lovey call and say she was moving back. And that's been a good twenty years now.

Sherry eases her SUV onto Interstate 40 and then into the left lane, and we begin to fly.

I say it's gonna be nice to be 'round my people when we ain't weeping over somebody that's lying dead in a coffin.

Sherry nods her head yes, and I see a smile tickling the corners of her mouth. '

I lean back in that butter-soft leather seat and watch the city streak by outside my window until it's just black highway and the hum of the engine. My eyes flutter and close and I'm dreaming of trees: sweet gum, white oak, sycamore. Flowers follow: lady slipper, May apple, bloodroot, and Cherokee rose.

I see the young me, before I hated the color blue, and the pain in my knees slip away, the gray in my hair disappear. Water come from the spring and not bottles, vegetables grow in rows and don't come in cans. Oil lamps and quilts. Loons sing us to bed at night and roosters wake us in the morning. Peaches, pecans, and guinea fruits that it seemed God put there for just us alone.

Romping, running. High, bright sun. No cares, no worries. Youth.

I hear Sherry's voice slip into my dreams. Dumpling? she says real soft. I feel her hand shake my shoulder. I uh-huh her but don't open my eyes.

Are we there yet? I kid, and try to recapture my dream.

She laugh a little and cut off the air-conditioning. The windows come down and she hit a button on the radio and all of a sudden there's the sound of cymbals and bells and a woman moaning.

Why she crying? I ask.

Sherry say, It's called chanting.

Whatever, I say.

Like I said, she is the strange one.

We been on the road three hours now. My mouth dry, bladder full, belly burning empty.

Nothing but fast-food places. Sherry's face twist up at the signs: fried chicken, hamburgers, pizza.

She say, I need some salad. Something fresh.

I look up and see Wendy's zip by. Salads, I say, and point to the sign that's already a blur.

Next one, she mumbles. But I see her eyes searching for something else, and I know that I won't be having a double cheeseburger with extra onions no time soon.

We pull into the Razzle Dazzle Diner. Diner food fine with me. I can have a cheeseburger. Better for me, I say. Steak fries good at diners, I tell her, and pull my wet wipes from my bag and start cleaning my hands.

Sherry watches me and says, How many times you gonna do that?

I say, As much as I need to, and pull another sheet out. Don't worry about me, go on ahead an' order your omelette.

Frittata, she corrects me.

All the same to me.

Now to the young, bored-looking waitress: Frittata. Spinach, please.

Uh-huh.

You just use the egg whites, right? she grills the waitress. Do you cook it on a separate skillet from the meat? she asks.

The waitress smirks and then walks away to find out. I see the cook stick his head out from behind the swinging door to get a look at what he's dealing with. He sees Sherry's pierced nose, pierced eyebrow, hair braided, tattoo on her left arm, T-shirt that says: Love Animals, Don't Eat Them—and knows exactly what he's dealing with. He makes a face and says something to the waitress. She come back and say, Yes, we use a different pan for the meat.

Liar, I think. But I wants my cheeseburger.

Sun starting to slip, sky going red and then a blue-gray by the time I finish my iced tea and Sherry her water with lime.

I guess we can do another two hours, she say, then we'll find someplace to sleep.

I say, Okay, and pull out another three wipes to clean my hands.

On the road again we don't talk about much. We ain't never really had much to say to each other, but decent music playing: Barry White singing, got me all warm inside and swooning.

Sherry know all the words to the old songs, we sing along, croaking like frogs but giving it our all as if we sound like angels.

Two hours later, one stop for gas, a bottle of water for her and a Pepsi for me, and she turn and look at me and say, I think I want to write a book.

Glad to hear it, I think. Anything better than cleaning toilets.

Really? I say out loud, but think, This something else she gonna start and not finish. 'Bout what? I ask, and then, Don't look at me, look at the road.

Well, I think I want to write about our family.

I laugh and think, Madeline would have a fit, and then I think, Sonny

Boy would want to star in the movie version, and then I freeze up some and wonder what skeletons might fall out of my closet.

Don't nobody wanna read about us.

I think so. Your mother, your grandmother. It's interesting.

Interesting?

Yeah, y'all have some real good stories.

We do?

Yeah.

Like what?

Like the one about Cora.

What you know 'bout that?

People talk. Uncle Beanie Moe, Auntie Lovey.

They talk too much, I say, and my mouth go dry.

What happened to Cora ain't such a nice story to write down, I say. This idea not sounding so good to me anymore, I think. If she know about Cora, what else she know about?

It happened, didn't it?

Well I ain't seen it happen, I just heard 'bout it.

You didn't see it? But you were there.

I s'pose.

We quiet for a time. She come back again. What about the story about your Aunt Wella and the wine and the wood chips?

My mouth kinda hinge on a smile. She was just an itty-bitty thing, had gotten into Vonnie's plum wine and was as drunk as a skunk. Grandma caught hold of her 'fore she went into the flames, I say, already remembering.

And the one about you in Harlem with Aunt Helen and the first time you saw hail?

I laugh out loud. Lord, I'd never seen such a thing, it 'bout scared the religion outta me; I stayed under the bed till Helen came home!

See, you got plenty of stories I can put down.

Can you just put down the funny ones?

Life ain't all fun, Dumpling, she say. And I feel she talking more about her life than mine.

We can write it together, she say.

I look at her like she got three heads. I can't write no book! I scream.

You the one been to three universities. Me, I didn't even finish high school.

She laugh. You tell me what you remember, what you heard, and I'll write them down, dress 'em up, and build a story filled with intrigue and mystery.

Her voice change up when she say "intrigue and mystery," making me think of everything slick—silk, oil, okra.

I don't know what the word "intrigue" mean, but I understand mystery.

Why you wanna know all of this stuff all of a sudden? I ask.

Sherry sigh, rest her hand on her stomach, roll her head on her neck, and say, I already told you.

Uh-huh, but why else? I push.

Well, she say, and put both hands back on the steering wheel again, Alice Walker said, "Black women can survive only by recovering the rich heritage of their ancestors."

Alice who?

Walker. Alice Walker, Dumpling. Now, you gonna tell me or not?

I don't know how much I remember, I lie.

Just start from the beginning.

Whose? I say.

Lou's.

The Book of Lou

A broad valley that fanned out at the foot of a sloping hill and was enclosed by a cluster of palmetto trees had been home to three generations of Yamasee by 1836.

Green-grassed and heavily scented by the climbing yellow jasmine that wrapped itself lovingly around everything that was still. Hummingbirds, mockingbirds, and wrens flitted through the sky above the valley, and speckled trout moved lazily beneath the waters of the babbling brook beyond it.

To the west of the valley a salt marsh was home to trees heavily bearded with Spanish moss, yellow-throated warblers, and egrets. A day away to the east, the blue Atlantic Ocean roared.

Nayeli had never been beyond the trees to the open land to the south and north of her valley home, nor had she been to the swampy edge of her world where loons serenaded the stars. But she had seen the ocean, had stood on the beach and tasted its salty spray on her tongue, digging her toes deep into the white sand as she watched the sleek black ponytails of the men brush at their backs as they worked at pushing their canoes past the surf.

She and the other children, attended by the women, gathered colorful seashells beneath a beating sun that pressed a polish into their copper-colored complexions.

It had been a wonderful day. A wonderful day that turned into a comforting memory that Nayeli clung to at night when she laid herself down to sleep.

Small in stature, with large almond-shaped eyes that were as dark as wells, Nayeli wore a jagged piece of blue granite that had been fashioned into an eagle, the wing pierced and a slither of leather hide laced through it tied about her neck.

A gift from her grandfather, Sahale, the medicine man of the Yamasee village and the father of her father, Yona.

"The eagle," Sahale told her when he presented her with the gift, "will take your prayers to the great spirit." Then he spread his arms and tilted his head up toward the sky.

Nayeli's older brothers, Dyami and Elan; tall and lanky boys filled with mischief. They amuse themselves by jabbing sticks into gopher holes and harassing their baby sister. They toss the severed necks of chickens at her feet, chase her around the camp with gator teeth and the stiff, dead bodies of praying mantises.

Their mother, Winona, a tall woman with sharp cheekbones, broad shoulders, and a narrow waist, swats at the boys with a switch, but the switch is slung without any real purpose and leaves a long dusty imprint in the earth. "Stop it," she warns them, but her words are lost amongst Nayeli's cries and the boys' hoots and hollers.

"Cease this foolishness now," the baritone authority of Yona commands, and the boys come to a screeching halt; their instruments of torture are quickly thrust behind their backs. Nayeli's mouth snaps shut and she rushes to her mother's side, wrapping her arms around her legs and pressing her face into her hip.

Three sets of young eyes climb Yona's long limbs, creeping over the necklace of shells, beads, and copper that hang from his tree trunk–wide neck until their eyes meet his, and the piercing fierceness those eyes hold sends shivers up their spines.

Yona is as tall as the forest that surrounds them, as tall and as mighty. His face is stern. It is like the rock that sits in the middle of the valley, the one the elders go to to smoke and discuss law. The rock juts up from the earth like a boil, except it is unmovable. Yona's face is like that rock.

He has been gone for three days, war paint still evident around his eyes, a gash across his forehead and one down his thigh. He has been to the South, fighting alongside his brethren against the Cherokee, but has returned victorious.

Winona's eyes soften and tear and she runs to him, throwing herself into his arms and burying her face in his neck. Yona's arms come up to embrace her, and his face softens until it no longer resembles the meeting rock, but the loving face of husband and father.

The children follow their mother's example and rush to him too, embracing every free space on him, even the parts that are bruised and painful.

Days later, wounds tended to and healing, Yona, the other warriors, the chief, and his advisers gather at the meeting rock.

"The pale ones have sticks that shoot fire."

"The Westo too."

"How?"

"They are trading with the white man."

"Trading what? Beads?"

"People."

"What people?"

"Our people."

"A young man for two guns. A woman for two more. A child for a pistol."

"The last settlement they hit was just four walking days away from here."

The men stand watch and send out Helaku to investigate. Helaku is small, but light and swift on his feet.

When he returns, he is not alone. He walks with Yamasee from slaughtered villages. Those Yamasee carry stories of torture. They talk about wild-eyed Westos dressed in the white man's clothes, with fire shooters at their hips.

They whisper the names of suckling children ripped from their mothers' breasts, and the old ones who were thrown down to their knees and beheaded.

"And the others?" Yona asks.

"Gathered into the backs of wagons and taken away."

"Taken where?"

His question is met with blank stares.

A month passes and still no threat visits the calm valley.

"Maybe the worst of it is over."

"Maybe they have all they need for now."

"Maybe." Yona's eyes bore into the woods that surround them. He has a strange feeling that something out there is looking back at him.

They strike just before sunrise. Not even the cocks have stirred.

Rivers of blood bubble beneath the heat of the flames that roar and lick out from the burning dwellings.

Sahale is dead. Yona is dead.

Yamasee women scatter, snatching up small ones as they move swiftly toward the salt marsh. Their feet against the ground sound like the drums the women beat, but this rhythm is frantic and Nayeli and her brothers cling hard to Winona as they shiver inside of the earthen walls of their dwelling.

Nayeli pushes her thumbs into her ears, trying to block out the screaming that sounds like the breaking Atlantic. But she cannot mute the pounding of fleeing feet, the screams of terror, and the shots from the fire sticks that cut through the last vestiges of the dark night.

Winona wraps one strong arm around her children, pulling them closer to her, the other she extends out into the darkness, and the fading light of the moon falls onto the sharpened edge of the spear she clutches.

Minutes pass and the Yamasee warrior cries give way to the lamenting moans of the dying. The moon's glow disappears, and Winona and her family are thrown into the purple light of dawn.

Westos rush in without warning, snatching the spear from Winona's hand and throwing her aside. The boys throw themselves against their attackers, who knock them down to the ground and then pummel them with their fists until they fall unconscious and their limp bodies are lifted and carried away.

Winona shields Nayeli with her body, becoming like the meeting rock—strong, hard, and unmovable. The Westos laugh at her; they mock her spirit, snatch at her hands held up like spears.

Finally, having had enough, they lunge. Winona lunges too, and for a few magical seconds she takes flight, her dark hair sailing behind her, her arms fanned out at her sides like wings. Winona soars through the air like an eagle, but her flight is cut short when they slice her throat in midair.

They snatch Nayeli up by her small arms; there is no time for goodbye, just a swift tearful look at her dying mother.

The Westos herd Indians like the Yamasee men herd horses; they herd them, dozens of them. They line them up, single file.

Metal chokers are clamped around their necks. Metal chokers with long heavy-link chains that connect them together like their bloodline, like their traditions. Then they are led south across the valley and out beyond the palmetto trees to the world beyond.

When they arrive, it's dark. Nothing much can be made of the place; the smells are different here. Strange, stinking.

They are shepherded into a stable, chokers removed, then left alone. It is night, and murmurs fill the air—frightened words, crying, and the sound of fists banging against the rotting wood walls.

Why? thrown out like the fists that pound.

Why? flung up to the heavens and the Creator.

Why? passed around among them and then tossed off to the side and stomped down into the earth.

Morning light seeps in from between the warped rafters of the stall. The women begin to weep all over again, and the small ones stir from their sleep, bat at their eyes, and then frantically reach out for their mothers.

The creaking sounds of wagon wheels and the strange, stiff British tongues of the men who have gathered outside the barn seep in along with the sun.

When the doors finally do swing open, the captives are temporarily blinded by the brilliance of the day, and they shield their faces with their hands and back away from what would have been welcoming on any other day.

A man—red like them, but dressed in European clothing with a black wide-brimmed hat, an eagle feather tucked into the felt band—speaks to them in their native tongue, demanding that they begin to file out into the daylight.

Nayeli has never seen a white man, and now her eyes fall on dozens of pale faces. Some are pinched and reddened by the sun, some pocked, others smooth and round like the moon. Blue-eyed, brown-eyed, eyes the color of rain clouds.

Red hair, yellow hair like the silky threads of corn husks. Black hair like her own.

The red man—a Westo, Nayeli assumes—presses a long stick against the smalls of backs and forearms, urging them forward and off into different directions, where other Westo men dressed in the same strange clothing wait with sticks.

Soon they are separated into three frightened groups: men, women, and children.

A white man with a hefty middle and brown, ragged teeth approaches each one, examining ears, teeth, palms of hands, and soles of feet. After this they are sent off to holding pens, where they are stripped naked, a bucket of water is dumped onto them, and they are made to scrub themselves clean with black soap.

One by one they are taken to a raised wooden platform and positioned next to a man who stands behind a podium. The man circles each subject, poking, prodding, and pointing to the Westo nearby to translate: "Lift your arms." "Open your mouth." "Lift your leg."

When the man is done, he moves back to the podium and the large leather-bound book that rests there and scribbles down the subject's new name and informs the crowd of that name, the approximate age of the subject, and what he feels the subject's abilities are. A beginning price is thrown out to the crowd and then the madness begins.

Shouting, hands being flung into the air, more shouting, pointing, screaming, and then quiet.

They auction off the males first.

Nayeli's heart leaps in her chest when she sees her eldest brother, Elan, dragged to the auction block. His wrists are bound tightly behind his back and his fourteen-year-old chest heaves. Nayeli breathes with him as she moves through the crowd of frightened children until she reaches the wooden gate. There she grabs hold of the posts and lets go of a blood-curdling scream: *Eeeeeeeeeellllllllllllllllaaaaaaaaaaaaannnnnnnnn!*

A Westo's hard stick comes from nowhere, barely missing her hands, the *thwack*ing sound it makes against the wood unlocks a dam inside of her, and the tears begin to stream.

Elan looks her way, but he does not call back to her. His lips tremble and tears spot his cheeks and dangle from his chin as he averts his gaze to the horizon behind Nayeli's small face.

Elan fetches three hundred dollars and will be sent to Barbados to work the Alleyene sugarcane plantation.

The second brother, Dyami, fetches two hundred and twenty-five dollars and will go to the Lucas plantation in South Carolina to farm indigo.

Whan Nayeli is brought to the auction block, the man looks at her, studies the brown spots that stare back at him from her bare chest. He snatches her deerskin skirt from her body, revealing her to the onlookers. Nayeli drops her head and uses her small shaking hands to cover her private place. Tears stream down her cheeks, come to meet at her chin, and then slowly rain onto the blue granite eagle.

"A girl child, six or seven years in age. Healthy. Fieldwork, housework. Fresh, untouched, sure to breed well!" The man lifts his gavel and shouts out to the sea of white faces and black top hats.

When the bidding is over, Nayeli is no longer Nayeli, daughter of Yona and Winona; she is the property of Henry Vicey of the Sandersville, Georgia, Viceys—cotton farmers.

Arizona

I say all that I can say and then stop talking and watch the scenery roll past. I guess I've said enough because Sherry ain't pestering me to say more. She quiet now too, staring hard at the road, thumping her thumb against the steering wheel while she chew on her bottom lip.

It's some pretty land outside my window. The mountains and rocks look like someone dragged a paintbrush across them. I laugh and think, Maybe the cactus did it. Maybe at night they come alive and paint the mountains. I giggle again and look around to see Sherry giving me an odd look.

You all right, Dumpling? she say.

I nod my head yes and then look at her face and ask, So what's new with you?

She flinch, like my question is a straight pin in her side.

I watch her, look at those big tits she got like mine, down at those hips that spread so far it covers the material of the seat. You gaining weight? I say.

Her head spin around, eyes big, mouth drop open and clamp shut again. No, she say, then, Well maybe a little.

Hmm, all them tortillas, I say.

Uh-huh, maybe.

Some more miles, five maybe, and then a sign.

I read it out loud: Flagstaff, Arizona, Twenty Miles.

Some more miles and then a sign.

I read it out loud: Best Western Pony Soldier Inn and Suites, Three More Exits.

Sherry make a sound in her throat and take the next exit. I look at her like she's crazy.

What you doing?

I got friends out here we can stay with.

Friends? What kind of friends?

The people kind, she say with her smart mouth.

The sun dipping and the mountains turn the color of stewed carrots and then the desert put on a show for us. Everything seem to light up and sparkle; it so pretty I forget that we been driving for almost an hour since we left the highway and the road ain't a road anymore, just a mess of rocks and sand.

Sherry's SUV tilt this way and that and she change gears and step hard on the gas while I press my hands over my heart and pray.

Who the hell live out here? Ain't nothing out here but cactus and snakes. But then I remember which one of my children I'm traveling with. She the strange one, which means she got strange friends. They probably tent peoples.

I look around at the backseat then, 'cause I ain't sleeping in no damn tent.

I look over at Sherry. Her face a mess of confusement.

You sure you know where you going?

She don't answer me, just bring the car to a stop, tell me to give her the road map out of the glove compartment. Then she lift her hand and flick at the space over her head and a little door flips down; from there she pulls out a pair of glasses.

I watch her put them on and I feel a pang in my chest.

How long you been wearing glasses?

Awhile, she say as she flips on the light, takes the map from me, and stares down at the place she has circled in red.

I just watch her, and them glasses make me realize I don't know her at all.

Oh, okay, she says out loud, and flicks the light off, hands the map back to me, and puts the car—I mean, SUV—in drive.

Just a little bit farther, she says.

Cabins.

Thank God, I think as we come to a stop and Sherry climbs out, throwing "Wait here" over her shoulder at me.

She walk to one cabin and knock on the door. She wait a minute before she knock again, and still nobody come. She look down at her watch and knock again, loud.

Someone must have asked something from the other side of that door, 'cause my child scream, Little Flower!

Little Flower?

Then the door open and a man as tall as a tree, dressed in a white T-shirt and pinstriped pajama pants, step out and grab Sherry around her waist and lift her up into the air.

He swing her around twice and then set her back down on the ground, step away from her, walk around her, and then give her another hearty hug.

He seem happy to see her; she beaming like the moon, I suppose she happy to see him too.

Sherry turn and point to me, grab the man by the arm, and then they start toward me.

I fidget in my seat, swipe at my hair, wonder if my breath smell, and then finally press the button on the door that make the window come down.

Elk, this is my mother, Dumpling, she say and then quickly, I mean Clementine Jackson.

I stick my hand out and he takes it.

Nice to meet you, he says, and smiles.

I think he got teeth like a mule. I grin back.

Little Flower has told me much about you.

I just nod my head and resist saying, I don't know shit about you.

Welcome to my home, he says.

The cabin is small, simple. A couch, a hearth, two chairs, colorful blankets here and there—hanging on the walls, thrown across the couch, rolled like logs and piled up against the wall.

Sienna and the children are sleeping, he says, and points at the closed doors. I look around and wonder where the bathroom at 'cause my bladder hollering. Where the kitchen at? my stomach growling.

Ten minutes later I find out the bathroom is outside in a box, behind the house. And ain't no kitchen; they cook on a split over rocks.

Jesus, Mary, and Joseph!

Elk take us back outside, take us to the other cabin.

It look the same as the first.

I hope you'll be comfortable, Mrs. Jackson, he say as he pushes open one *of the doors. Single bed, quilted coverlet, stool, piss pot on the floor, small window with something made out of sticks, yarn, and feathers hanging in front of it.*

I know I won't be, but I say, Yes, of course.

You want some tea?

I think that tea only going to run through me. I look out the window into the night, something howl off in the distance—No thank you, I say and then, Goodnight.

Elk smile, set the kerosene lamp down on the stool, say, I'll bring your suitcase in, then he turn around and take the keys from Sherry.

I watch him walk away, long black braid swinging, big calves bulging beneath pinstriped pajama pants.

Sherry step in, put her hands on her hips, and look around the room like it's the best place she's been in a while. Then she walk over to the window and say, It's nice out here, huh? Look at that sky.

I sit down on the bed. Look like the same sky in Nevada, I say, then I point and ask, What's that thing?

She touch the feather with her finger, smile a bit, turn around and look at me, and say, A dream catcher.

A dream catcher?

I just screw my face up to let her know I ain't pleased 'bout sleeping in no room that got hoodoo symbols hanging 'round the window.

It's supposed to catch the bad dreams and only allow the good dreams in, she say in a tone that make me feel like I'm supposed to know this stuff.

Uh-huh.

Sherry linger.

How you know that man? I whisper.

Elk?

Any other man getting the suitcases? I hiss.

Elk's an old friend. We go way back.

How far?

I dunno, ten years or more.

I ain't never hear you talk about him.

Well I have, you just weren't listening.

Elk walks back in before I can say anything else. He look at me, see the hurt in my face, look at Sherry, see the spite in hers, and then just set the bags down and ease back out the room.

Sherry fling good night at me and follow.

I look at the bed, poke it with my finger; the mattress feels stiff. I look around at the bare walls, at the dream catcher and the black sky beyond. I want to be mad, want to feel put out, but that dark sky and the billion twinkling stars set in it draw me in, and as mad as I want to be, I can't catch hold of the feeling and so put on my nightgown, climb into bed, and watch the sky until sleep take me.

I wake up to the sound of chattering children, adults, and Sherry's laughter. The sun is high and bright and the black sky is now a watery blue and cloudless.

Cool morning air sails through my window and I pull the quilt tighter around me. I look at the dream catcher and think that its yarned web has trapped all my dreams, because I had none at all last night.

A small face with dark eyes appears at my window. I can't tell if it's a boy or a girl. The face smiles and I decide it's a girl. Small finger come up and wave.

Morning, I say.

She blushes, sets a small blue flower on my windowsill, and disappears.

Later in the morning, I see that there are more than a dozen cabins, all spread out across the land. Women out front sweeping at the desert sand while children scamper about. Husbands backing out decrepit pickup trucks that cough, stall, and then find a life again, kicking up dust as the men wave and roll off to work.

"Come, come," say a short round woman in a white dress that is ringed around the collar, sleeves, and hem in red and blue stitching. I think that this must be Elk's sister, they look so much alike, but that may not be so, because the closer I get to her and the other faces that are seated around the picnic table, I notice that they all resemble—one look the same as the other—hard to tell them apart. I chuckle and think, They look to me like we black people look to the white man—all the same.

Sherry look different this morning. Her face look open, fresh. She smiling too, slide over on the bench, making room for my wide hips. Introduce me to everyone around the table, slide a plate in front of me. Someone else appear and place a metal cup of coffee near my wrist.

Everyone talking. Talking to me, over me, around me.

What's this? I try to ask, sly-like through my smile.

Fried bread, Sherry say.

And this? I use my chin to point at the reddish stuff on the side.

Wojape, she say.

Wo-what?

It's like a berry pudding.

I look a little closer.

Like jam?

Yeah, something like that.

I look around for bacon, grits maybe, some link sausage, but everyone got the same thing on their plates.

When in Rome . . . I think.

Madeline call? I ask after I gulp down my second cup of coffee.

Nope, Sherry say happily, then plucks her cell phone from her pocket and shows it to me. Across the face it says: NO SERVICE

What, you ain't pay your bill?

Sherry laugh. It means, she say, that there is no service in this area. Up in these mountains, out in this beautiful desert, she says, waving her arm through the air.

Elk seems sad to see Sherry go. He hug her tight and whisper something in her ear. He come over and hug me too. Say it was nice to finally have met me. Say, I hope you come back again.

I say, Thank you, hope to come back soon.

We drive off down the road. I look back and twenty people waving at us, then the dust kick up and they disappear.

They were nice people, I say.

Salt of the earth, Sherry mumbles and look both ways before turning left onto the highway and gunning it.

How you know them again?

I lived there for a year, after I left Berkeley.

You did?

I rack my brain and try to remember that year. Nothing comes. She done lived so many place, I can't keep track.

Uh-huh, I say. What you do there?

Worked the land, learned the customs.

What you want to do that for?

Because I found their way of life fascinating.

Really?

Yeah. For one, they don't hit their children.

I open my mouth to say something, then close it again when I realize I don't have anything to say. I'm sure there were other things fa-sci-nating 'bout her stay there, why she just tell me about that one?

I don't look at her direct, but can see her watching me from the corner of my eye. I say, Watch the road.

We ride along for a while and then she say all of sudden, I started writing the story.

I nod my head, blow at a tiny black bug making its way across my window; it hold fast, wait till I stop blowing, and then start moving again. I give up on trying to get rid of it, feel good that something else stuck inside this SUV with Sherry and her hurtful words besides me.

The notebook is in the backseat, she say.

I reach back and grab the red spiral notebook, flip it open, and see plenty of words jotted across the lines. I flip the pages, about fifty filled up—back and front.

When you do all this?

Last night.

Ain't you get no sleep?

I only need a few hours.

You sure?

I know my body. You gonna read it or just keep asking me questions?

I look at her, lean back in the seat, and begin with: A broad valley . . .

By the time I'm done, we running on empty and Sherry pulling into a gas station.

She tell the attendant to fill it up and then turn and look at me.

What you think so far?

I look back at her, tap the pages, and say, I ain't say all of this.

I know. I filled in the missing things.

With lies, I say.

No, with someone's reality.

How you know?

I've read enough history, heard enough stories to know.

I just humph.

It's good so far though, don't you think?

What I know from? I ain't much of a reader, you know.

The attendant come back and say, Twenty-two forty, please.

Sherry pay him, throw the SUV back in drive, and pull out toward New Mexico.

Tell me more, she say.

I think back and try to remember.

Henry Vicey was a short man with a soft, protruding middle. Brown-haired with shocks of white and ashy-brown eyes that were always smiling. A jovial spirit, with a booming voice and a corny sense of humor. He talked almost nonstop to the young slave boy named Hunt, who traveled with them.

Hunt drove the horses, fetched the water, skinned and cleaned the possum Henry shot and killed. Hunt had little more to say than "Yassa" and "Nossa."

Hunt pays little or no mind to Nayeli, but does as he is told and offers her peaches and bowls of corn mush and possum. Nayeli refuses everything except water.

She watches from the back of the wagon as the land changes right before her eyes. Mountains rise up in the distance and then shrink away. The dirt goes from brown to red. Green grass shimmers blue and then emerald. Oak trees are dwarfed by towering pines, the yellow sun turns white hot, and the sky is suddenly stripped of its blue.

On the seventh day, when Nayeli does not think she can take the *clippity-clop* sound of the horses' hooves, the rolling resonance of the wagon wheels, or the nonstop jabber of Henry Vicey much longer, they turn off the road and onto a narrow lane shaded by pecan trees.

It's slow going. Beating rains have pummeled Sandersville for three straight days, leaving the earth soft and yielding. Hunt uses his whip to urge the horses on.

An open space greets the end of the shaded path; there, a medium-sized whitewashed wood plank house stands. A porch, four beams, and a black roof that points and then goes long and flat at the back of the house, offering a resting place for the lazy limbs of the weeping willow that grows alongside it.

Potted flowering mimosa shrubs sit beneath the shuttered

front windows; rocking chairs, one on either side of the screen door, eerily sway in the slight morning breeze.

Guinea hens cluck around the steps of the house, pecking at the long tails of the sad-eyed hound dogs that lounge in the shade.

Nayeli stretches her neck and sees that off to the left and right of the house are rows and rows of cotton stalks that seem to stretch endlessly across the land. Just below the cotton rows are two clapboard shacks that look as if they will tumble down the slope they'd been hastily erected on.

To the right of the house is a barn and pen with two grazing horses and three mules.

"We here." Henry turns around and beams at her. "We home."

A week in and out of the back of a wagon left her smelling like the horses and the gunnysacks of yams and overripe peaches and the bottle of sweet-smelling bubbling bath liquid that broke and seeped when Hunt horribly negotiated a boulder that was embedded in the road. That and the road dust that first settled after the rains and then caked and browned on her skin in the beating heat of the sun. Nayeli smelled and looked anything but human.

"Couldn't get a chance to clean her up none," Henry Vicey yells down to the black faces that seem to float from everywhere.

"Mary, you clean her up 'fore April and the missus gets a gander at her."

Two pair of strong black hands grab hold of the horse's reins as Henry climbs down from the wagon.

"Yassa, Massa," the tall dark woman called Mary says, and reaches a hand out toward Nayeli who is huddled behind a bag of yams.

"What we callin' her?" Mary asks as she offers Nayeli a re-assuring smile.

Henry scratches at his chin and thinks about it for a while. "Well, I suppose we should call her Lou."

A quick glimmer of surprise streaks across Mary's face. "Like Missus's dog that died?"

"Yeah, she loved that dog something fierce," Henry says, and scratches at his stomach. "Yeah, I think Lou is a perfect name."

Mary shrugs her shoulders and shakes her head. "C'mon, Lou," she coos, and curls firm fingers around the frightened child's wrist, giving her a gentle tug. "C'mon, now. No need to fret."

Mary coaxes Lou out of the wagon and then down to the spring and a bar of lye soap. Curious young eyes gather to watch as Mary scrubs away the dirt, fingers the blue stone around the girl's neck, and moans something about "pretty."

Out now, and soaked through but clean and shivering like a wet rat, Mary throws an old sheet around Lou and guides her back up the hill and toward the slave quarters.

More faces. Old and young, male and female, watch silently. Some turn their backs and mutter.

The inside of the shack is dark, cool, small, and musty from the many bodies that live there. Pallets strewn here and there. Wooden bowls, oyster shells for spoons. Tin cups.

"Gimme that jar, boy," Mary says, and lowers herself down and onto a small stool. Her knees creek as she considers the child before her.

"Indian?" someone throws out from the corner of the room.

"Seem so," Mary mutters, as she uses one hand to scoop the jellylike substance from the jar the small boy is holding.

"What she called?" another inquires.

"Massa say she called Lou."

"Lou?" a harsh voice murmurs.

"What kinda name is that fer a girl?"

"Massa give her the missus's dog's name."

Heads shake in disbelief.

Mary pulls the sheet from the child's body. "Just a baby," she says, and begins to slather Lou with the mutton suet.

Before long, Lou is gleaming.

Turning her around, Mary begins to tackle the hair, but not without taking a moment to roll the silken strands between her fingers, coveting the texture; a mixture of admiration and hatred hits her way down deep and she gives Lou's hair a vicious tug.

"Ow!" Lou cries, and jerks her head forward.

And just like that, the insidious feeling is gone and Mary pats the girl's shoulder and purrs, "Pardon."

Still damp, but greased down, Lou's hair is parted, and plaited into two long braids that fall down to her waist. Mary calls for the frock that Henry passed off to her two weeks ago, telling her to "Keep this safe somewhere till I get back."

Mary slips the faded green dress over Lou's head.

The dress must have been a delight for some little girl a long time ago, but now the hem is tattered and the sleeves are patched at the elbows. It hangs pathetically from Lou's small body, imbuing her with an even more pitiful appearance than the caked road dust and dirt had.

The pitifulness reaches out and touches Mary in a place she has worked hard to turn into stone—but not hard enough, because her heart begins to ache.

It is April Vicey's tenth birthday.

Blond-haired and blue-eyed like her mother Verna, but having her father's height and hefty girth, April's mouth always seems to be working on something. April does not speak—well, not clearly; she either mumbles through a mouth crammed with food, or screeches.

An only child, April is more than enough for Henry and Verna. The two that could have been—one before April and one after her—came seven months too soon. Just blood sacks that Verna insisted on naming and burying down near the stream.

April blows out her birthday candle, greedily snatches at the brown paper that encloses her gifts: a small wooden doll, a jewelry case, a heart-shaped silver locket and chain.

Verna nods her head with approval and lightly touches April's hand. "You like it?" she asks, and the little girl fumbles with a word of thanks before she tosses it aside, looks at her father, and asks, "Is that all?"

Lou is a gift. Not like the one from God, not that type her mother always told her that she and her brothers were, but a gift just the same, and, as if on cue, Mary ushers Lou through the swinging door of the dining room.

"Well, and her." Henry grins and points to Lou.

Verna Vicey's eyes bulge and then narrow. Her lips curl and her nostrils flare as she begins, "You didn't tell—"

"Hush, V," Henry throws at her, then turns his attention back to April. "She your very own slave."

April digs her hand into her cake and shoves a hunk between her puffed pink lips, then declares, "She all mine?" White icing spurts through the air and settles on the table and the front of her new dress

"Yep!" Henry exclaims.

"How could we afford—" Verna begins again, but Henry's hand comes, up halting her words.

"Mary, bring her on over here so April can get a good look at her."

Mary gives Lou's shoulder a little nudge, but Lou does not move an inch, she just stands there staring at the faces that stare back at her. "Go on now," Mary leans in and whispers in Lou's ear.

Lou does not understand these words, this place, the strange scents, the dark people, the white people. None of it.

Mary nudges her again and Lou takes one cautious step after another, and soon she is standing just a foot from her new mistress.

April's mouth smacks at the cake as she considers Lou's copper-colored skin, sleek black hair. "She don't look like none of the darkies I ever seen."

"No, that's right," Henry Vicey begins, but then is suddenly distracted as he begins to pat at the breast pocket of his shirt. "Shoot. Mary, get me one of my cigars from my humidor," he says, then leans forward so that his face falls between April's and Lou's. "You right, darling. She ain't no regular darkie, she an Injun. I betcha Fannie Gibson ain't got one of these!" He laughs and slaps the table hard with his hand.

April rubs her hands together in glee. "She sure do got some pretty hair." April sighs longingly and reaches for one of Lou's braids.

Lou shrinks back a little.

"Oh, don't be afraid. I ain't gonna hurt you," April coos.

Mary hands Henry his cigar and moves into the background.

"Oooh," April moans, her eyes sparkling and latching onto the blue stone. Lou shrinks farther away. "Gimme it!" April squeals, and quick as a flash her hand comes up and snatches the stone from Lou's neck.

Verna eyes the stone. "What in the world do you want with

a rock?" she spits at April. "Give it back to her," she orders before returning her attention to her husband.

April holds the granite out to Lou and then quickly snatches it from her reach. The teasing goes on for a few seconds and then April tires of the game and allows the granite to drop to the floor, where Lou hurriedly retrieves it.

"We cannot afford her, Henry." Aprils words are strained and stern.

Henry waves his hand at her and lights his cigar. Leaning back into his chair, he puffs and then releases three smoky circles that April squeals with delight over before breaking them with her pudgy index finger.

April's room is white-walled. Delicate pink curtains hang from the three small windows, a pink-and-green quilt covers the bed, and a rocking chair graces one corner with a pink sitting cushion and a pink-cheeked ceramic doll on top of that. It is a welcoming space with a fireplace and woven throw rug.

Lou sleeps on a pallet at the foot of April's bed. The dogs, on the other hand, have small wooden houses behind the main house. She eats with them on the back porch though, seated on a small stool: a bowl of buttermilk and bread in the morning, a plate of corn bread, beans, and salt pork in the afternoon, corn porridge in the evening.

She is a gift, but also a playmate and servant, forced to stand alongside her mistress swaying a fan made of peacock feathers to keep April cool and to shoo the bothersome flies away.

It is a pitiful existence that is made worse by the tears that spring from her eyes when she has a moment alone to long and grieve for her family.

The dark people try to talk to her, try to comfort her when they see her tear-stained cheeks and swollen red eyes. They speak slowly and use hand gestures to try and make her understand, but for the first few weeks she just drops her eyes away from their thick lips and they chuck her chin and blanket her with reassuring smiles.

Their eyes are sad for her, and she sees the weight of their existence in the slump of their shoulders and the bend of their necks.

Lou sits picking over her plate of food, eyes moving over the land, always searching for her mother's spirit even as her mind tackles the new words that are quickly replacing the old ones she grew up with.

"Loooooooooooooooooooouuuuuuuuuuuu!" Her new name cuts through her daydreams, and quick fast she is on her feet, the plate and the remnants of her meal clattering to the ground. Like lightning the dogs are on it, hungrily devouring every last morsel.

"C'mon, now. Let's go play."

April romps through the tall stalks of corn, laughing and giggling. She slaps at Lou's arm and runs off. Lou remembers this game with her brothers, but her feet do not skip along; there is no smile resting on her lips as she moves slowly toward the quivering stalk to her left.

By the time April is fourteen and Lou is ten, she has outgrown her place at the foot of the bed and is given a cot in the kitchen. She is no longer needed for April's amusement. There is water to haul, furniture to dust, corn to shuck, and beans to snap.

The cook—a large burly woman called Naples—sings her instructions and always smells, it seems to Lou, of clabber and peaches. She talks all the time, even when there is no one there to listen or respond.

Four years now, and Lou's Yamasee language is practically gone. She remembers the words for *nose, eyes, sky, mother, father, family,* and *love,* but little else.

It is on a Sunday that Lou is sent out of the house altogether.

Sunday is the day that Verna spots a red stain on the back of Lou's skirt. To Verna, it is a blinding red smudge against her character, a reminder that yet another piece of property could and probably would produce a bastard child. There were already three running about. Three yellow-skinned, hazel-eyed reminders that her husband was as unfaithful as he was foolish.

"Come here," Verna orders.

"Yes, ma'am." Instantly Lou halts her stride, turns on her heel, and comes to where Verna is standing.

"Turn around."

Lou does as she is told.

"You dirty heathen," Verna whispers between clenched teeth, then her palm falls like fire across Lou's cheek and she is sent flailing to the floor.

This is not the first assault. This is one of many. The last one came when Verna stumbled across her husband watching from the upstairs veranda as Lou was bathing in the stream.

For that, she was slapped and her hair cut down to the scalp.

"Don't you have any decency, any respect?" Verna cried, and leapt on Lou, levying blow after blow across her face.

"Out, out of my house, you!" Verna screeched, rising to her feet and kicking Lou in the ribs.

"Why?" Henry asked later that night.

"Because she stinks."

"No, she doesn't."

"Well, she's a bkye."

"Lou?"

"I found April's locket on her cot."

"You did?"

"And a shilling. Where would she get it from if she didn't take it?"

Henry eyes his wife and pulls at his beard. "What Naples say?"

"You gonna take a slave's word over mine, Henry?"

* * *

Lou is banished to the slave quarters and to the field where she is outfitted with a gunnysack and beaten straw hat. She is given a pallet on the already overcrowded floor, a plate and cup, and instructions on how to handle the blood that is flowing from between her legs.

"It'll come every month from now on," one of the women tells her.

"Every month till Massa get to you," another one says.

The first time Buena Vista came, Lou was fourteen years old and she had calluses on the palms of her hands, had tried and failed at picking cotton, and had been assigned to assisting Naples in the kitchen and washing clothes in the spring.

"Buena Vista?"

They roll the name across their tongues. Saying it aloud quick and then slow. Running it together in their mouths and then picking it apart with their teeth.

He arrives with Oswald and Cora Joseph, the speckled white man and his ailing-looking wife. Oswald is Henry Vicey's distant cousin from Kentucky, recently relocated to Macon.

Buena Vista drives their carriage and helps the missus down with his strong hands. Oswald don't seem to mind, and the missus, well, it seems to the onlooking faces that being helped down from the carriage is the best part of the trip.

"Buena Vista?"

His name is repeated and the black faces fold in on themselves. "What kind of name is that?

"Don't know," he says as he fumbles with the reins.

"You drive the carriage and what else?"

"Pick cotton, same as you."

They eye him. His hands look too clean to be cotton-picking hands. Too smooth. Can't be doing much else than holding reins.

"Sure 'nuff?"

"Ay-yuh," he says, and pulls an apple from his pants pocket. He looks over the crowd again, and his eyes fasten on Lou. He is smitten right then and there.

The women watch as he slides the apple up and down the front of his shirt, considers the shine, and then bites in.

Second time he comes, his eyes are swimming with the memory

of bronze skin and slick dark hair. Eyes black, but sparkling.

A voice comes from the rear. "Y'all back here so soon?"

Buena Vista strains his neck, his eyes eager, hand fingering the apple in his pocket. "Can't see ya. Y'all come a little closer."

The crowd rolls and then parts.

Nellie appears. Stout, but tight. Dark. Strong. Good teeth, he thinks, but she not the one.

"They just visitin', I guess," Buena Vista says, and his hand rolls across the apple in his pocket while his eyes ride her hips. She smiles, pulls her stomach in, and her breasts swell up and touch her chin.

"Y'all don't get no passes?"

"Nah." It is a collective response.

"Oh," he moans. "Too bad, lotta country to see beyond here."

"You all get a pass?"

Buena drops his eyes and studies the dirt. "Nah."

"No matter; you here now. Seem like you be coming regular," Nellie spouts, taking another step closer.

"Ay-yuh, seem so." His eyes pick over the faces that gather around him, but there is no bronze among them; plenty of black, though, and a sprinkle of yellow. "Missus say we be making the trip every other Sunday," Buena adds, and then, "Look here, where are all y'all menfolk at?"

The three that are there, right up in his face in fact, grunt.

"No disrespect," Buena Vista spews out with a little laugh. "But y'all kinda long in the tooth for all these young womens."

The men exchange glances and try to stretch themselves into the youth they remember.

"I means to say, I just wonder who with who," Buena Vista says, and rocks on his heels.

"Why you wanna know?" Nellie blows at him, lips pursed, tongue flicking. "You looking for something other than conversation?" Nellie come to stand alongside Buena and rests her hip against the fence. "A woman, maybe?" she purrs.

"Maybe," Buena gushes, and his hand squeezes the apple.

A cry goes up from behind them. "She the massa's whore; got three sons from him already."

Every head turns, and Mary is standing there, broad and stern, hands on her wide hips.

"True," someone whispers, and they all turn back to Buena.

"And?" Nellie throws back at them. "I ain't had a whip on my back since." Turning to Buena again, Nellie stretches a finger out and runs it along his bicep. "So what y'all looking for?"

"Where's the slight one with the pretty skin?"

Nellie pulls her hand back. "What y'all want wit her? She ain't nothing but a chile." And then her mouth opens and her tongue runs the length of her bottom lip. "I got pretty skin."

"Sure do," Buena says, but his eyes don't alight on her.

Nellie's back stiffens. "She ain't our kind."

"What kind is that?" someone laughs.

"Human?"

"We ain't even that, 'cording to the white folk."

"Mind your damn business!" Nellie barks at the crowd.

"Hush up, Nellie, with that type a talk; it's Sunday."

"Where she at?" Buena Vista asks again.

"Down in the field, I s'pose."

"On a Sunday?"

"Not a-pickin', just a-sittin'."

They come every other Sunday for three months.

Buena riding high, grinning, two apples stuffed into the pockets of his overalls, his heart thumping in his chest.

Those eyes, that skin.

It's all he can think about. And every other Saturday night he can barely sleep—up before dawn, horses hitched, and waiting while his owners sit at the dining room table and tap delicate spoons against the shells of soft-boiled eggs.

He drives the horses, double time, while the missus hangs on tight to her hat and the master calls out over the thunder of the galloping horses, "Goddammit, Buena, slow down!"

Once there, he paces. Paces so hard, his feet pound out a trench in the dirt before he finally catches sight of Lou and Nellie moving across the lawn and toward the back of the house.

"Hello, ma'am." Buena Vista moves beside them in a flash, quickly removing his hat.

Lou looks at Nellie, who is smiling smugly back at her. "Go on and speak to him. You the one he want."

Want?

Lou does not understand what is happening here. Henry Vicey wanted her, and so he purchased her. This man standing beside her—all teeth and rolling the brim of his hat between his fingers—didn't look like he had the means to buy her, and even if he did, he couldn't; he was a slave too.

Lou's head swiveled between Buena Vista and Nellie.

"Don't she speak?" Buena's voice betrayed his sudden disappointment.

Nellie dug her finger into Lou's shoulder blade.

"Oooooouch!" Lou cried, and swatted Nellie on her shoulder. "Quit!"

Nellie rubbed the place where Lou had landed the blow and laughed. "She sure do," she said, and sauntered off.

The worry lifted from Buena Vista's face. "My name is Buena Vista," he said, and presented her one large, dark hand.

Lou looked down at it and then back at him, but said nothing.

Buena Vista's smile wavered, and he threw a desperate look at Nellie's retreating back. "I—I," he started as he dug desperately into his pocket. "I brought you a gift," he said cheerfully, and presented Lou with a shiny red apple.

Lou eyed it, and then with a sigh removed it from the palm of his hand

"Thank you," she whispered, and dropped the apple into the pocket of her dress.

Buena Vista grimaced. Didn't seem that there was any way to get through to this woman. Buena Vista looked down at his shoes, thinking hard about something else to say. He thought about the long ride home, about the excitement that had fueled him in getting here. What if she offered him nothing else, turned her back on him and walked away, or just came right out and said, "You black and ugly." What then could he count on getting him back home?

Buena Vista was deflated. He had stupidly assumed that this woman would find him irresistible, but it seemed as though she didn't even find him interesting.

"Uhm . . . so they call you Lou, huh?"

"Uh-huh," Lou said, and rubbed at a crick in her neck.

"Pretty name."

"I'm glad you think so." Her words dripped with sarcasm.

"Oh, you don't think it's pretty? What would you rather be called, then?"

Lou bit down on her lip. She hadn't said her given name in so many years. She didn't even think about it, because what came along with the thought was far too painful to bear.

"Never mind. It's all right, I guess."

Buena Vista considered her. The sadness that now shadowed her face was not lost on him. He'd seen it on his own face when he stooped to stare at himself in a puddle of water.

"Well, I think it's a right fine name for a right fine lady," Buena said, and puffed out his chest.

A small smile crept across Lou's lips. She didn't thank him, but she did give him the benefit of a head-to-toe examination. Her eyes moved shyly over his body. He was a good-looking man. The way he carried himself reminded her of her father.

Buena looked up at the sky; the sun was moving west. "I'm sure the massa gonna wanna get going soon, so's we can make it back 'fore dark."

Lou nodded.

"I just wanna know if'n I can visit with you again?"

"Gal, them sheets gonna have to come off the line 'fore the sun sets!" Mary yelled from the porch.

Lou jumped at the sound of her booming voice. "I gotta go," she said, and turned and scurried toward the house, leaving Buena Vista standing there.

"Can I visit with you again?" he yelled at her back.

Lou turned her head toward him and threw him a look that didn't look like "no" to him.

He jumped jubilantly into the air and slapped his hat against the palm of his hand. Then he placed it back on his head and started off toward the waiting carriage.

That look gave him all the fuel he needed, with some left over to spare.

Oswald remained on his steed and spoke down to them all. Henry and Verna on the porch. Lou and Buena standing shoulder-to-shoulder below.

Henry had barely heard the part about how Oswald's wife was not getting any better, and how it looked as if her days were numbered, and they'd never sold the property off back home, and so Kentucky was where they were headed back to . . .

He'd heard some of that. But what his mind was stuck on was the part about Buena Vista and Lou getting hitched.

"He claims he loves her," Oswald had said with a laugh. "Well, you know I don't believe they know anything 'bout that. But in any case, they wants to be together and old Buena here has been a mighty good slave. Not a moment of trouble." Oswald beamed.

Henry's mind was still stuck on "hitched."

Henry just looked at them. "Something's wrong here," he said as he rocked on his heels and chewed on the tip of his pipe.

"What's wrong with it?" Verna asked. "He wanna marry her—or whatever it is they do down in that clearing—so let it be."

"She an injun and he a darkey. T'aint right."

"So what? You talking about them like they're actually part of the human race, for chrissakes," Verna spat.

"Well, they ain't of the same race. He a nigger and she a savage. Like trying to mate a cat with a dog." Henry chewed on the end of his pipe. "Just might be against the law," he added thoughtfully.

"I assure you, it's not," Verna said and, throwing her knitting needles down into her lap in frustration, she jumped up from her chair and quickly moved to her husband's side.

Henry spat over the porch railing, sending a glob of saliva to land on the toe of Buena Vista's boot.

"Look, Henry, I hate to lose Buena; he's a strong buck, damn good carpenter, quick in the field, and his seed is top-notch."

Verna's eyebrows went up. "'Seed'?" she repeated.

Oswald nodded his head and laughed. "He a stud, sure 'nuff. I done bred him with four of my best nigga womens; all of them had boys first time around—last girl gave me twins!"

Lou flinched, but her eyes did not move from her bare feet.

Naples had told her that it was time for her to choose a man, and the pickings were next to none there. "That man sure do believe in you," Naples had said with a laugh. "Got it bad, from what I see."

Lou had just blushed and continued shucking peas.

"You of age now anyhow. Time to make some babies, continue where your mammy and pappy left off."

Lou had just looked at Naples.

"You hear me, gal?" Naples pressed.

Lou had heard, and nodded her head yes. And so when Buena Vista spoke his intentions for the third time, she'd nodded her head again and said, "Yes."

"So, you see, I can't let him go for less than nine hundred dollars. And that there is a bargain," Oswald said.

Henry opened his mouth to speak, but Oswald threw his hand up, halting his words.

"Or, I'll tell you what else I'm prepared to do because we're family," Oswald boomed. "I can give you three hundred for the girl and take her back to my place."

Henry's head started shaking even before the words began to spill from his mouth. "No, no, no."

"Don't be a fool, Henry, that's more than what you paid for her. She's sickly, anyway. Always bedded down with one thing or another. Can't work the field past eleven, 'cause she faints in the heat. She's a waste; get rid of her," Verna hissed.

Henry stepped away from his wife and leaned over the railing of the porch. His eyes fell on Lou who stood coyly by, head bowed. She was his. He bought her, nurtured her, and watched

and waited patiently for the years to shepherd her into womanhood, and now she was here—beautiful, glowing, and ripe for
the picking.

Every man who'd ever stepped foot on his property had
commented on how beautiful she was, how exotic looking. "I
had one once. Like fire, they are," one man had said.

"Careful—one time and you'll be lost to the world forever,"
another had warned with a sly grin.

He wanted to be lost to the world forever. He couldn't let
her go, at least not before—

"Nine hundred dollars, you say?"

"Henry!" Verna erupted, then caught herself and threw a
shamed look at Oswald. "Oswald, will you excuse me and my
husband for a moment, please?"

Oswald nodded his head but let out a heavy breath of irritation.

Once inside, Verna caught Henry by the elbow. "Have you
lost your mind? I can't believe you're even considering purchas-
ing that Negro. We cannot afford him; we're already up to our
necks in debt. Did you forget about our bill at the feed store
and the land taxes?"

Henry's face twisted in anger. "Don't you tell me about my
affairs. I know what I can afford and what I can't," he said, and
pushed past her and out the door.

"Oswald, let's take this conversation into the drawing
room."

Oswald gave him a puzzled look. "Well, I—"

"I have some French cognac I'd like you to try."

"Well, that sounds quite inviting." Oswald grinned and
climbed down from his steed.

The sun was setting a fiery orange when Oswald mounted his
horse again. Head spinning from the cognac, he waved at Buena
Vista and gave him a loose smile before he clucked his tongue
and hollered, "Git on, Moses!"

It had been a fine day, he thought to himself as he galloped down the road toward home. One strong black buck for a string of fine pearls and the promise of Lou and Buena's firstborn child.

It had been a fine day indeed.

Albuquerque, New Mexico

Two stops for gas and lunch. Arizona eight long hours behind us, Albuquerque, New Mexico, sprawled out ahead of us.

Sherry cell phone ring. She pick it up, glance at the number, pluck the earpiece from her ear, and hand the phone over to me.

It's for you, she say.

Hello?

Dumpling! Madeline, screaming.

I grab my chest, say, Oh Lord, what's wrong?!

She say, I been trying to reach you for hours!

We fine.

Why didn't Sherry answer the phone?

No service, I say.

What?

We were in the desert, on a reservation.

On a what?!

Reservation, with Indians.

Madeline suck her teeth, blow some air. What y'all doing on a reservation?

Uhm, we spent the night there. Them people some of Sherry's friends.

Figures, she say, and then, Let me talk to her.

I pass the phone to Sherry. She hesitates but takes it.

Hello, Madeline, she say, and not much else except some throaty sounds and then she just pull the phone away from her face, look at it like Madeline done said something off-color—like she been known to do—and then Sherry just hit a button, a little music play, and then nothing. She done. The phone is off.

She toss it down in her lap, wiggle her butt in her seat, screw up her face, and shake her head like she talking inside of herself and the conversation ain't good.

I don't even ask what Madeline said. I know my children.

Sherry move right and slide that SUV between a blue Volkswagen Beetle and a brown Ford that look like the one my husband sold off two years before he died.

The traffic crawls and we inch our way down the Fourth Street exit. I point at a sign and say out loud, University Boulevard, Downtown.

Sherry look at me. Why must you do that? she say.

What?

Announce the signs.

I just shrug my shoulders.

We drive some and then I see a sign that says, SUPER 8 MOTEL— MIDTOWN.

I open my mouth, then snap it shut and wait.

We drive some more and pull into the parking lot of the Super 8. Anything better than a cabin, I think as Sherry cut the engine and open her door.

We step into the lobby and Sherry's face frowning 'fore I can finish reading the words on the small plaque set on the front desk that say, WELCOME.

I look around. Lobby seem okay to me. Purple carpet, a few places to sit, Glade in the air, smiling young girl asking how she can help us.

In the room now, Sherry look around and already I know she see something wrong.

She particular and peculiar.

Mattress too thin, she say.

She pull the blankets off and toss them onto the floor, bring in two quilts from the back of her SUV.

They don't wash them after every stay, she say. Full of other people's germs. Like sleeping with twenty people.

Okay, I say. I just want to eat and go to sleep.

Can we order room service?

Sherry pick up the menu, flip it over, flip it back, toss it down on the bed. If you want to eat that stuff, she say, and pull out a bag of granola.

Yes, I do, I say to the closing door, and pick up the phone, press the button with a picture of a little man carrying a tray, and order me a cheeseburger, onion rings, and two Pepsi colas!

Sherry leave the room and come back with a small fountain with blue marble rocks. She look behind the beds, the dresser, and the nightstand until she find a socket that suit her. When she plug it in, night sounds come out the back.

Nice, huh?

I shrug my shoulders. I usually fall off to sounds of the television.

She smile, go into the bathroom, come out with a glass of water, and pour it into the fountain. Now we got water sounds too. I think I'm going to be up pissing all night long!

The food come and Sherry turn her nose up at the smell of it. She also turn the air conditioner on high, so's I have to eat my food while I'm wrapped up in one of her blankets to keep from freezing to death.

After I'm done, all showered and clean and wrapped up tight in my bed, Sherry turn off the lights, move to the middle of her bed, and fold her legs Indian-style.

She start making sounds like the woman on the CD in her car. I mean, SUV.

What you doing? I cry.

Meditating.

I turn over, punch my pillow, and think maybe the next stop I can hop a plane.

In the morning we drive into town, have breakfast at a little café. We sit outside and I order pancakes and bacon; Sherry order a bowl of fruit and ask the waitress to bring her just hot water, she have her own tea bags.

What's wrong with the tea they got here? I ask. She say she only drink organic green tea.

I pull the wet wipes from my bag and clean my hands.

Sherry watch me and then ask, How many times a day do you have a bowel movement? She say this as I stuff a forkful of pancakes in my mouth.

I'm eating, I say. What you wanna know for anyway?

You know, she starts, and rests her elbows on the table, you should go like a baby does.

What?

After every meal. That's the proper way.

Shut up, Sherry, and let me worry about how many times I shit.

She huff, but drop the subject.

We sit for a while after our meals are finished and watch the world around us. Plenty of Mexican-looking peoples around here. Red chili peppers draped across almost everything like Christmas lights.

You ready to hear the rest? she ask.

What?

Sherry waving the red spiral notebook in my face.

Oh, yeah, why not.

She call for another cup of hot water.

I say, And another coffee, and lean back into my chair and listen.

Only two slave quarters, each with one large room. No privacy at all for a man and his wife after they say "I do" down in the clearing.

It's midday anyway, and a Thursday at that, so Henry hustles everyone back out and into the field and sends Lou off to the kitchen.

"Later," Buena whispers in her ear, catching hold of her hand before Meade the nigger slave driver pushes the end of his whip into Buena's back, hurrying him along.

Lou walks off to the kitchen. The honeysuckle necklace Nellie had draped over her neck is already going limp in the heat, the blossoms wilting and turning brown.

"Naples, you go on down to the quarters and rest some." Henry didn't know what to say to get Lou alone.

Naples turned on her heel. "Sir?" She hadn't seen the inside of one of those shacks in more than seven years. Her place was in the pantry, right below the shelves laden with jars of preserves and bags of flour.

Henry avoided Naples's eyes and looked off to his left. "You heard me."

Naples took a deep breath, and her whole body shuddered. She let her eyes fall on Lou for a moment and thought to mouth some word of warning to her, but didn't.

"Yassa, Mr. Vicey sir," Naples said, and exited the kitchen through the back door.

Lou had never been uncomfortable in Henry Vicey's presence. In fact, she'd felt safe with him. He'd never raised his voice to her, had never struck her, had allowed her to continue to wear the eagle-shaped granite around her neck, had even given her a longer strand of hide for it when the one she had became too small for her teenage neck.

He'd been kind and decent to her. But now, standing there, Henry not looking at her, his eyes darting here and there and his hands picking up things—salt shaker, paring knife, plate—and then setting them back down again, made her feel nervous.

"So you got a man now. How that feel?" Henry suddenly said.

"Lou found herself jumping at the abrupt sound of his voice. "F-Fine, I guess."

"Uh-huh," Henry said, and moved toward the cast-iron stove. "You ain't give yourself to him 'fore you all said them words to each other down in the clearing, did you?"

"Sir?" Lou replied, her eyes low, watching his feet shuffle in place and then take a step or two closer to her.

"What you know about God, Lou?" Henry asked.

"I—I don't know."

"The Bible?"

"Nothing, I suppose."

"Well, let me tell you about God and the Bible. God wrote the Bible, and said that a woman must remain virtuous until she takes a husband."

"Yassir"

"That apply to the white men and women, but you all—I mean the savages and niggas—that don't apply to you."

Lou said nothing.

"It don't apply to you like it don't apply to the cattle and chickens and such." Henry moved closer. "God put you all here to serve us. Do you understand what I'm saying, Lou?"

He was in her face now. His stomach brushing against hers, his breath warm on her cheeks.

Lou nodded her head. She understood. This is what Nellie and the rest of the women talked about, warned her about, and sometimes sat back and cried about.

"The Good Book say a slave is supposed to honor and serve his master." Henry bent and whispered in her ear. "Are you a good slave, Lou?" His hands were on her, everywhere. His breathing labored. "Are you, Lou? Are you?" he said again, breathless as he ripped the necklace of honeysuckle from her body and tossed it to the ground.

"Are you, are you?" He pressed and tore at her dress.

Lou let go a choked scream.

"Don't you scream, Lou; don't you do it or I'll whip you good," he said, some of his fingers crawling across her breasts, the other ones down between her legs.

"Stop that crying. You stop it now." A red-faced Henry steps away from her. "Shhh," he warns, and points to the ceiling above his head. "You want the mistress to hear?" Lou covers her mouth and weeps. "She'll have you hung if she find out what you done."

Henry shoves a naked, scared, and trembling Lou into the pantry and down to the floor. He shuts the door behind them and blocks it with a pickle barrel.

In that dark space that is dank with the scent of pounded wheat and jarred peaches, Henry Vicey takes.

He helps himself, over and over again, to her innocence, youth, and virtue. He gorges himself until his mouth has tasted every part of her, sopping up every bit of what she had managed to hold on to from the valley.

He takes.

He takes.

He takes until he is sure that he has depleted her and that there is nothing much left over to bring to Buena.

Later, Naples sweeps the curled and brown petals of the honeysuckle across the floor and out the back door. She pushes the pickle barrel back into its corner, touches the sacks of flour, rearranges the jarred preserves on the shelf, and eases her aging body down onto her knees. There is a slight thought to the job at hand—just slight; she's careful not to ponder too long. All pondering does is confuse her head and make it hurt, so she gets down to it and begins to push the wet rag over the specks of blood that are drying dark in the grooves of the wood flooring.

Her eyes have always been dark, but never empty.

She's always worn a wistful expression, a longing look, sad sometimes—but now there was nothing.

He reaches for her and she shrinks away, and right then he knows. He stands up, takes a few steps toward the house, balls his fists, pushes them into his temples, and coughs out a sound that could have been a scream. The hounds perk up when their ears get wind of it; the overseer grabs his whip and waits.

But Buena just kicks at the dirt, goes off and punches at the bark of the dogwood behind the quarters, goes down to the stream and dunks his head.

The women try to comfort Lou. Standing over her, hands folded in pity across their stomachs, they say, "Dis here is our life, what you gonna do? Worry yourself into tomorrow 'bout it? It's already done."

"It ain't like you the first—"

"Or the last."

"You got a husband now. Pick your face up off of the floor."

"Straighten your back."

"Dis our life, what you gonna do?"

The men gather around Buena, eyes focused on the horizon as they skip pecan shells across the ground and say, "Sure is a pretty sky."

"Right fine sunset too."

"I smell rain, though."

"Ay-yuh, it coming all right; gonna wash everything clean."

What should have been theirs right after the exchange of words in the clearing comes a month later, in the middle of the day, sixty pounds of cotton in a sack across his back, the sun pressing down on his neck.

He's careful with her down in the dirt beneath the watching sun. Gentle as he slips into her and thankful in the end, even though he is just a nigger and white men tell him the only thing he and the other niggers have to be grateful for is them.

Now at night, she curls into him, and they touch each other as the others sleep their hard days away. Sometimes they sneak out into the cotton rows, away from every shut eye that ain't asleep, and share secrets with each other before they make love.

"My real name is Nayeli," she whispers to him through the darkness. He strokes her cheek and then her neck.

"Na-ye-li," he repeats slowly, allowing her name to coat his tongue. He closes his mouth and swallows it; now it is as much a part of him as she is. "It's a beautiful name."

Lou wants to cry. It is a beautiful name. She'd never thought of it that way. "If it's so beautiful, why does it hurt so bad?"

Buena pulls her closer to him and cradles her in his arms. "They cut your finger off, it hurts. They cut your toe off, it hurts," he begins, then takes a breath and squeezes Lou into him. "Same with your name; they cut it from you, and it hurts." Lou nods her head.

"What does it mean?" Buena asks.

Lou sniffs. "It means I love you," she whispers.

Lou has many secrets, while Buena seems to have next to none, and the few he does possess are more sightings than secrets. More gossip than confidential.

"Once, after Massa Owen and his wife had a disagreement, I saw him piss in the pail of well water the girl had set aside for the missus's bath," he says, and then muffles his laugh.

Lou whispers back, "I can read."

The years she'd spent at the foot of April's bed had not been pleasant ones. April was a brat; that much was true. But she was smart as a whip; her favorite game after hide-and-seek and tag was teacher and pupil.

For the four years Lou shared April's room, she was not only her slave and playmate, but her student. "You sit there, Lou, and I'll stand over here and you do what I say and now hold that book properly and sit up straight and what letter is this, have you forgotten, what, are you stupid or something?"

Lou was far from stupid, but she was a great actress and so always looked at the arithmetic and spelling words with a confused face.

"Lou, Lou! I just told you how to spell that word. Now, try it again." And Lou did, over and over again, looking at the letter F and sounding out an E. Looking at the word "boy" and saying, "Dog?"

Sometimes her acting abilities got her a slap across the face or a book bought down hard on top of her head. April would storm away from her, red faced and cussing. "Mama, Lou is as stupid as the damn dogs!"

"Don't say 'damn,' sweetheart," Verna would start, and then, "Didn't I tell you that it was against the law to try to teach a slave?"

"I'm not breaking any laws, Mama, 'cause she ain't learning nothing," April would say with a pout.

"True enough; how could she? They're all so stupid."

Lou had learned plenty.

She practiced writing her alphabet in the wet dirt around the stream's embankment. Counted the petals of the wildflowers. Listened close when Verna went over April's lessons with her, and even managed to steal a book or two, which she kept hidden beneath a loose floorboard on the back porch.

Who was the stupid one now?

Lou teaches Buena Vista.

First by the moonlight and then by candlelight. The alphabet scrawled into the dirt, so easily erased.

"A," he whispered in her ear before snatching a nibble of her lobe. "You taste like honey."

Lou pushed him gently away and pointed to the next letter. "T," Buena Vista said, allowing the tip of his tongue to tap at the roof of his mouth. "T-t-t-t-t-t. Sound like old Massa's pocket watch, huh, Lou?"

Lou smiled and nodded her head. "Okay now, Buena. What this here word spell?"

Buena Vista stared down at the letters scrawled in the dirt: C-A-T.

Buena cleared his throat and looked around their little cabin before he laughed and reached for her again. Lou slapped his hands away. "Not till you tell me what the word is, Buena."

Buena Vista shrugged his shoulders in frustration and leaned heavily against the small wooden bed he'd made for Lou as a wedding present.

"Look here, woman. Plenty of gals right here on this here plantation would love to have a big ole buck of a man likes me, and you here pushing me this way and that." Buena laughed.

Lou snuffed at him and pointed her index finger at the word.

Buena Vista flexed his biceps before pulling himself up and prancing around the tiny space like a rooster.

"I ain't got all night, Buena." Lou's voice was tired.

"All right, woman," Buena said, and dropped down to his knees. "C-C-AAAAA—" He turned puppy-dog eyes to his wife as he struggled.

"You doing fine, baby," she said, stroking his arm, urging him on.

"C-C-C-AAAAT. C-C-AAAT. C-AT. CAT!"

"You did it, baby. You did it."

"I did, didn't I?" Buena said, and felt his chest inch wider with pride.

Beneath the cover of night Lou teaches Buena Vista, and will do the same for the children they produce together, with the hope that their children will be able to do the same for theirs—but in the light of day.

A piece of the newspaper found itself wrapped around the hitching post. Buena had just meant to retrieve it, crumple it in his hands, and deposit it into the trash bin. But he found himself staring at the words, surprised at himself when he recognized at least a dozen of them and then even more astonished when he found his lips moving, sounding out each letter, piecing words and then whole sentences together.

It had happened; he had crossed the line that separated him from his master. The excitement filled him; he could feel every vein in his body begin to bulge with it.

A dam broke loose inside of him and knowledge washed through him. He shuddered. He thought he knew what power felt like. But what he experienced on that day did not compare to felling a pine or wrangling a steer.

This strength that surged through him did not radiate from his hands, but pounded in his mind.

Albuquerque, New Mexico

The first few lines she speak I miss, 'cause my mind is drifting, but no sooner than I know it, I'm all caught up in the story again.

I see the fields and Lou's face, and I smell Buena and he smells like fresh-plowed earth. I feel them inside of me, even though they both dead and buried deep in the ground.

No marker, no mound of dirt.

As soon as I'm all dug in, her cell phone ring and I'm back again.

She look at the name, press the button, say, Hello, yes, uh-huh, New Mexico, me too, okay, bye.

She press the button, look over at me, and ask, How you like it so far?

Was that Madeline? I ask.

She just make a face that say, Now you know that wasn't no Madeline. Then she say, No. So what about the story so far?

A friend of yours, then?

She smirk, lean back in the chair, and blow air through her lips. She say, Yes, Dumpling, it was a friend of mine.

Boyfriend?

Sherry just watch me.

Well? I say.

I guess I'm talking too loud, 'cause people turn and stare.

Sherry ain't even fazed by it; she look bored, point to the book, and say again, How you like it so far?

I just shrug my shoulders.

Sherry smirk again, throw some money on the table, and jump up out of her seat.

I guess it's time to go.

The slaves try not to stare, try to go about their business, but April is a sight to behold. Busting out of her wedding gown, every which a-way, so big now she walks with a cane.

Twenty-five years old, an old maid, all of the other girls her age have been married for eight years or more, with families of their own.

"Massa had to go as far as Washington County to finds a husband for her," the slaves whisper.

"Who all would want her anyhow? She as fat as a cow and mean as a witch's tit."

The slaves snicker amongst themselves.

"I hear he ailing, ain't got much breath left in his body."

"Massa knows that, figurin' he gonna get hold of the land the husband drop dead and leave behind."

"He ain't got no kin?"

"Son died of the malaria some time back."

"Really?"

"Oh yeah. Down in Florida."

"So he ain't got no kin to leave it to. It just gonna go to his wife, and so that mean it just gonna go to Massa."

"He a slick old dog."

April wobbles down the steps, her mother trying desperately to snatch corn bread from her pudgy hands.

"You getting crumbs all over your dress. You just had breakfast, for God's sake, April!"

"Ah, leave her be, Verna. This here is her day." Henry beams as he climbs into the wagon. "Sara, Jenny," he calls, and two women appear from their watching places behind the shed.

They pop out quickly, exchanging guilty glances before approaching, heads bent, eyes sweeping the floor.

"All y'all hands clean?" Henry asks.

They look at their nutmeg-colored palms. "Yassir."

"C'mon on, then, and help me hoist Miss April up in this here wagon."

Sara and Jenny exchange looks. They are only twelve and fourteen and reed thin.

"You sure do look pretty, Miss April," Sara says, and takes her place to the right of April. "Sure 'nuff," Jenny agrees, and takes her place to the left.

"All y'all ready?" Henry calls down from the wagon.

"Ready," Sara and Jenny answer uncertainly.

"Ready, baby?" Henry whispers down into his daughter's moonlike face.

April's mouth is still working at the corn bread, and so she just nods her head.

Henry grabs hold of April's arms, and all of the watching faces suck in their breath as Jenny and Sara move to a crouching position and wait for the go-ahead.

"Heave!" Henry yells, and Jenny and Sara straighten their legs, bringing the tops of their shoulders deep beneath April's armpits, pushing themselves up until they are on their tiptoes. Their hands try to find anchor somewhere on April, but it's futile—their fingers slide off the silk of the dress.

"Ho!" Henry yells, and pulls with all of his might, which is not much. April rises less than an inch off the ground.

It goes on like that for at least twenty minutes. It goes on like that until Jenny drops down and Sara's eyes are tearing up from the pain that's ripping through her back.

Henry snatches his hat off in frustration, slapping it against his thigh as he bawls, "Dammit, dammit, dammit!"

"Can I have another piece of corn bread, Daddy?" April asks, more concerned about her stomach than getting to her wedding on time.

"Sure, baby," Henry answers absentmindedly as he looks desperately around for some other means of getting her up into the wagon.

"No, you cannot!" Verna yells. "Next time you eat, you'll be a married woman!"

Jenny hides a chuckle in the palm of her hand, and even Sara's tearful face registers some amusement.

"Buena, Joe!" Henry calls out. "Y'all gonna have to help me hoist April up into this here wagon."

Verna's face ices over and then shatters. "Have you taken leave of all of your senses?"

"What?" Henry's face is a mess of befuddlement.

Verna looks at the approaching men and takes a step closer to her husband, dropping her voice an octave and hissing, "I will not have no nigger men handling my daughter."

Henry looks at his wife, his daughter, and the men standing a respectful distance away awaiting further instructions.

"Well, how else we gonna get her up in this wagon?" Henry's voice is full of defeat. He tugs at his hair, then balls his right hand into a fist and shakes it in his wife's face. "How else, Verna?"

Verna folds her arms across her breasts and huffs. "You just find some other sort of way," she says, moving off to the shade of a peach tree.

Suddenly, Henry turns and grabs hold of the reins. "Hiya!" he yells.

"What the hell?" Verna's jaw drops as she watches the wagon start to move off. "What are you doing, Henry?" she screams.

"Where's Papa going?" April asks as she waves at the swirling dust the wagon wheels have kicked up.

"To hell, I hope," Verna mumbles beneath her breath.

"Where?"

"Hennnnnnnnnnrrrrrrrrrrrrrrrrry!" Verna cups her hands around her mouth and screams as she rushes out into the clearing.

"Is he coming back, Mama?"

"Shut up," Verna says, and storms toward the house and straight to the bottle of brandy.

* * *

An hour later, Henry was pulling back onto the property, the minister sitting alongside him, Bible pressed against his chest, face stiff, and lips pinched so tightly that they appeared bone white.

Three other wagons followed, filled with wedding guests who did practically nothing to hide their irritation.

The groom came on horseback, his old tired face long and void of expression.

"We gonna have the wedding right here," Henry said as he climbed down from the wagon.

Verna approached. She tried to give her best and brightest smile, but it came across crooked and uneven from the three glasses of brandy she'd consumed. "Welcome, welcome," she slurred.

"Please go in, into the parlor. Let's get out from under this wicked sun," she said. "Mary, get these fine people something cool to drink."

The guests murmured and moved toward the house.

"Well, this is all good and fine, Henry, but they ain't gonna live here now, are they?" Verna seethed between clenched teeth as she linked her arm with Henry's and followed the guests toward the house. "Either way, she gotta get in that damn wagon."

"Yeah, well, by then she'll be her husband's problem." Henry coughed. "Where is she anyway?"

"Knee deep in buttermilk, I suppose."

Albuquerque, New Mexico

When we get back to the hotel I begin to feel bad about how I acted at breakfast, so while Sherry in the bathroom I pick up the book, read the words again. My lips begin to tremble and before I know it, I'm laughing so hard I think I'm going to wet myself.

I throw the book down on the bed and hold my sides to keep them from splitting. Sherry come out of the bathroom, her face confused. Then, not confused, she start laughing too and say, Oh, you think that was funny?

Sure 'nuff you got some 'magination, I say, and wipe at the tears.

Grin is all Buena Vista can do when he sees his wife wobbling along, belly low and blooming larger with every day. Grin is all he can do, because this baby won't be sold away like the others he'd watched over even before their mothers pushed them out and into the world.

This here baby, he thinks, will call him Papa and stretch small fingers out to him. This one, he'll walk and talk and run and play with.

"Won't be long now," Mary says when she catches him staring and smiling.

"I hope not." Buena Vista laughs.

They have at least a dozen names: Perry, Vance . . . "I heard once that my father's name was Mingo," he tells her.

Lou smiles. "That's an Indian name."

"Sure 'nuff?" Buena Vista muses on this information. "So's I got some Indian in me too, then?"

"Seems so."

Buena strokes her hair. "If it's a boy, we can call him Mingo, or maybe Yona after your pappy."

"Maybe," Lou says sadly, and looks out across the fields.

"You go on outside and wait!" Nellie shouts at him as she rushes past him with the tin bowl filled with steaming water. "This ain't no place for a man to be."

Buena looks down at his hands again and then at the feet that just won't listen. He wants to leave, but Lou's moaning and wailing keep him welded to the spot as the women move furiously around him.

Lanterns burning everywhere, the smell of the oil making him nauseated, and Lou, screaming now, and the men pushing open the door, beckoning him, "C'mon now, Buena, let them take care of it."

Buena ignores them.

"Get him outta here!" Mary bellows when she turns to wring out a blood-soaked rag and catches sight of him standing and staring.

The door slams shut and Lou's screams become muted.

An hour, two, five, and Buena remains.

"Gave us a hell of a time," Nellie says, eyes weary, head rag askew. "You been here all this time?" In the darkness she almost bumps into him.

"Yes." Buena's voice is even.

Nellie considers him. "On your feet, all this time?"

"Yes," Buena responds, looking over her shoulder.

"Humph," she says, and pats him on his back as she moves past him. "Go on in, they waiting."

Buena hesitates and his eyes find Nellie's in the darkness.

She can feel his apprehension, even though the murky shadows mask his expression. "It's yours, don't you worry none," she says, and reaches to lay a comforting hand on his shoulder. "Go on, now. Don't you keep them girls of yours waiting."

Buena's feet listen now, but it seems to take him ages to get to the doorway. He slowly pushes the door open and sees

Mary, slumped over and snoring in the chair beside the bed he built for Lou.

And there is his wife, propped up and smiling down into a bundle of squirming limbs.

Their eyes meet and Lou brings up her hand and weakly beckons him with her fingers. He moves as if on a cloud and is suddenly at her side, looking down into the most beautiful face he has ever seen in his life.

His heart galloped inside of his chest and then exploded and flooded his being with an emotion he'd never experienced. His legs threatened to buckle and he was suddenly lightheaded—everything in him seemed to be coming undone.

"This is what it's all about, isn't it, Lou?" he choked out beneath the flood of tears as he reached for his newborn daughter.

"Yes, yes," Lou said, weeping with him.

Buena took the tiny baby and pressed her face against his cheek. He had thought he knew love. He thought that Lou was all the love he'd ever wanted, and then when he finally got her he thought that she would be all the love he would ever need.

But right then . . . he knew right then that this wasn't the case at all. There was room left for more, so much more.

He cradled his daughter in his arms and realized that as full of love as he thought he was, this little one suddenly let it be known that he had been missing out and, clutching her to him like he did, something in him told him he could never be without it again.

"We gonna take your name back, Lou," he croaked. "We gonna take your name back and give it to her."

Lou nodded in agreement.

Buena looked into the baby's face and whispered, "Your name is Nayeli."

Amarillo, Texas

We pulled out of New Mexico at noon, hit Amarillo, Texas 'round five. Sherry say, We'll stop for some gas. You hungry, Dumpling?

No, I say, and am surprised.

Sherry laugh, point to my stomach, and say, Them pancakes still laying on your gut; you better watch it.

I look down, poke my belly with my finger, then use that same finger and point at her stomach and say, You better start doing the same.

Sherry kind of blushes. Just bloated, I guess, she say, and pull at her T-shirt.

I guess, I say.

I'm going to go to the bathroom. You need to go?

Nah, I'll just sit here and watch the attendant pump the gas.

As soon as she come back, the phone start to ring, she look at it, toss it back down, and start the ignition.

Madeline? I ask.

Who else?

Ain't you gonna answer it? Something could be wrong.

Other than her being crazy?

We laugh together, and it sound like sweet music, like instruments meant to be played together. She hear it too, and she look surprised.

Let me answer it, I say when the ringing start up again.

Go ahead, but I don't want to talk to her.

I pick up, say hello, hear Madeline screeching on the other end. I can't get a word in, try over and over again, my head beginning to hurt. Finally, I push the phone back to Sherry, and she shake her head at it and whisper, I told you I didn't want to talk to her.

But I don't move the phone. I keep it in her face until she take it.

Sherry take a breath and say, Hello. Fine. Yes. No. And then her voice tightens and her face kind of turns to stone. I did not, she starts, and grabs hold of her hair and tugs real hard. I just look. No I didn't, she sings in that voice that reminds me of when she was small and still ate meat.

She twirls her index finger by her temple and then pretends to strangle herself. Her eyes roll up into her head and her tongue dangles out of the corner of her mouth, then she say real loud, Okay, Madeline, bye!

What she accusing you of this time? I ask.

She said that I knew all along that I was going to take this cross-country trip and had I given her notice, she could have sent her husband and the kids on the plane and she could have come along too—to bond.

Bond?

Yes.

Is that what we're doing? I laugh.

Sherry laughs too.

Route 40

Sherry say we got to make up some time, should have been on the road straight after breakfast instead of right at lunchtime. So we pick up some food and eat in the car while she do eighty down the highway.

She handle this SUV like a man, I think. Sherry a driver like her daddy. Madeline can't do more than fifteen minutes before she start complaining about the people on the road, the way her legs feel, how tired she is, just everything!

The more I think about it, the better I feel about Madeline not coming. She would have just whined and complained the whole time and Sherry might have killed her.

The sun starting to dip, starting to change from yellow to orange right before my eyes. The road feel like a rocking chair. I try to keep my eyes open but can't, see the first signs of night slipping across the sky. My eyes flutter and I fall asleep.

I dream I'm on a rowboat, stretched out on my back, my eyes in love with the sky above me. I hear Lou's voice calling to me, I feel the water lapping over the side of the boat, it falls on my face, my arms, and I laugh 'cause I don't even feel afraid being out in that big blue sea all by myself.

I sit up and stare over the side of the boat, and there are a million fish swimming alongside it, a million fish in all the colors of the rainbow! Jesus mercy! What a sight!

One fish jump in, then another and another, until I'm up to my knees in squirming fish. I still ain't scared, trying my best to toss them out as fast as they jump in, but they too quick for me and too heavy for the boat and the boat begins to tilt . . .

My eyes fly open and I pop right up in the seat.

What happen?

The car is half on the road and half off, dirt settling around us, and Sherry's eyes wide, both hands gripping the steering wheel, knuckles white.

My heart beating in my chest. What happen? I say again.

She can't even speak, just keep gripping the steering wheel tighter and shaking her head in disbelief.

The night is heavy; can't see nothing beyond the reach of the headlights. You doze off?

Sherry don't respond.

See something in the road?

Sherry just stare and then she throw the car in park, jump out, and puke.

After she done, she climb back in her seat, wipe her mouth with the back of her hand, wipe the tears from her eyes, and clear her throat like she going to make a speech, but don't say nothing.

You okay?

She nod her head yes.

We can sleep right here, you know, I say. Just pull a little more off the road.

Her eyes fill up with water again.

It's okay, we all right, just a little shook up, I say, and pat her hand.

Her flesh feel good beneath mine; feel strange, though. I don't know when last I touched my middle child. I stop patting and start rubbing. Stop rubbing and just let my hand rest on hers. She don't push it off; I guess it feel good to both of us.

No, no, we can't stay here. I'm okay. We're just a few miles away from a motel.

You sure, now? I say.

She nods her head and jerk the SUV back onto the highway.

You better believe my eyes don't close again until I'm laid out flat on my back in a bed.

Oklahoma City, Oklahoma

The Westin Hotel.

A man in uniform greets us when we pull up. He young, good-looking, smiling. I nudge Sherry in her side, say, He a looker, ain't he?

Sherry look at him, shrug her shoulders, hand him the key to the SUV. He give her a ticket, then snap his fingers and another nice young man come a-runnin'. He say, Evenin', ladies. Welcome. And then he remove our bags.

How long are you going to be with us? he asks, looking at me.

Well, I ain't the one running things, so I tilt my head toward Sherry.

Just one night, she say, and I let out a sigh so heavy Sherry spin around and look at me. What? she say

My legs swelling, they old like me, you forgot?

Sherry look down at my legs.

I say, Can't we stay here a spell? More than overnight, maybe?

Sherry a woman always wanna be on time. I guess she pride herself in never having kept someone waiting. She look at me and then down at her wristwatch and then up at the sky.

Well, she say, and bite down on her lip, I guess we can spend two nights here, but make sure this the place you wanna stay, because this ain't gonna happen a second time.

The man say, Wonderful! Glad to have you and your sister with us!

I blush and say, She my daughter!

Sherry just roll her eyes.

A pulled-pork sandwich for me, salad and salmon for Sherry, and then we both out like lights. No fountain, chanting, or meditating—just sleep!

I stop myself from singing out, "Ooooooklaaaaaaahoma!" in the morning when I wake up.

Glad to be alive for one, happy that I'm sleeping on something called a featherbed, thrilled that we in a part of Oklahoma City called Bricktown that beat like my heart.

I ease out of my bed and move to the window, which is really a terrace. I slide the door open and step outside and inhale the Oklahoma air. It's fresh, sharp, and wet. There's a canal right off the street; I ain't never in my life seen such a thing. Taxis that run on water! Have you ever?

Sherry say it remind her of Venice.

I say, Where's that?

Italy.

You been there?

Yes.

I feel bad that I can't remember everywhere she's been. She don't say nothing 'bout me not remembering, but I think inside she saying what she said before: I was hearing but not listening.

Folks seem nice. They speak to you when you walk down the streets. Say "Evenin'" and "Noon" and all. Reminds me of Sandersville somewhat, 'cept the square bigger than the one I remember, and of course we ain't never had none of the fancy shops they got here. No outdoor cafés and such. Maybe they got 'em now, but not when I was living there.

Sherry and I stroll the streets, pop in and out of shops. I buy the grand-kids some T-shirts, a magnet for Madeline's fridge, a baseball cap for Sonny Boy.

Let's stop at this café, she say. Rest our feet, take a load off and have some iced tea, something to eat?

Sure, I say, and plop down in the chair

This nice. Small round wrought-iron tables. Little vase with white flow-ers. Market umbrellas to keep the sun off, cool breeze coming off the canal. Nice.

A young woman comes toward us.

She smiling, give us two menus, set a pitcher of water down, asks if we need something to drink besides water while we look at the menu.

I say I'd like some sweet tea. Me too, Sherry say, but without the sweet.

The woman just look at her and then say, Pardon me?

Just iced tea, no sugar. Just a wedge of lime, if you have it.

Lemon'll do you? the woman say.

Sure, Sherry say, and pull her shades down from her head and over her eyes.

What about your organic tea? I say, and snicker.

Sherry cock one eyebrow. Well, just this once won't hurt, she say.

I'm sippin' away when the phone call come. Sherry pull out her cell-u-lar and smile down at the numbers,

Who's that? I ask.

The smile gone as quick as it came.

Wrong number, she say, and drop the phone into her backpack.

You ain't gonna answer it?

She don't even shake her head no, just look out across the square at the people who walk by.

Madeline call next.

It's to the point that Sherry don't even say hello, she just hit the Answer button and pass the phone to me.

It's not that she don't want to talk to you, I say, but she busy right now . . .

Oh, we just fine. Making a lot of headway, seen a lot of things. We here in Oklahoma now, sitting out having some sweet tea, looking at the canal.

Uh-huh, canal, like the one they got in Venice . . .

What I know 'bout Venice? A few things. I laugh and wink at Sherry.

How the kids? Your husband? Have you heard from Sonny Boy? No? Oh, me neither . . .

No, I ain't worried about what he doing. He a grown man, why you always trying to mother everybody in the world? You got three kids of your own to mother, I say, and then suddenly the conversation is over.

She'll call back before our food is even cooked, I tell Sherry.

Sherry nod, lean back in her chair, and then lean forward again and say, Tell me some more.

Two months. Just as Lou was getting the baby to take her nipple without a fuss.

Just as she was getting used to saying her name and not crying behind the memories it evoked. Nayeli.

Comfortable with Nayeli sleeping between Buena and herself. Liking the feel of squirming fingers in her mouth, the taste of them, sweet like muskmelon. Getting used to that new laugh Buena had—a soft chuckle, like an old man.

Secure and confident in sunup and sundown and everything that fell between, but not at all prepared for Henry Vicey stepping through the door, sheepish grin in place, a flick of the hand sending the other slaves shuffling outside. Except Buena. He jumps up, grins, says, "Afternoon, Massa."

Henry ignores him, walks right past him and straight to Lou.

"How you doing there, Lou?" he says, heavy boots walking across the floor, tiny cabin shaking, cold chill where hot air had been hanging.

"Fine," Lou says, and moves the baby from one arm to the other. She wants him to see her, see that she ain't his.

Two other men come in, heavy boots; dirty, caked mud falls off their heels as they step in.

"How do," Buena says, voice uneven and then surprised when he recognizes one of the faces. "Mr. Oswald?" Face breaking into pieces of confusion, throat bulging with questions he ain't allowed to ask.

"Buena," Oswald says without looking at him. The other man eye him, though, sums him up slowly, deliberately.

"She sure is a fine baby," Henry says, stepping a little closer, making sure he can't see any of himself in the child Lou holds.

"Yassa, thank you."

"Uhm," Henry moans, looking over his shoulder at Oswald

and the stranger before looking back at Lou and asking, "Can I hold her?"

Lou can't see Buena, can't find his eyes to know if this is right or even real. "Sir?" She feigns hard of hearing.

Henry took a breath and reached out to Lou. "Hand her over, Lou," he said, and his face went red.

"Massa . . . Mr. Oswald, sir, what's going on here?" Buena's voice was full of fear now, so full that it lapped against the walls like water.

The stranger pushed his jacket aside and turned to Buena so that he could see quite clearly the leather and the gun it held.

"Give her here, Lou," Henry said again, and then his hands were on the baby tugging her from Lou's gripping fingers. Lou never said no, not out loud, but her head shook back and forth as she tried to hang on to Nayeli—it shook back and forth until the baby cried out in pain and Lou let go.

"Massa, what you think you doing?" Buena screamed. Then a stool tumbled over and the tiny shack shook so hard Lou thought the walls would fall in on them, and there was the sound of the stranger's gun being cocked and Oswald saying, "This here completes your sale, Buena." Then they all turned and walked out.

Buena hollered, right there on the floor where the stranger had knocked him down and brandished a gun in his face. He curled himself into a ball and screamed like they were pulling Nayeli out of him instead of just carrying her away from him.

Lou just sat there staring down at her empty hands. She had nothing left to let go of.

She'd left quite a bit of herself in the valley, and another chunk on the floor in the pantry, and now the rest of her was gurgling and squirming in the arms of a white man.

She had nothing to let go of, but something new to hold on to.

The "*This*"—Oswald had spoken.

"This?"

Inanimate, without life, no mother, no father—wood, maybe, a stone, a cow chip. Those things were a *this*, a *that*, and an *it*. Not her daughter, not her sweet Nayeli.

She closed her empty hands, and a hollow laugh escaped her. Lou foolishly thought that the first cut was the deepest, the most damaging—losing her parents, her brothers—but this, her child ripped from her as she suckled . . .

Lou knew then the first cut is *not* the deepest; it's just a sample of the deeper ones yet to come.

Buena is not the same.

He withers into something that is bent and shuffling with eyes that hardly ever reach for the sky.

Nothing can ever be the same again, not even their love for each other.

Lou says nothing, but her eyes accuse him. *Maybe if her name was different. Maybe if you'd never come on that wagon and caught sight of me. Maybe if we both were never born.*

She says nothing, but her body pulls back when he climbs on top of her and presses his flesh against hers. It pulls back but something stick and, less than a year later, Lou is standing in the slow flow of the stream at the point where it is the clearest, where the sun seems to swim, and thinking for the umpteenth time about killing herself and her twin boys.

One strapped to her back, the other cradled in her arms. Identical twins dug in deep after the tears dried up and her body began to yield to his again and they were all the other had left to cling to.

A mother again, Lou watches the road for wagons, though Henry had assured her, "You don't have to worry; nobody taking these two from you. They yours and here to stay."

They weren't hers and she knew they weren't here to stay. They could be gone with a blink of an eye.

Lou had to protect herself against the next cut and so she

looked on her sons as the white people did. Thinking of Jeff and Jim as *this* and *that*, as chattel; it was less painful that way.

That was June, and by late autumn April is back home, mourning the death of her husband and feeding her misery with cakes and pies.

Nothing much different from what she did before she was gone; she's just wearing black now.

Henry is so happy, he's bursting. A hundred acres of land has just fallen in his lap. A house, three slaves. He can hardly contain himself, and heads off to town and the local saloon to blow smoke and talk loud about all he has. But unbeknownst to him, twenty-five acres and two slaves will soon disappear when Charlie Lessing turns his cards over to reveal three aces.

By the time Jeff and Jim are two years old, Lou and Buena realize that as identical as they are, they are more like night and day than mirror images.

Jeff was the first to walk, to run, to talk, while Jim crawled until he was almost twenty months old, and didn't cut a tooth until his second birthday. Talking was a chore for him and so he pointed his way through questions and answers while his eyes remained vacant and muddied.

His debt mounting, Henry Vicey had mortgaged all of the land and most of the chattel, leaving just four adult slaves and the twins.

April was bedridden, ulcers eating through her legs, and soon bedsores covered her back and buttocks because Verna still would not allow a strong black male hand to touch her daughter, not even to turn her. Meanwhile, all of the women together couldn't even budge her, so she remained on her back, like a beached whale.

"I tell you what: I'll take it all off of your hands and let you remain on."

"*Remain on?*" Henry tried to focus his bleary eyes on Charlie Lessing, a tall, broad-shouldered man with piercing green eyes and thin blond hair.

"Whatya mean, *remain on?*" He slurred as he lifted the shot glass of whiskey to his lips.

"I mean, I'll pay off all of your debts and let you stay on the land and in your house."

"Whaaaaat?" The whiskey burned his throat, and his tongue quivered.

"Sharecropper," Charlie said, and tilted the whiskey bottle for the umpteenth time.

Henry straightened his back and slapped the bottle from

Charlie's grasp. The other men in the saloon abruptly stopped their conversations and turned their attention to the two men who had been huddled at the corner table for most of the night.

Henry leapt from his chair, sending it tumbling noisily to the floor. "No Vicey man has ever sharecropped no land. We's owners. We's kings!" he bellowed, and slapped at his chest.

Charlie just smirked, reached into the breast pocket of his jacket, pulled out a silver coin, and tossed it to the barmaid who was quickly clearing away the broken pieces of glass.

Henry stood swaying and patting the empty pockets of his pants.

Charlie called for another bottle of whiskey as he stood and righted Henry's chair. "Sit down, Henry," he said before taking his own seat again.

Henry plopped down into the chair.

"I'm offering you a way to save your family's land"—Charlie lifted his shot glass and drained it—"and your name." He belched and then slowly relit the snubbed black nose of his cigar. He puffed until the tobacco glowed orange. "You can work the land and buy it back from me, acre by acre," he said, leaning forward.

Henry said nothing. His eyes were on the young mulatto girl who was curled up in the lap of a man who reminded Henry of who he had been before that day.

Strong, confident, a ladies' man. He shook his head in remembrance.

Charlie followed Henry's eyes across the room. "She is something, ain't she?"

Henry nodded.

"Go on, Henry. It'll be on me. Sometimes it takes the arms of a woman to make a man think straight."

Henry licked his lips.

"Go on," Charlie urged.

Henry was supposed to drive them.

Henry was no longer "Massa" now, just a piece of poor white trash. Common labor. A sharecropper. An overseer.

He was supposed to drive them, but he spent most of his time drinking in the back of his wagon or underneath the shade of a tree. When his bottle was empty he'd try to bury his misery between his wife's breasts, but she had stopped allowing him into her bed. So now he took his misery and the few coins he had, and found some whore to lay on top of.

Charlie Lessing was "Massa" now and had a hundred men come in and clear the land three hundred feet behind the Vicey home.

He would build a mansion—a grand home that would match the one he owned in Myanmar, where he lived with his wife Anne Marie and their children. This house, though, would house his mistress, Delia Hampton—a fiery buxom vixen with a forked tongue, wild black hair, and jagged sapphires for eyes.

The house was completed in a year. Lessing had men working night and day. The constant banging, sawing, and raucous behavior of the men frayed Verna's nerves. She couldn't sleep at night, and during the day all she could do was stand and watch that magnificent structure bloat and rise up into the sky, casting a mocking shadow over her scant saltbox of a home. It was more than Verna could stand.

She hated Lessing and his house, she thought as she turned away from the window and her eyes fell on her husband who was sitting half-dazed and still caught in the vestiges of the previous night's drunken stupor.

Their eyes met and Henry muttered, "What?"

Verna just scowled at him and stormed out of the room.

Yes, Verna hated Lessing with all his money and smart business sense, but she hated her husband more.

* * *

"I don't want to go."

"But Verna, what will we look like if we don't attend?"

"What will it look like if we do? *Fools!*"

Henry stood in front of the mirror wrestling with his tie. "Well, we're going and that's that."

It was all Verna could do to control her anger when she and Henry arrived for the grand unveiling party Charlie was having for the mansion.

Double wraparound porches, main hall with marble floors and oak moldings . . .

"This banister is carved from a two-hundred-year-old African mahogany tree," Charlie pointed out to his guests.

The insistent "oohing" and "aahing" was more than Verna thought she could take, and so she pressed her kerchief against her mouth to keep from screaming.

There was a humongous crystal chandelier hanging from the ceiling in the entry hall as well as in the parlor, the library, the drawing room, and the dining room.

"Twenty slaves to staff the house," someone whispered.

"Twenty-three, to be exact," Charlie laughed as he led his guests up the curvaceous staircase and to the first of six bedrooms.

By the time Verna saw the third bathroom, she was dizzy.

"It takes twenty buckets of water to fill this tub," Charlie said proudly as he glided his hand across the rim of the copper tub.

"Oh my. That's a lot of boiling to do," someone said.

"Yes, I suppose. But we have two cast-iron stoves."

A sigh of surprise.

Finger sandwiches. Wine. A violinist and pianist. Verna swore if she heard the statements "*How lovely*," "*How beautiful*," or "*Simply magnificent*" ever again, she would kill herself.

The shame was complete. Verna was the wife of a nobody. How would she ever live down the disgrace? Where would she go?

Her parents had been dead for years. Her mind whirled as they made their way home.

"Verna?" Henry's voice squeaked when the wagon came to a stop and she leapt off. "Verna?" Henry called to her again, but she just kept walking.

"Bastard," she whispered under her breath as her hands grabbed hold of the door handle. The screen slammed back on its rusty hinges, shuddered, and then fell to the ground.

I will not live like this, Verna thought to herself as she paced in circles around her bedroom. The laughter from the party members sailed down off the hill and settled into the space around her. It bellowed in her mind and she imagined that they were all laughing at her.

She caught sight of herself in the mirror. When did her face become so lined? She stepped closer. Her skin looked like parchment paper. When did her hair start to turn gray?

And then she heard it, like a blowing horn in the corner of her mind: "Oh, isn't this house just amazing!"

It wasn't the word *lovely*, *beautiful*, or *magnificent*—none she promised herself to take her life on—but *amazing* was close enough, and she knew for as long as she remained in that house, on that land, she would never stop hearing those declarations. And so she went to the closet and pulled out the only rifle her husband still owned, checked the chamber for bullets, and then walked slowly to her daughter's room.

"Mother, is it as wonderful as everyone is saying it is?" April asked enthusiastically, lifting her heavy head as far up as her thick neck would allow.

"Yes it is, darling. It is." And with that, Verna raised the shotgun and blew her daughter's bright eyes right out of her head.

Route 40

*Bricktown was nice, sorry to leave it. Sherry say, Maybe we can stay again,
on the way back.*

*Sure, sounds good to me. I ain't got no job, no small children, no place
to go but home. What about you, ain't you got something and somebody to
get back to?*

*Sherry let out a heavy sigh, fiddle with the radio knob, and stare out at
the car in front of us.*

I watch her from the corner of my eye.

Ain't you got a boyfriend?

Sherry's body flinch a bit, she say, We going back down this road again?

A girlfriend, then? I say, and prepare myself for the worst.

*Sherry turn her head a bit toward me and say, I got plenty of girlfriends.
You know what I mean.*

No, I don't.

I think, Why it always got to be a fight, then I say out loud, You gay?

*A noise come out her mouth that sound like a laugh and a cough all
mixed up together, and then she say, Hell no!*

I feel a little relief.

But there is somebody, right?

Uh-huh, she say, and a little smile dance across her lips.

I seen that smile before, feel despair come over me, say, He white?

*Sherry face go dark, she shake her head no, grip the steering wheel tighter,
and say, Get the book from the backseat and read what I wrote last night.*

I watch her. He's black, then?

Can you please just read?

*She annoyed now. Shit, I'm annoyed too, and reach back and snatch
the book from the seat and begin flipping the pages hard so she knows that*

I'm annoyed. I huff, stare at the words, and then start moving them across my mind.

When I'm done I'm breathless. I don't know what to say. I close the book and clutch my heart and then my head and check to see if there's a hole between my own eyes. Because it's lit up there, on fire. I look for blood on my hands.

You okay, Dumpling? she asks, and I say, She killed her baby and herself. I didn't think she would do it.

Well she did, Sherry say, and switches lanes.

She did it 'cause you wrote it that way, I say, even though something inside of me believes that she really did.

I say, This is getting too serious. I don't know if I can take any more. Maybe we should stop.

Sherry turn her head and give me a hard look. We'll stop when we get to the end, she say, and I wonder, What end? And then I think, Whose end?

Naples ran screaming from the house, her crude braids stiff and at attention atop her head as she tore down the front steps, frantically waving her bright blue head-scarf in the air.

"Lawd, Lawd, Lawd!" she cried, streaking past a startled Henry who was still seated, openmouthed atop the wagon.

Henry couldn't seem to move; he just sat gaping at the house, so Buena Vista went inside to investigate, and when he came out, bloody footprints followed him down the steps and into the dirt clearing where the slaves huddled together waiting.

"They dead. Both of them," he said, looking up at Henry.

Henry's face went slack and then his eye moved slowly over the land his family had owned for generations before him. His lips trembled, but no one could hear a word of what he mumbled.

"Mr. Vicey?" Buena Vista took a few steps closer.

Henry's eyes slowly found him; they were ringed red and puffed. His bottom lip sagged now, and a slow tic climbed up the right side of his face.

Buena Vista continued, "Missus and the daughter are dead."

Henry said nothing, just snapped the horse reins and cried, "Hi-ya!"

They watched as the wagon rolled out and into the night.

Come sunup, the horses had returned—Buena found them grazing around the porch and gathered them and put them in the stable.

Days later the wagon was found abandoned near Swallow Lake, miles away from Sandersville. They supposed Henry had either drowned himself or jumped a barge headed out to sea and back to Mother England to reclaim his rights to a long-vacant throne.

They were Lessing's now. The lot of them.

Two hundred and twenty-six slaves between his two plantations, ten horses, and more than five hundred acres of land.

Charlie Lessing would not be the owner Henry Vicey had been. The whip that had remained coiled just inside the door of the barn would be joined by four more, and the tan leather of those whips would soon turn black with blood and skin.

Charlie Lessing liked to consider himself a gentleman's gentleman, but he did enjoy shoving his bare hands into the rich soil of his land. He found great pleasure in biting into the lush peaches that grew on it; he adored the rows and rows of cotton that seem to stretch endlessly—but his real guilty pleasure was sparring with the young slave boys.

More than a decade passes and Lou manages to avoid the whip. Buena and some of the others are not as lucky. Sometimes they speak too loudly or move too slow. Other times the gunnysacks come in too light or too full of unusable buds—whatever is wrong, Malroy the new slave driver and his whip are always there to punish it.

Since the twins came, Buena has found his spine again; he walks erect and talks loud, his eyes spit fire, and his lips are always drawn back across his teeth. Sometimes he listens, most times he doesn't.

"Wild," Lessing says, and signals Malroy to bring the whip across Buena's back again.

He won't cry out, no matter how many times that whip cuts across his back. Not a tear falls, and the fire does not go out in his eyes but burns brighter, and Malroy swears Buena's eyeteeth are pointed and curled like a mongrel's.

Lessing breathes and with a nod of his head the whip cracks skin again.

"I think he fi'n to bolt," Malroy confides in Lessing.

"Is that what you think, Malroy?" Lessing laughs smugly and brushes a speck of brown from the white cuff of his shirt. "Personally, I think he's contemplating murder."

There seems to be no breaking Buena Vista. The hate is dug in deep. Not even the joy he gets watching his sons romp and play or Lou's giving ways at night can pull him back from it.

Not even when she takes his hand and presses it against her stomach and says, "Two months gone and no blood."

So much hate pulsing through him that he can't get excited about the new life growing in Lou's belly. He looks at his sons and his wife and can't even remember what love feels like, what food tastes like. "Is water cool?" he asked Lou one day when her lips were still wet and glistening from the ladle of water handed to her in the field.

No sensation, no emotion, no taste—just the hate.

So Lessing sells him off. Cut-rate price. He's tired of dreaming about shadows rushing at him in the dark, black hands reaching for his throat.

Goodbyes are for white folks.

Hand-holding people crossing dew-drenched meadows. Stargazing people whom the years have bound together so tightly, the two become one. Gray-haired people with creased faces and shared memories.

Goodbyes are for white folks and not for slaves, so Lou watches from the field as Buena is hauled away in the back of a wagon.

"C'mere, boy," Malroy called to the thirteen-year-old Jim. He was long and lean like his twin, but slower in mind. Strong though, he could swing an ax better than a man twice his age, and seemed to find pleasure in cotton picking. Liked the cool waters of the stream, but had been whipped twice for frolicking in it during the hours he was supposed to be working. Smiled a lot and laughed out loud for no reason, held conversations with people no one but him could see. Slow.

Jim, who had been chopping wood, handed the ax off to one of the other boys, sauntered over to Malroy, and presented him with a wide grin.

"Massa Lessing say he want you today," Malroy said, his lips peeling back to reveal three empty spaces in his gums.

Jim looked over Malroy's shoulder and spotted Lessing striding toward them. Jim waved.

Malroy huffed in frustration. "Take off your shirt," he commanded.

Jim slowly removed his ragged shirt and dropped it to the ground. "All right now, get on in there," Malroy said, indicating the fenced-in space that Lessing liked to refer to as his "boxing pen."

"Malroy!" Lessing called from less than twenty feet away.

"Yessir!"

"You count how many licks I get in, ya hear?"

"Yessir!"

Lessing approached the fence and, instead of walking through the opening, he hoisted himself up and climbed over. He sized Jim up, took in his lanky arms and narrow waist. The boy looked near starving. Lessing could see the bones of his rib cage with almost perfect clarity.

"Okay, boy, put your dukes up," Lessing commanded as he raised his own fists and started churning them in Jim's face.

At first Jim just grinned and watched as Lessing made a slow circle around him.

"I said put your dukes up, boy!" Lessing yelled again.

Jim giggled and pointed at him.

Annoyed, Lessing dropped his fists and turned his attention to Malroy. "You didn't pick me a worthy opponent, Malroy!"

Malroy shook his head and started toward the pen. Halfway in, and almost as an afterthought, he turned to Lessing and asked, "May I, sir?"

"Yes, you may," Lessing responded with a little snicker. Malroy stepped forward and brought the coiled whip from behind him, pulled back his arm, and then threw it forward. The whip unfurled like a deadly tentacle, whistling as it cut through the air. Then came the awful snap as it split the top of Jim's right shoulder.

Jim stumbled, then collapsed to his knees, holding the bleeding, burning part of himself and screaming, "Mama, Mama, Mmmaaaaaaaaammaaaaaaaaaaaaaaa!"

"Massa say put your dukes up. Now, get up and do it!" Malroy bellowed.

Lou had to stop for a moment. Pregnant again and not due for another month, the relentless Georgia heat beating down on her and not even the memory of a breeze to cool her burning brow.

She looked around to see if anyone was nearby, but the others were a good hundred feet ahead of her. She looked behind her, and the rows of cotton bucked and swooned, so she slipped her sack off her back and laid herself down onto the hot earth and dug back to a time she rarely allowed herself to visit: a moment in her life when she stood at the edge of the world and a blue sea rolled over her small feet and sprayed her young face cool.

"Lou."

Her name came, but her little-girl self did not drag her eyes from the ocean, because that is not what she was called in that place. Instead, the little-girl part of herself took a step forward and watched the water climb her calves and lap at her knees.

"Lou." More urgent now and someone shaking her shoulder. The dream burned away as Lou opened her eyes and looked into the yellowed ones of the slave woman called Vessa.

"You sick?" the young girl asked.

"Tired," Lou said as she struggled to her feet.

"Your boy getting ready to fight Massa," Vessa said out of the corner of her mouth as she quickly bent down and retrieved Lou's sack.

"My boy?" Lou felt her heart whip in her chest, and she grabbed hold of her belly and looked toward the place where the pen was. "Which one?"

"Jim."

It wasn't a run but a sort of awkward gallop that got her there just in time to see Malroy bring the whip down across Jim's left shoulder.

"Please!" Lou screamed as she lunged into the pen and threw herself between Malroy and a screaming Jim. "Please stop," she begged as she reached one hand behind her back to touch her son.

Jim's face was caked with dirt and tears. "Mama! Mama!" he cried and wrapped his shaking hands around her ankles.

"Ain't you supposed to be in the field?" Malroy asked.

"Please, please," is all Lou could find in herself to say.

Malroy shoved Lou out of the way, coiled the whip, and positioned it to strike again, when Lessing muttered, "Enough. These creatures are cowards." He kicked at the dirt. "Is there not one among you that will spar with me?" he cried, his hands up, palms facing heaven.

No one said a word.

There were plenty of men who would step into that pen, but Lessing did not want a man; he wanted a boy, because any one of those men could have beaten him blind and Charlie Lessing knew it.

He was the coward.

"I'll do it."

Jeff made his way through the crowd and set the heavy pails of water down at his feet. He was slightly wider in the back than Jim, an inch taller, and had all his senses. "I'll spar with you, Massa Lessing."

"You won't do no sucha thing!" Lou screamed, and reached out and snatched at his wet pants. Jeff walked past her like she wasn't even there.

Lessing considered the boy who came to stand less than a foot away from him. He really wasn't much different from the one who lay weeping in his mother's lap.

Lessing circled Jeff. "Uh-huh. Hmmmm," he said. "Well okay, then."

Lou helped Jim to his feet, and together they moved from the center of the pen to its perimeter.

"Put your hands up," Lessing instructed, and Jeff did.

Lessing began his dancing, kicking up dirt and boxing the air between them. Jeff narrowed his eyes and moved his hands up and in front of his face.

The first blow caught Jeff on his right cheek, sending him stumbling backward and into the fence. The second blow clipped his chin and hurled him to the ground.

Jeff knew that he was there to be a punching bag. That was an unspoken rule. But the third blow opened up something inside of him, and Jeff found himself punching back, catching Charlie Lessing squarely on the nose.

Lessing's eyes bulged with surprise as he stumbled sideways and then came to a halting stop, bringing his hand up to inspect his nose. Taking advantage of the opportunity, Jeff stepped in and laid another shattering blow to Lessing's cheek, then one squarely in his gut that sent the man tumbling to his knees, where he curled up into a shuddering ball of flesh.

The sun had blocked the first blow, and all Malroy caught of it was the sharp jerk of Charlie Lessing's head and then his hand as it rose to investigate. It wasn't until the second blow had been delivered that Malroy finally moved.

By the time Malroy drew back his arm, Jeff had landed the third punch that sent Lessing to his knees, spitting bright red blood all over his bare chest.

The whip missed Jeff by an inch and fell dead near his feet, where Jeff caught hold of it and began dragging Malroy toward him.

Lou knew that look in Jeff's eyes. It was the same one Buena had kept at a simmer inside of him, but here it was boiling over and out of Jeff.

Jim began to clap and cheer his brother on, and Lou turned and slapped him across his face, then pulled him to her and buried his weeping eyes into her bosom.

She watched Lessing slowly gather himself, using the fence to pull himself into a standing position, blood glistening on his lips, his eyes on fire, and his skin a pulsating red. She watched him straighten his back and curl his fingers into fists and knew that the next time she would be able to hold Jeff in her arms, it would be after they cut his swinging corpse down from a tree.

Route 40

I slam the notebook closed.

What's wrong?

I can't take any more. It sounds too real.

Well that's a good thing, she say. That's how a novel is supposed to sound. Real.

Ain't you got no heart?

Oh please, Dumpling, stop being so dramatic.

I want out of this SUV. I need to walk these visions out of my head. I look up and catch sight of a sign that says, LITTLE ROCK, 120 MILES.

I need to walk it off, walk off the worry I got for Jeff and Jim.

But ain't no place to walk right now. I look down at the red cover of the notebook, and then back at the road.

I hear Jeff calling to me from the pages. I hear Lou crying.

Turn on the radio, I tells her sudden and loud.

Sherry give me a strange look and then press the button that make the music come out.

I lean back, try to let Diane Reeves's voice sing over the wailing and whispers going on inside of my head, but Diane lose out, and I shake my head and say, Okay, okay.

What, Dumpling?

Nothing. Turn off that damn radio, I say, and flip the book open again.

Charlie Lessing licked the blood from his lips and spat it into the ground as he watched Malroy get the better of Jeff, catching him by his throat and squeezing so hard that Lou felt her own breath thin.

"Git down, boy!" Malroy demanded, and his grip tightened.

Jeff's eyes rolled, and his tongue bulged as he struggled to remain standing.

"Git down, I say!" Malroy screamed again, and applied more pressure until Jeff's body bent.

Malroy gave Jeff's throat another good squeeze and then let go. He turned proudly around to face Lessing, whose face was a blanket of boredom.

"Now I . . ." Lessing started, and then his face contorted with surprise. Malroy couldn't turn around quick enough, and so the blow caught him in the neck and sent him stumbling forward and into Lessing's chest.

"Jeff!" Jim screamed, and took off behind his fleeing brother.

The hole was thirty-six inches deep and thirty-six inches wide. Just large enough to cradle Lou's swollen belly.

"Get on down there, Lou," Malroy ordered after he'd snatched the shovel from the young boy he'd ordered to dig the hole.

She got down on her knees.

It was late afternoon by then, and the sun was making its slow move west.

"Move closer," Lessing commanded, then turned to Malroy. "She's got to get closer," he sputtered in frustration.

Lou bent over on all fours and crawled to the edge of the hole.

Lessing chewed on his bottom lip and watched. "You—you're going to have to help her, Malroy," he said, throwing his hands up. "She's as big as a cow, for God's sake."

Malroy positioned himself on the opposite side of the hole, bent down, and, hooking his hands under Lou's arms, took a deep breath and whispered, "Just relax."

Lou let her arms go slack, and Malroy dragged her forward until her stomach was perfectly positioned over the hole and then eased her down.

Tiny, sharp stones dug into her knees and the side of her face as the baby she carried rolled and kicked in protest inside of her.

"I don't want to do this, Lou, but them boys you got don't know how to mind," Lessing said in a voice that dripped with mock sympathy. "Now they gone and run off." He looked out across the land. "Won't get far, though, that's for sure," he added thoughtfully. "That's for damn sure. Now, someone's got to get whipped." Lessing rubbed at his bruised chin. "They ain't here to take their punishment, so you the next best thing."

Lou squeezed her eyes shut.

"If it could be any other way, it would be," Lessing said,

and walked a safe distance away before giving Malroy the go-ahead.

She expected some sort of announcement, a statement that would begin the torture, but all that came was the crack of the whip and then her own high-pitched screams for mercy ringing in her ears.

Her cries cut across the field and reach out to the boys who are balancing themselves on the crooked limbs of the magnolia trees. In the darkness they are almost invisible behind the waxy, emerald-colored leaves.

Lou's cries strum their heartstrings as they grip the limbs tighter and squeeze their eyes shut.

When the crack of the whip is no longer heard and Lou's cries fade to nothing, the boys climb down from their hiding place and move in circles in the thick of night in search of food.

Every night is like the night before until Jim looks at Jeff, rubs his eyes, and says, "Want Mama."

Freedom is not sweet, Jeff decides, as he takes Jim by the hand and they start toward the twinkling light of oil lamps.

Jeff's heart is beating so hard in his ears that he does not hear the snapping of twigs when Malroy steps out of the darkness and wallops first Jeff, then Jim, with a cast-iron pan.

"They back." The whisper nudges its way into her dream.

"Huh?" Lou says, but does not move. She is on her side, a sheet thrown across her stomach and naked breasts. Her back is bare and the moon clings to the gaping scars that are lined with a greenish-brown salve made from stinkweed and sassafras.

"Malroy got 'em, both of dem," the voice says.

"They ain't dead?" Lou's voice is almost sorry.

"Not yet."

When Jeff regains consciousness again, he's on his back, spread-eagled, wrists and ankles tied to a wagon wheel. Jim is tied to a tree, legs stuck out in front of him, head lolling on his chest.

Malroy is perched on a barrel a few feet away, smoking and sipping whiskey from a jar.

The dark sky hangs above them, the dim quarter-moon glowing somewhere off to the right while the blinking stars look down on them.

Jeff's throat pulses with pain and he can feel the ropes cutting through the skin of his wrists and shins. He twists this way and that, and the ropes slice deeper, sending fire through his wounds.

"This gonna be the last night you boys see." Malroy's voice comes to him first and the footsteps follow. "You the one who did it?" he asks, bending down so he can get a better look at Jeff. "Was it you or him?" he asks, his hand coming up and pointing toward Jim, who is just beginning to stir. "I could never tell the two of y'all apart." Malroy grumbles and tips the jar to his lips again.

Jeff says nothing.

"The devil musta got ahold of you." Malroy's face swims above Jeff's. "'Cause I can't think of one good reason why you would do what you done." Malroy shakes his head with dismay, then shuffles over to Jim. "Thought one of you had some sense," he says, and kicks at the soles of Jim's feet. "You the one who did it?"

Jim's eyes flutter.

"Well," Malroy mutters in resignation, "I guess it don't matter which one of you did it. When Massa get back from Myanmar, both y'all going to swing."

It scratches at the back of Lou's mind as she eases herself into a sitting position and her back screams out in pain. It's there, even though she pretends it's not. That thing she will have to do. Her God-given right, the only one the white people haven't found a way to take from her.

It is a necessary act; she's seen it played out day in and day out for as long as she can remember. The weaker is always destroyed. Sometimes pounced upon and eaten by its own mother, other times tossed from the nest and left to die.

Rubbing her stomach with one hand and reaching for her shift with the other, she forces herself to focus on the situation at hand, even though her mind is trying to drag her to a safe place—that place in time that is frozen inside of her, bright and colorful and full of yellow sun and a cool blue sea.

"Can't right this minute," she chastises her mind aloud, and eases the smock over her head.

Shuffling over to a shelf, she reaches for the small paring knife she uses to gut chickens and skin taters.

"The strong have a better chance of surviving," she whispers as she starts out the door. "The strong have a better chance of living to fight or run another day."

"What you want?" Malroy slurs when his bleary eyes catch sight of Lou.

"Just wanna see my boys before they taken away from me is all," Lou says, and shuffles forward.

Malroy eyes her and then pulls the small bottle of whiskey from his pocket, unscrewing the lid and swinging it in Lou's direction. "Want a taste?"

Lou says nothing. Malroy laughs and takes a long gulp before replacing the lid and pushing it back into his pocket.

"Go on," he spits. "But don't take all night."

She knows just who is who. Jeff is slightly taller, stronger around the chin, while Jim's eyes droop a bit and his mouth is soft like woman's. Both boys are as still as corpses, but the slight rise and fall of their chests lets Lou know otherwise.

She moves toward Jim, who is roped to the trunk of an ash tree. She watches him for a while, takes in his features, but stills herself from reaching out to touch him. The night blows around her and the stars glitter like silver in the black sky while the moon frowns down on the earth and the mess the white men have made of it.

"I believe I'll take you up on that offer," she throws over her shoulder at Malroy before turning to face Jim again.

Malroy, his chin resting on his chest, back barely scraping the round wood of the water barrel, lifts his head on a weak neck. "Heh?"

"I believe I'll have that drink now."

Malroy's face goes blank and then a sinister smile swells on his lips before he clumsily removes the bottle from his pocket and passes it over Lou.

Lou inhales, presses the glass lip to her mouth, throws her head back, and drinks.

Back with Jim now, she settles herself down on the ground

in front of him, folding her legs beneath her, and places one hand flat on the cold ground. The other she wraps tight around the paring knife and rests her fist in her lap.

She waits.

Before long, the muttering and drunken chuckles from Malroy come to an end and are replaced by loud snores. It is then that Lou moves onto her knees and crawls forward.

She allows herself to touch him, to stroke his leg, caress his young face, before grabbing hold of his chin and pulling down gently until his tongue is visible.

He stirs a bit, weakly moving his head left and then right, trying to climb out of the blackness the blow from the pan hurled him into, but Lou holds fast, reaching in and catching hold of his tongue. Fingers nimble, hand swift, she slices into the pink flesh, severing it and tossing it flapping to the ground.

Then she presses her lips against the crying, screaming ones of her child and spits the whiskey she's been holding in her own mouth down into his.

Lou jerks her head back, and Jim sprays the night air blood red. His eyes are wild and his lips flap helplessly as Lou takes his face and presses it against her bosom, rocking him until the pain and the shock pull him back into the darkness again.

Just before dawn and before they are even heard, Jeff feels the vibrations of the horses' hooves. Then the galloping sounds cut through the purple-blue haze of the new day.

Malroy, groggy and head still spinning from the whiskey, pulls himself up and hurriedly brushes at his clothing as he tries to shake the dullness from his mind. His eyes fall on Jeff and then Jim, whose chin is resting on his chest, which is caked with dried blood. Before Malroy can move to investigate, Lessing and two of his cronies gallop into the clearing.

One is potbellied and blond and carries a jug of whiskey, and the other is tall like Lessing, but thinner, with puffed cheeks and dark hair. Lessing carries a whiskey jug too, and is the first to dismount. The other two follow. None of the men are steady on their feet.

The potbellied one comes to stand by Jeff's head. He lifts his boot, balancing it over Jeff's face. "Watch out, now!" he screams, and Jeff squeezes his eyes shut, bracing himself for the hard sole and the pain. But the boot comes down a half-inch from Jeff's cheek. "Okay, okay, my aim is off." The man laughs and raises his boot again.

It goes on like that at least a dozen times, until the man tires of the game and walks away.

"Malroy, fetch his mother," Charlie Lessing instructs, then turns the whiskey jug up to his lips.

Three minutes later, Lou appears.

"Yassir?" she says, careful not to look at Jeff or Jim, whose head is still hanging limp. Her eyes hold fast to the tops of Lessing's shoes.

"One of these boys did a very bad thing," Lessing says, his hands laced behind his back. "But, of course, you already know that." He snickers.

Lou says nothing.

"If you were raising them right, they would know their places." Lessing shakes his head and drags his hands through his hair. "I can't have no niggers of mine stepping out of their place."

Lessing's eyes swing between the boys. "Which one done it, Malroy?"

Malroy's eyes follow suit. "I—I don't know, sir," he mutters.

Lessing's face flinches and his eyes bore into Lou. "Which one done it, Lou?"

Lou raised her hand and pointed a shaky finger at Jim.

Jeff's eyes bulged and his mouth fell open, but the words he wanted to holler out seemed to be caught in his throat. It was only then that Lou allowed her gaze to brush over him; it was a cold and sweeping look that chilled Jeff and forced his mouth to snap shut.

"Jeff. He the one that done the bad thing to you," Lou said, and finally turned to look at the child her words would hang.

Lessing nodded his head and walked a crooked line over to Jim. "Hey, boy, hey!" he said as he kicked at the soles of Jim's feet. "Get up, now; it's time to die!" He laughed.

Jim slowly raised his head.

"What the hell happened to him?" Lessing said in disgust, taking a few steps backward.

Jim's lips were bloated purple and crusted with blood.

"Malroy, what you do to him?" The sight of Jim's face snatched Lessing's drunkenness right from him as he turned to confront Malroy.

Malroy straightened his back. "Nothing, I ain't touch 'em, 'cept to knock 'em down and bring 'em here," he nervously sputtered.

"He gets fits, sir," Lou said quietly.

Lessing spun around. "What?"

"He gets fits," Lou said again.

Lessing looked back at Jim. "That true, Malroy?" he asked over his shoulder.

Malroy scratched at his head and looked hard at Lou. He'd never heard of either of the boys having fits. But there were a lot of things kept from him. And then again, he thought as his eyes fell on the discarded whiskey bottle, there were things he just couldn't seem to remember.

"Yassir," he said, his voice a bit unsure.

Lessing picked up a broken tree limb and jabbed at Jim's cheek. Jim opened his mouth to scream, but only a choking sound emerged. "Jesus, the boy bit his tongue clean off," Lessing said in disgust as he tossed the limb aside. "Well, let's string him up."

The horse brays and shuffles restlessly as Malroy sits behind Jim, holding him upright with one hand while working to loop the noose around his neck with the other.

"It is up to you," Charlie Lessing screams and points a scolding finger at the crowd of slaves that huddle and watch, "to make sure your offspring know that they are slaves and the white man is the master!"

Lou watches as the potbellied man's hands tighten around the reins as Malroy climbs down.

Jim's eyes lay on her, pull at her, ask her, *Why? Why?*

Some of the women turn away, some of the men walk away, but Lou remains, eyes open and clear. She will watch Jim leave the world the same way she watched him squeeze into it.

"Those who can't hear will feel!" Lessing bellows, and with the drop of his arm, Malroy slaps the mare on the behind, sending her tearing out from beneath Jim's body.

Jeff screams as Jim's face is streaked with terror and then panic when his air is cut off. His feet flail and kick, and his mouth opens and spews nothing.

The nothingness is so loud and heavy that it knocks Lou to her knees.

She remains there until Jim is still. She remains there inhaling the scent of the good earth, feeling God's gentle breeze against her face. Then she rises, laughs, and begins to dance, hopping from one foot to the next, spinning and chanting the song of the dead: *Return to Mother Earth and become joyful in the light beyond the living. Return to Mother Earth and become joyful in the light of the living . . .*

Everything she thought she'd lost or forgotten is returned to her in Jim's last moments of life: the scent of her grandfather's pipe, her mother's soft hand protectively wrapped around her own, her father's strong back, the kind eyes of her brothers . . .

Everything.

Goodbyes are for white folks.

Hand-holding people crossing dew-drenched meadows. Stargazing people whom the years have bound together so tightly, the two become one. Gray-haired people with creased faces and shared memories.

Goodbyes are for white folks and not for slaves, so Lou looks past the limp body of her dead child and toward the new day.

Route 40

When I finish I just look at Sherry, try to figure out what's broken inside of her.

Why you looking at me like that? she says, then does that thing with her eyes that make you think you're the strange and peculiar one, not her!

I say, A mother would not kill her child, and I toss the nasty red book into the backseat.

Really? she says, and looks out ahead of her for a while. Well, you didn't seem to feel that way when Verna killed April.

That was different.

How?

White people do things like that, not us.

We do it too, now, and we did it then.

That's what she say, but I feel like she want to say something else. Feel like we ain't talking about this story anymore.

Women do it for a number of reasons. Verna did it out of shame, Lou did it to save one, I—

I hear the "I," but then her voice stall and her eyes glaze and then she all of a sudden snaps the car to the right. I don't have time to hang on or scream or shut my eyes when I see the nose of the tractor-trailer barely miss the tail end of our car.

When we climbing the ramp that say REST STOP, I finally find my voice again and scream, Have you lost your ever-loving mind?

She can barely put the car—I mean, SUV—in park before she out and puking up her lunch.

I grab my wipes from my bag, jump out, and run—best my stiff legs can carry me—around to her side, but she hold up a hand, keep me at bay.

She say, I'm okay, Dumpling. I must have eaten something bad.

I hand her the wipes.

Little Rock, Arkansas

We just sitting there, staring at the school.

I look at the clock; it's been twenty minutes. She ain't saying nothing, just staring.

Then she jerk, push the door open, and jump out.

I think she gonna throw up again. Think she might have some type of virus. Wonder how in the world I'm going to drive this SUV when I can barely handle my Pontiac.

But she don't bend over and hurl, she move quick as lightning across the street and toward the building. I don't know whether I should follow or stay. She walking fast, so I snatch the keys out of the ignition and start off after her.

People looking. Sherry's face set, intent on doing something. I don't know what. I call out to her, Sherry!

But she don't slow up at all until she standing right in front of it.

I come up beside her, breathing heavy.

Sherry stretch out her arm; her fingers brush against the stone, then press into it. Then her eyes begin to water.

I don't understand none of it. What? I say. It's just a school, what's wrong? I say, and put my hand on her shoulder.

She say, This is Central High School.

I look up at the building. Okay, I say.

She look at me, she say, Nine black students walked through these doors in 1957.

I think back to where I was and what I was doing in '57; I can't remember. Then I look at her and say, Only nine?

Dumpling, don't you know about the Little Rock Nine?

I press my hands against my ears. You sounding like your sister now! I scream back at her, and start toward the SUV.

Sherry follow.

I ain't stupid, you know.

I know.

I'm older now; you think my mind quick like yours?

Sorry. I didn't mean to yell at you.

I know all about what happened down here, just couldn't grab hold of it right quick.

I understand.

You got me telling you stories, dragging me up and down the highway, Madeline calling every hour like she crazy, ain't heard from Sonny Boy, my legs swelling—I'm tired!

Dumpling, I apologized, what more do you want?

I look at her. What more do I want? *I say, and slam my hand down on my knee.* I want to do some of the listening for a while. I'm tired of talking. Ain't you got something to say? You come out of me and I don't even know you! You hardly ever call or come home. This time on the road is the longest I been around you since you were in high school. You like a stranger to me.

I feel myself shaking all over. Reach down in my bag, pull out some wet wipes, wipe at my hands, drag them across my face. I'm on fire.

Turn on the goddamn air-conditioning, *I say, and pull at the collar of my T-shirt.*

Sherry turn it on, roll up the windows, stare straight ahead.

Well? *I say when I feel the sweat drying up on my face.*

Sherry sigh and say, What you want to know?

I wanna know why the man on the other end of your cell-u-lar phone is such a secret. I wanna know his name, if you love him, what he look like, what he want from life. I wanna know if you're happy with him, if y'all talking marriage or living together maybe—I know you young people like to shack up instead of walk down the aisle.

You want to know a lot, she say.

She so difficult, this middle child of mine.

I just want to know enough to make me feel like I got a middle child, *I say.*

Sherry look at me and her eyes dig deep into me before she take a breath and say, His name is Falcon; he sells umbrellas on the beach.

My eyes widen, and her hand go up.

She say, Don't say nothing bad about that, Dumpling. Don't jinx me the way you always do.

I wonder what she mean, but my mouth shut.

She goes on and say, He's eight years younger than I am. Her face blush for a second. He's one of three children too, she say, and her whole body seem to glow.

I don't have to hear her say she love him, 'cause I see it all over her. Don't have to ask if she happy, 'cause as soon as she said his name, happy start spilling out of her.

Falcon, huh? I say, and she beam and nod yes.

Route 40

Mama, that you? Sonny Boy say after Sherry hand the phone over to me. He the only one of my children call me Mama.

Hey, baby, where you been?

I been here and there, you know how I do.

I shake my head and smile. Yeah. You all right?

Uh-huh. How 'bout you?

I'm okay.

From what Sherry say, you all been a lot of places.

Sure have, seen a lot of things.

That's good. Mama, where the emergency money at?

I sneak a peek at Sherry, turn my head toward the window, say, Where it always is.

I checked there, he say.

In the coffee can, behind the cornmeal? I whisper.

When you start putting it there? I thought it was in the coffee can in the freezer.

Oh, I moved it. Thought I told you that. What you need it for anyway?

Aw, Mama, he say like that suppose to answer my question. I miss you, he say.

He just like his daddy. He as slick as oil, know just what to say to make me melt.

I miss you too, Sonny Boy. You coming down?

Don't know yet.

When you gonna know? It's already Wednesday.

Soon, Mama.

Meet-and-greet happening on Friday.

I know.

Okay, now.

You heard from Madeline?

Now, boy, what kind of foolish question is that!

He laugh, say, Be safe. I love you, Mama.

Memphis coming up.

We gonna stay there? I ask.

Sherry look at the clock on the dashboard. It say just after one.

If you want to, but I'd rather head down to Birmingham and stay the night there.

I shrug. It don't matter to me much. Okay, I say, whatever you wanna do.

She look out at the highway for some time, fiddle with radio buttons, adjusts the rearview mirror, and then say, Then Willie came?

What? I say.

Willie, Suce's husband.

Oh, yeah.

What you know about that?

Some, I guess.

Was it Kentucky?

Some say Louisiana.

New Orleans?

I dunno.

Creole?

What?

Fair-skinned, nice hair?

Yeah, yellow nigger, I say, and laugh. Sherry make a face. She don't like that word. I fold my bottom lip in and say sorry with my eyes.

Now, he was your uncle Vonnie's father, right?

I cringe up when she say Vonnie's name, go straight for my bag, my wet wipes.

Yeah, I say under my breath, and wipe at my hands.

Willie and Suce

By the time the Union army fell Savannah, Charlie Lessing's land had shrunk, had borders—sold off for one thing or another: gambling debts and taxes.

So as far as the eye could see was no longer Lessing land. Beyond that, something so wonderful loomed that it felt too good to think about for long periods of time.

North.

North, where slaves were men and women, holding down jobs, making money, owning property. Children learning. New clothes and places to go and wear them.

The folks who listened to the old slave named Paps shuddered. Sometimes they held themselves and sometimes they held each other as they listened; hearts clamoring, feet planted, but souls already stealing away.

Paps had been there. Five years. Two babies—boys—walking and talking, learning their ABCs. He, Paps, tended the horses for a white family. His wife Margaret cooked their food, washed the clothes, and kept the house clean.

Happy?

"Every day of my life. Not a care. Not a worry, not slave, but a man," Paps said.

"But you here now."

That he was. Back in the devil's clutches.

"How did it happen?"

Stolen, right off the street. Knocked in the head with a rock. Woke up in Virginia. Chained up, blood dried and crusted on his forehead. Shit in his drawers.

He had never been put up on a block. He had been born on Seymour land.

"Where that?"

"Kentucky."

"How you get free?"

"White people bought me, said they were farming in Arkansas, then took me north with four others. Burned my sale papers right in front of me and said, *Paps, you's a free man*."

"What kind of white people are they?"

"Amish."

"Am-a-who?"

"Fire burn the sale papers away, but your skin still black. Nothing can change that."

"Yep, so there I was, thirty-two years old, stinking, shivering, head hurting like hammers banging inside. White man asked me, *What your name, nigger?*"

"What you say, Paps?"

"I just looked at him and said, *Free*."

The women smile and clutch themselves tighter, while the men shake their heads in disbelief.

"That white man laughed. Gavel went up, numbers called, hands raised, shouting, gavel went down, and here I be," Paps said with heavy resignation.

Jeff had heard the story told the same way for more than ten years. He thought about it—all of it. Dissected it the way he split logs—with precision. And so one morning he just ran. Barefoot and without food.

Ran until he could feel the land change under his feet, ran until his chest burned and his heart begged him to stop, ran until night fell and the woods came alive with sounds he'd never known on Lessing land. Ran so hard that he ran right into the paddy rollers.

His back told the tale. Nothing but bulging skin that had healed rocky and then on the second run was peeled open again and healed into molehills that shouted through the material of his shirt.

His face was still beautiful, though—beautiful enough to make the women still grieve over the one that swung.

How they wanted him, lusting behind him, using their eyes to tell him how much they wanted to scale his back, conquering every peak, before huddling themselves in the valleys beneath. But Jeff (now called Brother, so as to never forget the sacrifice made for his sake) had warm words only for Lou.

He bathed her feet and he was the one who attended to her meals. He had smiles only for her. The women milled around to see those strong white teeth and hear his laughter, like clapping thunder. They tried to prod Lou for the words she used to make the thunder roll out of Brother; maybe they could use it for themselves and be dampened by the tears that had to follow laughter that powerful.

But Lou just smirked at them.

The baby Lou had been carrying when they strung Jim up came a week later and she named her Suce.

Everyone came to see, expecting Jim's face to be pressed into some part of that newborn. Anywhere—her leg, her stomach, the soft wrinkled cheeks of her behind—she had to be marked. God would not allow a woman—a mother—who had made a choice such as the one Lou had made to live the rest of her years and not be reminded of it every single day.

But that child was perfect. All ten fingers and ten toes, perfect.

And now, twelve years later, Suce had grown into a beautiful girl. And happy too. Seeming to walk in sunlight no matter the hour of the day. Her laughter, songlike, magical, and generous, was always giving the people who heard it the courage to imagine palms as smooth as cream and fingers long, brown, and unblemished by the scars that came along with picking cotton.

Already wintertime and still they labor. Lessing thinks that he is the luckiest man this side of heaven.

All over, niggers strolling like men. Real men. Backs straight, arms just a-swingin'. Heads held high. Mercy! Who would have ever dreamed it?

But not there, not on the Lessing plantation. Niggers there remained stooped over and shuffling. Shows how stupid they were. Freedom so abundant, you could smell it. Charlie Lessing could. Freedom so pungent that he'd taken to walking around with a handkerchief pressed up against his nose. So ripe was the scent of it, it kept him up at night.

Five months and still his property remained just that, *his* property!

He had decided that no lost war or nigger-loving president was going to just say a few words, sign his name on parchment, and declare that his property—property that he had bought and paid for—could just stroll off and be free.

Not there. Not ever.

Lessing had seen the signs and started the fence just before Atlanta was taken. The fence enclosed the remaining forty acres of land he owned.

There were dogs posted on the borders and a man on horseback who patrolled the grounds.

Malroy was dead now. His sons were dead, killed in battle, but Lessing had his shotguns and two new whips with steel tips to keep them slaves in line. And how he used them, whipping them just because.

Because he hated them.

Because he'd lost so much in so little time.

Because he hated them.

Because he'd lain down with the females and loved it.

Because he hated them.

Because the war was over and his side had lost.

Because, because, because.

He started picking them off with his shotgun. Sunday afternoons, Saturday mornings. His feet propped up on the porch railing, chair tottering on two legs, drunk. Even in that precarious position, he pulled the trigger and was able to fell the unsuspecting target. Even shot dead his horseback-riding man, but that had been by accident.

Suce rose just as dawn started breaking through every place it could find to slip into. Careful, she thought, Lessing don't like no sunlight before his eyes can clear and catch hold of something familiar, so she's careful at night to make sure the shutters are closed tight and the drapes are pulled closed.

Since October he's been tied down. One leg, one arm, just in case he needs to scratch or wants a drink of water from the glass Suce keeps filled on the nightstand.

When he shot his own man and still no white men came, Brother had walked right into the house, knocked Lessing down, and dragged him upstairs.

Lessing was crazed, that was for sure. A raving lunatic, and if the killings didn't prove it, well then, him cradled in Brother's arms like a baby did.

His arms were wiry and pale, those he threw around Brother's neck, and it disgusted him; he'd seen women wrap theirs around Lessing in the same way. But that was before the war and before the money dwindled to nothing. Before the madness'd started eating at his mind. The women took what they could after they'd drowned him in gin and pussy, then cut and ran north just like some of the Negroes did.

Brother's skin had crawled beneath the feel of Lessing's arms, and when he threw him down on the bed, he restrained himself from pummeling him with his fists, the walking cane propped in the corner, and anything else that would leave that white man pulped and bloody.

Brother's eyes took in the room—velvet drapes, silk-covered chairs, crystal this and crystal that. "Umpf!" he snorted, and punched his palm with his fist.

Here he was, living like a pig: mother dead, father probably dead too, twin brother lynched, burned, and buried. Friends gone. Just him, Suce, Laney, Hop, Tenk, and Spin left.

Brother could have killed him, but things come back and haunt you. Lou had warned him of evildoings early on in his life; she said it was Jim who'd started picking away at Lessing's sanity.

Not too long after Jim swung, she'd seen two shadows walking alongside Lessing. He'd seen it too, she could tell by the way his feet came to a halt, the confusion on his face, and then the horror before he jumped and ran. After that day, something in his eyes changed. She knew that look, had seen the same change in Buena's eyes after they took Nayeli away from them.

"Jim ain't too happy with me, neither," she'd said, pointing at the swell of her stomach.

Lou's belly bulged out beneath the tattered gray fabric of her shift. Suce was ten years old by then, and Lou hadn't had the hand of another man on her since Buena was sold off.

But you couldn't tell Laney that. She looked at Lou's growing belly and then at her husband Tenk, who had always seemed to forget himself in Lou's presence—stumbling over his words, blushing beneath his dark eyes, and grinning like an idiot.

"What you saying, Laney?" the people she confided in asked.

"You know what I'm saying."

"Well, Tenk may have been a wolf once, but he an old dog now!" they laughed.

"What that mean?" Laney turned on them.

"It mean he may have the heart, but not the might!"

The rumors had floated back to Lou and she had laughed before the hurt set in. She approached Laney. "You think I would do such a thing? We like sisters, almost," Lou had said, taking Laney's stiff hand in her own. "You think Tenk would do you like that?" she pressed.

Laney had snuffed and snatched her hand from Lou's grip. "Well who it belong to then?" she sneered, indicating Lou's bulging stomach with her chin.

Lou cradled her belly and rocked a bit on her heels. She smiled, but the smile was heavy with grief, and then she turned those sad black eyes on Laney and said, "Oh, this here is my Jim."

Laney's eyes widened. "You got fever, Lou? The sun getting to you again?"

"Nah, I knows it's him," Lou said, and rubbed her stomach.

Laney shook her head in dismay. "How you know that?" she asked in a mocking tone.

Lou rolled her head and pressed her hand into the small of her back. "I knows it's him," she whispered as she patted Laney's shoulder and began moving past her, "'cause the way out is back through."

Whatever it was, it remained in her for three years, eating Lou from the inside out. At the end all she was, was hallowed cheeks, sunken eyes, and stomach.

The slicing pain came late one night, cutting through her middle and gnawing at her back. Lou sprung up right in her bed and howled. The hounds' ears shot up and they began yelping and pissing until finally they huddled against one another and curled their tails between their legs and shook.

Lou howled again, curdling the blood of everyone who heard it. Lessing turned over in his bed and pulled the shotgun he slept with into him like a warm woman. He squeezed his eyes tightly shut and prayed.

Brother rushed to his mother's side, as did everyone else who had heard that horrible noise.

Someone lit a lamp and the darkness was shattered; Lou's eyes bulged and Brother and the rest of the onlookers gasped in shock when the lamp was brought closer and they saw that Lou's hair was completely white.

Laney had stumbled where she stood, but Tenk got hold of her arm and steadied her.

"Mama," Brother started, and placed his hand on Lou's exposed thigh. Her skin made a rustling sound beneath his palm like dried leaves, and he snatched it back in terror.

Lou pushed, and her belly bucked and writhed beneath her shift. She howled again and, God forgive him, Brother backed away from her.

Lou, up on her elbows and legs as wide as they could go, snarled between howls now, her lips skinned back on her teeth, eyes wild as she bared down,

There was praying going on, sacred words being thrown out into the air, someone humming a favorite spiritual they sang down in the clearing on Sundays, someone else pleading for it to stop, another urging someone to do something, anything.

But no one was stepping forward (too scared) or stepping out (too curious).

Another howl, another push, a sudden gust of air, and the lamplight flickered and then faded. "Git it lit, git it lit!" someone demanded. Fumbling, a cuss word or two passed, and then the sound of water, of breaking waves.

In the darkness they turned bewildered faces on one another and then the lamp finally gets lit again just in time for them to see a blue ocean rushing out from between Lou's legs.

That was three years ago, but the memory of it was planted in Brother, dug in deep and rooted like a stubborn weed. That recollection and the feel of his dead mother in his arms, soft and wet and smelling of seawater, her legs grainy with sand.

Thinking about it just made him angry all over again, and Brother balled his fists and turned on Lessing, who was curled into a ball of whining white flesh in the center of his bed. Eyes unfocused and watering, he looked up at Brother and pleaded, "Please, Papa, don't hit me."

Laney had followed them into the house and, against her will, she felt some pity sprout in her chest for the old man. She made herself known at the bedroom door, brought to a stop what was about to happen by saying, "What us gonna do with him?"

There was bread and all types of jam and some pork in the cooler, and ale. Little else, but that was a feast for them. At first Hop and Tenk wouldn't come past the porch. But Spin stepped over that threshold like it was his house.

So frightened were Hop and Tenk that their kneecaps jumped and their stomachs churned with gas.

Brother came to the door a third time, his mouth chomping contently on something. "Where Suce?" he said.

Hop nodded toward the left of the house. Brother stepped out onto the porch and called for her: "C'mon, Suce."

Suce slipped slowly from the shadows.

"C'mon now, it's okay," he said, looking off into the dark woods and then over at Tenk and Hop. "Y'all too. C'mon inside 'fore someone sees y'all out here."

Hop and Tenk exchanged fretful looks and then followed Suce through the door.

At the kitchen table they ate like men and women, Laney dabbing the corners of her mouth with a linen napkin and gushing at the absurdity of it all.

Tenk guzzling down ale so fast, he burped his words out. Hop and Spin roaming through the parlor, Spin scared to touch anything, just staring openmouthed, and Hop greedily snatching up everything that caught his fancy and quickly shoving it into his pockets.

Suce trailed behind them, careful to keep her hands at her sides.

When they were full and Brother told Laney to "sit back down; you don't have to clear no table here," the question was asked again: "What us gonna do?"

Death would have been the best thing for Lessing, but Brother knew if he killed him, he would be condemning the lot of them. He leaned back in his chair and the others leaned in and waited.

No one had been by the place in months. Lessing had run some off, screeching like a banshee, rifle swinging in the air, sometimes dressed just in his drawers, other times in one of his fine suits.

Brother supposed that when Atlanta was taken, a right good amount of people had just run off, carrying as much as they could handle, leaving the rest behind for the looters who were roaming the countryside.

Not a soul had come a-knocking since September, and by the time Brother had knocked Lessing to the floor, it was just after Christmas.

Brother leaned forward, resting his large forearms on the table and blanketing the waiting faces with an earnest look. "We gonna keep doing like we been doing."

"What?"

"Laney, you gonna wash and hang the sheets every day, just like always."

"But—"

"Hop, you, Tenk, and Spin gonna build that pen." He paused then and pulled at his chin. "Not on the south part where Lessing wanted it, but in the north, where you can be seen from the main and back roads."

Hop and Tenk just stared while Spin walked in circles, trying to get at an itch on his back.

"In the spring, we gonna work the fields together, just like we always do," Brother said, and leaned back in his chair.

Laney cleared her throat and scratched the back of her neck, getting herself ready to speak her mind, but then Brother sat up again.

"We gonna keep Lessing in this here house"—and he tapped his index finger on the table—"up in that there room and"—he pointed up to the ceiling above their heads—"quiet."

They all stared at Brother. It all felt wrong to them. Hop could already feel the noose around his neck, could smell Tenk's body burning. He looked at Brother and his head was gone. Spin would swing too. Laney and Suce would probably be the only ones to get away with nothing more than a whipping.

"And we gonna move into Vicey's house," Brother went on matter-of-factly, and his eyes rolled to the window and gazed down on the old saltbox.

Laney's eyes bulged. "You done lost your ever-loving mind," she said, and stood up. "Just 'cause you got some book learning don't mean you got sense." She spat and pushed her fists into her hips. "What you 'gestin' gonna get us all lynched."

"Ay-yuh," Hop said, and ran his fingers down his throat.

"Maybe," Brother said, and folded his hands.

"I wanna move into this here house!" Tenk exclaimed, reaching for the jar of jam. "And take me one of those bubbly water baths I heard about." He laughed and Hop found his laughter too and joined in.

"Like I said," Brother continued, his eyes narrowing, "we gonna move into the *Vicey* house. It got four bedrooms. A mite better than what we living in now." And then his voice tightened when he said, "Only one gonna be 'lowed in this here house is Laney."

Their faces went long and they looked down at the table.

"Why me?" Laney asked, and threw her weight into one hip.

"'Cause he like you, and 'sides, you gonna have to bring him his meals, keep him clean, and—"

"I ain't gonna wash that man's dirty behind!"

Hop and Tenk laughed out loud and then clapped their hands over their mouths.

"You'll do it," Brother said, and the tone he took told Laney that that was that.

"Fine."

* * *

January, and the ground cold and stiff, the sound of horse hooves, faint at first and then closer. The hounds send a signal, howling and already standing at the far end of the property, ears alert, tails at attention. Brother drops his hammer and takes a moment to blow warm breath into almost-frozen hands.

Laney comes to the door, and Brother nods her way before picking up his hammer again. There's banging along with howling and hooves, clearer-sounding now, just around the bend.

Hop is the skittish one, and his hands won't hold the nail in place. It falls and he pulls another one from his pocket and tries again. The point wobbles against the wood while his eyes watch for the horses and the wagon he's sure they're pulling. He feels the wheels cutting through the earth, slicing through the green that's waiting for spring beneath it.

A small figure shoots out and across the land, so swift it's almost unseen. If it wasn't for the hounds, the turning wagon wheels, and Brother's hammer, the day would be quiet enough to hear the screech of the hinges and the click of the lock.

They pretend not to notice, but Brother's heart is galloping and Hop keeps dropping the nails. Both of their backs are to the road, hoping their coats hide the twitching of the skin there.

The hooves and wagon come to a halt, and now it's just the snorting of the horses. Then, after a moment: "Hey, nigger."

Brother takes a breath and turns his head slowly around; his body follows and Hop just grips the wood of the fence and wills himself not to faint.

Brother does not offer a smile, just the placid face of slavery. It is a look that is beaten, untaught, and unthreatening. "Yassa?"

The white man is short and stout and climbs down from his wagon with a puffed chest, keeping his distance so as not to have to look up at Brother.

"Who the owner of this property?"

"Massa Lessing," Brother says, careful to keep the hammer still and stiff at his side.

The man smiles at the word "Massa."

"He home?" the man asks, and looks up toward the house.

"Yassa," Brother says, and then drops his head a little. "But he sickly."

The man's eyebrows climb.

"Is there a missus?"

Brother stumbles on this one, but he camouflages the hesitation with a cough and then a quick wipe to his nose with the back of his hand. "Nope. She passed last winter."

The white man studies him. "Children?"

"No sir."

"How many niggers?"

Brother is careful with this one. He can't be too swift, seem too smart.

"Well, sir, it be me and Hop here." Hop supposes he should turn around, but his neck won't move so he just keeps his eyes trained on the nail. "Laney," Brother continues, and uses his chin to point at the old woman who is slowly making her way up the hill and toward the house. "A girl," Brother says, and then adds quickly just in case the stranger got any ideas, "she just a child." He takes a moment and then says, "Tenk and Spin, they in the barn, and that be it."

The white man watched Laney until she disappeared behind the house.

And then he grunted and spat into the dirt before looking off across the land and then back at Brother. "Y'all tell Lessing I'll be back when life's feeling a mite better."

"Yassa."

"Tell 'em Pinkerton come by to see him."

"Yassa."

Brother waited a few beats before he turned back to his work. He heard Pinkerton's boots crunch against the ground, and then the sound abruptly ceased.

Brother's heart pounded and he found himself gripping the hammer tighter than he ever thought possible. Hop heard the silence too and just went on ahead and threw his body weight against the fence; otherwise, he would have fainted straight away.

Brother waited another few beats and then turned back around, fully expecting to be looking down the barrel of a shotgun, but instead, he saw the man's hand up and waving. Brother swallowed and turned his eyes toward the house.

Up in the window, behind the lace curtains, was a small figure in a white gown, waving back.

Brother's throat closed up.

"He look frail," the man said as he lowered his arm back down to his side. "What's ailing him?"

Brother couldn't answer; his throat was locked shut. His eyes were stuck too. His lips just flapped, but words floated from beside him: "Yellow fever."

"Jesus, Mary, and Joseph," the man said, and hurriedly climbed up and onto the wagon and drove away.

After the hooves and wheels faded, leaving just the sounds from the fussing warblers and the now-and-again yelps from the hounds, Brother and Hop exchanged astonished looks.

"Don't know where that came from!" Hop laughed nervously and wiped away the sweat on his brow.

Brother dropped his hammer and started toward the house. Hop finally found the strength to turn around, but his might left him with one move and he found himself on his knees, his face resting on the cold ground, snorting loose dirt like a hog.

Brother passed Tenk and Spin, who were stepping out of hiding from behind a tree. Tenk set his mouth to say something and then snapped it shut when he saw the determination in Brother's face.

Laney met him at the door, her eyes stern, but there was worry etched into the lines of her skin, and if she hadn't moved, she was sure Brother would have knocked her out of his way.

Taking the steps two at a time and leaving small mounds of dirt on the green carpet runner, he found himself at Lessing's bedroom door, his hand clutching the brass doorknob.

He shoved the door open and was greeted by scurrying sounds. Then his eyes fell on Lessing, who was propped up-right in the bed, both hands bound above his head to the bed railing, eyes wide and staring, handkerchief balled and stuffed into his mouth.

To the right of him was another figure—small, white-haired, pale-faced, shrouded in a gown that was a dim gray in the leaving light.

Brother's breath caught in his throat and he thought, like a man named Willie who would come months later, *Haint*, when he saw that the dressing gown had no feet poking out from un-der its hem and no hands dangling from the sleeves.

"Brother?" The voice was familiar and now the haint floated toward him, and he felt his feet move two paces backward.

"It was a good idea, right?"

Suce, dipped in flour maybe or dusted down with powder? Something sweet-smelling in the air. Oh yes, and there was the puff and the container wide open, lid resting beside it. Pow-der. And the dressing gown was three times her size which explained her missing limbs.

He laughed then. A thunderous laugh that let loose all of the tension he had been shouldering since the night he knocked Lessing down. He laughed until his sides hurt and then he grabbed Suce up by the waist and swung her through the air. "It was a very good idea," he said.

Hop must have put a curse on himself because he fell sick, just three days after the white man came. Fever so high, Laney's fingertips practically sizzled when she touched him. Brother carried him to the big house and laid him to rest in one of the many bedrooms. Hop had smiled at the gesture, but Brother was more concerned with keeping the rest of them well than with Hop's comfort.

"He's dying for sure," Laney cried as she worried holes in the carpet, pacing night and day around his bed.

Then Tenk disappeared or up and left or was eaten by coyotes.

"White man got 'em," Laney mumbled as her eyes swept the road.

"White men don't take just one; they got to have it all, and we still here, ain't we?" Brother said.

"Bad sign, no matter how you look at it," Laney replied, and shuffled away.

Brother stayed quiet. He couldn't deny that. It was a very bad sign.

Time came when Hop's eyes turned yellow and he couldn't take any food or water in. Laney boiled pots of water and filled the porcelain tub, spilling in the bubbling liquid, and Brother set Hop down inside of it.

Hop didn't even have the strength to laugh, but he smiled himself silly. By the time the water went cold, he was dead.

So that's the way it remained.

Just the four of them.

Lard running low, sugar just a memory, and Suce dusting herself white and waving from the window whenever someone came to inquire, which was almost never. Building the pigpen, over and over again.

Taking down one side and then putting it up again.

Sheets on the line, billowing in the air.

Normal.

Winter in Georgia sneaks in under the cover of night, blanketing the earth in a white frost that burns away beneath the rising sun, leaving behind a crisp coolness. Just the evergreens remain that way (green); all else turn orange and red and then brown before curling and floating down to earth and leaving only bare, crooked limbs that point toward the back of the departing season.

Tattered clothes are layered upon tattered clothes in an attempt to keep old bones warm; shoes are mended and kindling burns throughout the short winter days and deep into the blue-black nights.

It is the winter sky that is most beautiful of all during that time. Wide, high, and pale during the day, and at night the stars move a little closer to earth, burn a little brighter.

And the moon, a great big beautiful sphere, sometimes white like the soft flakes that drop from the sky and melt away on the young tongues of those who stop between chores to tilt their heads back and stretch their mouths wide open.

And sometimes the moon is yellow like the eyes of the old ones who have seen much and tell tales over campfires.

That sky made heaven a believable place, a place that could possibly one day welcome niggers, criminals, and ornery types of men—even one such as Willie.

It was just a name.

A name on a forgotten piece of newspaper: MYANMAR.

He couldn't read, but had remembered the sound of it just in case he found it in him to leave the safety of the woods and back roads and stop someone, present the paper, and ask, "How many more miles?"

But he had searched and searched and hadn't been able to find that bit of him that would allow him to travel in the day or walk the more heavily traveled thoroughfares, even though months earlier Argyle Elliott had told him he was a free man. "Man" is the word that made him smile. Free, he felt, was something still a long time coming.

That day, months earlier when Elliott came running in—hands just a-clapping, him kicking his feet up and doing that stupid jig that he did around the fire during Christmas—the menfolk just shook their heads. But Elliott had found a warm place in the hearts of the women and no matter what it was they were doing, they would stop, watch, ask, or fuss over him.

A man near forty, but standing no taller than a five-year-old. He was toothless and gray at the temples, but was swift on his feet and, as short as he was, he could jump a mile up into the air and talk louder than any tall man there.

"What you so happy 'bout?" Rosa asked, and folded her thick arms across her heavy breasts.

Elliott coming from midleap, came thudding down to earth, kicking up a cloud of dust. "We's freeeeeeeeeeeeeee!" he wailed, and started again stamping his feet, slapping his thighs, and chucking his shoulders up to the heavens.

"Free from what?" Rosa asked, laughing.

"Free from being enslaved. Free from the *yes Massas* and *no Massas*. Freeeeeeeeeeeeeeeeeee!" Elliott did a spin on his heels.

"You a fool if there ever was one," Willie remembered saying.

Even though now it all felt like a dream. But it was true, 'cause he found himself replaying that day over and over in his mind, even as he walked those Alabama roads.

It wasn't a dream, because every day he opened his eyes, he was right where he'd laid himself down and not back on the Miggs plantation with clucking chickens and fatback crackling in Rosa's pan. He missed the fatback, though.

"Fool enough to know what I heard," Elliott had said, and offered Willie a large toothless smile.

The women gathered, and even the men drew a little closer. There had been rumors, nothing else.

"Sumter come back—"

"Massa Miggs wit 'em?"

"Sumter say Massa Miggs fought the good fight, yes he did, but he took a bullet in the chest and died right there on the battlefield."

The women clutched their chests and sucked the air out of the room. The men just grumbled.

"Missus a whole heap of sad. Sure 'nuff, wailing like the wind right about now."

The women cocked their heads and listened. Sure enough, sorrow as light as a sun shower sailed through the air around them.

"You seen him, Sumter?"

"Yes ma'am. He come marching up the road, got the massa's medals in one hand, jacket in the other." Then Elliott's eyes went moist, the women were sure of it. "He look direct at me and say, *President Lincoln say slavery is 'bolished*."

"'Bolished?"

"That mean done wit. Over!" Elliott said, and stooped his body back into his jig pose.

"Wait," Willie said just as Elliott was about to slap his palms together. "What the missus say?"

Elliott straightened his back, and a shade of annoyance darkened his face. He clenched his fists and pressed them against his round hips. "She say she *knew it was coming and now it's here. So where's my husband?*"

Everyone's eyes bulged and they waited.

"And Sumter told her, and she fall down on her knees and begin to wail."

"What us gonna do?" someone asked.

"Where us gonna go?"

"How us gonna eat?"

By evening, Elliott's news was confirmed. Paul Archer, the missus's brother, brought the news to them directly.

"If any of y'all want to stay and work the field, you're welcome to it. You will receive wages every first of the month. If you want to leave, that is your prerogative. You are free to go as you please, but we would appreciate if you'd at least stay on until the crop is harvested."

Mouths slipped open.

"What's a prerogative?" someone whispered.

"Sound like it might mean freedom to me."

June passed, and a fiery July beat down on them as they each stared at the two silver pieces Paul Archer pressed into their hands. August saw the same heat and another set of silver pieces and so did September and October, when the fields were bare and the freed men and women looked at one another and their silver and asked, "Now what?"

Willie didn't have any questions, only dreams.

He remembered well the last night he spent on the Miggs plantation. He could barely sleep—him and about a dozen others. There was plenty of tossing and turning. Plenty of whispered questions and murmuring—murmuring so loud, the birds lifted from the trees in search of a piece of space they could actually snatch some shut-eye in.

Willie was up before dawn, up just as the moon became translucent and the stars were nowhere to be seen. He had a piece of old tablecloth, dumped the few items he owned onto it, and tied it to the end of a fallen tree limb. He hustled down to the river, washed the crust from the corners of his eyes, and rinsed his mouth clean. The freezing-cold water rattled his teeth, and his whole body shook against the chill.

And before he could get far up the embankment, he pulled the piece of paper from his pocket and lovingly fingered it. It was old, worn, and yellow, tattered around the edges, the letters fading—but still, anyone with good eyes could make out the word: MYANMAR.

Once, many years earlier, before the mice had made a meal out of it, there was another word that said GEORGIA.

That slip of paper had kept him going. He preferred it to the warmth of a woman, could go without a meal as long as he had that piece of paper close by.

He didn't know what had attracted him so to that place. A place as foreign to him as another country. Some little town carved out of a state he had never visited.

Willie's mind had painted pictures of Myanmar: green flowered fields, cloudless skies, fruit trees always bearing, and a brook that made music against the rocks beneath it.

Just a piece of paper with letters that could have said anything, but he knew it was Myanmar because the young Miggs girl had ripped it from the newspaper and had slowly sounded out the word over and over again until her tongue stopped jamming up against her teeth and the elder Miggs girl looked over her book, smiled, and said, "That's perfect."

Willie, pulling weeds and patting earth down around the porch was trying not to listen, but the little girl's slight voice and the word, over and over again like the awkward scales the young Miggs boy played on Saturday afternoons, stuck in his mind.

My-an-mar. Myyyyyyyyyy-aaaaaaaaaaaaaaaan-mmmmmm-aaaaaaaaaaar.

Later, when the girls were called in for supper, the wind caught hold of the paper and brought it right to Willie's feet.

The word looked up at him, beckoned him, and Willie plucked it from the ground and jammed it into his pocket.

He was near seventeen by then and had had it for nearly twelve years. That paper was magical, painting dreams where there was once just darkness.

Dreams of him walking a road, the sun high and lemon-colored, its rays warm against his face, new shoes, and Willie high-stepping like the white men—neck straight, eyes savoring all the land that lay ahead of him, not just the dirt road and the grass that grew at its edges—all of it.

And then the stone wall, covered in creeping honeysuckle, and her.

His heart always skipped a beat at the first sight of her, and fear struck him someplace deep, but he'd confused that feeling with excitement.

Her hair was the color of glowing embers and wild about her head, not moving at all in the wind that suddenly picked up out of nowhere and wrapped itself around him.

Willie knew, before he even saw her face or any part of what she was below her neck, that her hip was pressed against the stone wall—had been pressed against it for a long time, maybe even years, while she waited for him. Everything in him wanted to run to her, raise her skirt, and kiss the purple bruise that he was sure the stone and the years had left there.

He wanted to do that for her.

When he gets to where he can just make out her cheek-bone, beautifully chiseled and high, he's honored with an eye—just one—beadlike and black, fixed on the future even though Willie is approaching from her past.

Her left arm is stretched out on top of the wall, her chin pressed into the fleshy part of her arm just below her shoulder. It is a lazy pose. One that betrays the ardent look that rests in her eyes.

He always wakes just as her head begins to turn slowly toward him.

Five years he'd been dreaming about that woman with the fiery hair, languid stance, and eager eyes.

He'd also been in love with her for just as long.

And so at the drop of a word Willie set out in search of a place called Myanmar and a woman with chiseled cheekbones and hair the color of a burning sunset.

He traveled at night, walking through the mouth of darkness without too much worry. There were others moving across the land just like him. Some he thought that didn't need to. Some were as white as any white man he'd ever seen. So white they were easy to spot in the darkness, like snowflakes on a pitch-dark winter night. But he knew they were Negroes. The nose gave it away—sometimes the lips too; other times something in him just told him so.

"Spooks were right," he'd chuckled to himself one evening when a man called out to him from behind a tree. High moon and night sky blotched with clouds that threatened to drop something—snow, sleet, rain—something.

The voice cut through Willie's thoughts and triggered the need to pee.

"Psssst. Hey you," the voice came again, and Willie quickened his pace, preparing for the full-out hauling-of-ass type of run he would need to break into if the calling voice was unfriendly.

"Hey. Slow down, friend."

Friend?

Willie threw a slow look over his shoulder, and his gaze collided with bulging, yellowed eyes sunk deep into a black face.

A wave of a hand and then the "Hey you" again.

Willie forced his feet to come to a stop; even though the command was swift, his legs took four more strides before halting, and even then his calf muscles pumped away beneath his skin.

He turned and started reluctantly toward the man.

The man himself popped back behind a tree. Willie stopped a foot or so away from the tree and called out, "Yeah?"

The man's head reappeared, and then a whole body stepped

out from behind the tree. He was a lanky something, this man who had a nervous twitch tugging at the corners of his mouth and rapid blinking eyes. "You . . . uhm, going north?"

Willie didn't know which way he was going. For the past week he'd just been walking, sometimes strutting when the mood hit him, traveling along and putting all his trust in his dream and the slip of paper he carried in his pocket.

"Headed to Myanmar."

The man's shoulders jumped a bit and he brushed some nothingness off the top of his head. "Myanmar? Ain't never heard of the place. Where that?"

"Georgia."

The man's head bounced. "Can't be too far; Georgia right here where we standing." The man's eyes rolled and he snatched a quick peek over his shoulder before stepping closer and dropping his voice a bit. "I'm heading to Philadelphia. My sister there already. Just awaitin', I s'pose," he said, his eyes glazing over. "You got some food?"

Willie took an unconscious step backward. He had exactly two pieces of slab bacon, one and a half hardtack, and an apple.

"Nah."

The man took another measured step forward. "What you carryin', then?" he said, pointing a shaking finger toward the bundle that swung from the tree limb Willie had hoisted over his shoulder.

"Clothes," Willie said, and gripped the limb tighter.

The man glanced over his shoulder again and his voice dropped to an inaudible whisper, forcing Willie to lean in a bit. "I sure am hungry. Been on these roads for nearly a month," he said, rubbing his stomach and moving steadily toward Willie. "Anything you got would help some. Anything."

Poor nigger, Willie thought. Well, they were all in it together, weren't they? All in this mess called life and bound together by one thing or another.

Willie's own mother had farmed indigo in South Carolina before she was sold off to the Miggs plantation. She was just fourteen years old and had a baby hanging from one tit and fingertips stained blue that would remain that way until death. His memory of her was faded, but the teardrops that were etched below her eyes and the foreign way in which the American words rolled out of her mouth stayed with him—that and the cool feel of her blue fingertips on his body. He was the youngest of eight children; all the others had been sold off one by one over the years. The day she died was a scene in his mind that had begun to blanch, but if he thought hard enough he could see the wild horse break loose from its corral, he could hear the steady gallop of its hooves as it cut through the field, and he could see his mother's blue fingers reach up into the air, just before the horse struck her and she was trampled beneath it.

The memory came as a bright white light that set his forehead to burning even as the cold winter night wrapped its icy fingers around him.

He shook the memory away and looked at the haggard man who stood before him. Yes, he thought, they were all in it together.

Willie didn't say a word, just stepped off the road and farther into the woody darkness. The man followed.

"They call me Sammy," the man said after they'd covered a few feet.

"Willie," Willie said, and presented his hand. Sammy gave it a blank stare and seemed not to know what to do with it, so Willie pulled it back in place at his side.

"Been running for a month," Sammy said as his eyes crawled eagerly over Willie's sack.

"No need to run. You can walk now," Willie advised him, dropping down to one knee and undoing the knot. "President Lincoln done set all of us niggers free," he explained as he pulled out a hardtack and handed it off to Sammy.

"Sure 'nuff?" Sammy said, fingering the bread and suddenly

breaking down, crying so hard that the hardtack went soft in his hands and then melted on his tongue, and still the tears ran.

Willie couldn't remember crying a tear out of hurt, longing, or shame. The only time his eyes teared up was from a troublesome wind or a menacing bit of dust.

But now he felt like he might cry too; Sammy's piteousness, weeks of running, black skin, and nervous ways rubbed against him and he felt tears welling up.

He hurriedly wiped them away and dug once again into his bundle and presented Sammy with a piece of slab bacon.

They sat, backs resting against a tall pine, whispering their lives to each other until Willie's words were replaced with even sleep-breathing and the only eyes still open were Sammy's.

When the sun broke through the night shadows, Willie found himself alone. His small bundle was gone and so was Sammy.

He was headed for Myanmar, but never did get past Sandersville. Dead on his feet, the front of his shoes flapping and licking up dirt. His back aching and throat dry. Starving and seeing double when he stopped to lean against the wooden post.

No sun on that day, just a whipping wind, cold rain, and the memory of the last best place: two days in a farmer's barn, hidden behind hay that had been pressed into blocks, and Willie wrapped in a forgotten quilt that stank like he didn't know what, but serving its purpose and keeping the chill at bay.

No food and his hunger was bottomless, open and spreading into his dreams, devouring the red-haired beauty. And then the sound of horses, voices, and the "yuk yuk" laughter that told him the voices were white. Also, something about stoning, lynching, and gutting some "nigga baby" and then the "yuk yuk" again.

Willie could hardly wait till nightfall before slipping out of his hiding place and hitting the road.

That was two weeks ago, maybe three. He couldn't quite

remember, all his senses tuned now to what was coming up fast behind him. Death had been tailing him for at least three days. That he was sure of.

Walking closer to the road, hunger nudging him there, planting hopeful thoughts in his mind, coating his tongue with the memory of fatback and sweet corn, making the clouds look like biscuits and the soft insides of baked potatoes.

Stumbling along, passing a worn sign that meant nothing to Willie but stated, TOWN OF VALENCIA—his ears clogged from hunger, Willie didn't hear the sound of the approaching horses, but felt the beat of them in the earth beneath his feet and scurried off and into the woods where he threw himself down to the ground and laid still. Very, very still.

There, pressed into the frozen earth, he watched as the horse-drawn carriage approached. It slowed as it took the bend and Willie could see the pale-pink face and the hoofed foot of the driver.

Death himself, riding high and capped.

Now Willie stumbled along again, careful to keep watch over his shoulder. He'd left a bit of his sanity back there in the woods of Valencia—either that, or he picked up a touch of madness.

Coming into the town of Ennis, he found shelter beneath a grove of chinaberry bushes. There he gathered dead leaves around his feet and tried to hug himself warm.

Dozing, dying—he wasn't sure which, but when he shifted his weight and pulled his knees closer in to his chest, his eyes fluttered open and there staring back at him were eyes as pink as azalea blooms.

"Ooooh, Scratch, you done found me," Willie whispered, his mind already failing him. And he squeezed his eyes tightly shut and mumbled words he'd heard the old women whisper on Sunday mornings.

"Baaa-aaaa," responded the creature.

Willie, perplexed, slowly opened one eye and then the other.

"Goat? A goddamn goat?" he said out loud to the pink eyes that blinked back at him.

Broad daylight, and Willie walking right out into the open found himself surrounded by twenty goats grazing on the dead grass.

Some looked at him and scurried a few feet away, switching their tails as they went.

Willie propped his hands on his hips and laughed. "Goats!"

More scurrying and pink eyes watchful as Willie walks slowly toward a kid whose mother has allowed fear to force her more than ten yards away from it.

Willie bends toward it, extends an empty hand, and begins making kissing sounds with his mouth.

The kid's tail switches nervously and it skips closer to its mother.

Willie can wait. He looks at the sky, and the sun promises him at least three more hours of light. Willie peers down the road, listens hard for hooves, and hears nothing. He can wait. Patience, he knows, is a virtue.

An hour of just sitting as still as a stone until the goats wander back toward him, skittish though, hunger outweighing their fear, and they drop their heads and attention away from Willie and begin chomping at the dead grass again.

Another hour, the light fading fast, and Willie's heartbeat is so slow, it can't be felt in his chest or heard in his ears, and his toes are frozen—those and his hands—and he prays that his fingers won't fail him when it comes time to act on the plan he's put together in his mind.

Another thirty minutes and a kid close to Willie's shoe is sniffing at the sole, licking at the leather before it takes its first nibble of the worn hide.

Willie's mind says, *Now!* but his body takes its sweet time, and it's a full minute before his hands spring out and grab hold of the kid's neck.

The snapping sound sends the other goats scrambling toward a mound of dirt that Willie thought must be a beautiful sight in the spring, carpeted in green and bursting with color. He smiles and pulls from his pocket small knife, which he uses to slice open the goat's belly.

Steam rushes out of the open carcass and turns misty in the cold air; then Willie shoves both of his hands into the kid's bloody, hot organs and sighs with relief.

Hands warm now, his hunger jumps up and kicks him in the gut and, God help him, Willie bends his head and dines on the intestines, the heart, and the liver like the animal his slave master had constantly reminded him he was.

Little good it does him—the blood, the taste of the flesh, the very act alone makes him puke up every bite he's taken in. Not to mention the "Whoa!" from close by and the "Hey, nigger, what the hell do you think you're doing?" along with the bullet that cuts the dirt by his shoe and sends Willie running.

Now here he is, looking back on four days of walking, goat's blood stiff on his clothes and flaking off of his hands, hunger beating at his stomach. Frigid cold tearing at his skin, stealing all the feeling out of him, and death somewhere close by watching and waiting to pounce.

Willie is aware of all of these things but not the curl of smoke coming from the chimney of a small house to his left.

Not aware of or even imagined before his eyes flutter closed and he falls face forward to the ground.

Waking to warmth made him think of hell, and he knew he would die another death if he opened his eyes and saw the devil looking down at him. The murmuring he heard could be words, but Willie didn't know what language was spoken in hell and so he concentrated on the smells that swirled around him: beans, salt pork, fried bread.

He couldn't tell where his hands were, if he even had hands, and what of his feet? His head hurt and his mouth pulsed. His eyes remained shut.

"Suce, heat up some water and let me get at these here feet again."

"Yessum."

Kindling being stirred in a hearth. A woman's voice, words he knew.

Heaven, maybe?

A door opens and a rush of cold air passes over him.

"He a sight, ain't he?"

A man's voice.

"Sure is."

"Them his shoes?"

"Yep."

"Look like he walked clear 'cross the country in them."

"Seem so."

"Gotta name?"

"He was passed out cold 'long the road."

"Who found him?"

"Spin."

"What he doing out? I thought he had the fever."

"Can't say. Fever left him days ago."

"Hmmm."

Willie chances it. He understands the words, smells the beans and salt pork, feels the warmth. He opens his eyes.

Two faces, both lined and dark.

The man wears a beaten, wide-brimmed straw hat. Big man, broad nose.

The woman is small and old, time chipping away at her spine, leaving her stooped. Head-tied and pink-lipped, she looks down on him with wary eyes.

"You got a name, boy?" The man touches the woman's shoulder and she disappears behind him.

Simple space. A tin roof; Willie supposes that it points, slopes, and then goes flat for four or more feet.

He opens his mouth, but only squeaks.

"Get him some water."

Willie hears the footfalls off to his left. Sturdy floor, he thinks. The wood plank walls end in sharp corners. A saltbox house. He'd helped build one of these when he was on the plantation. His eyes flutter with the memory.

"Here." The man's big hands are gentle as they ease Willie up and help him to drink the water. The first few sips burn his throat, but then a whole desert comes to light in his gut and he has three more glasses before he gives his name.

"Willie."

"Where you all come from?"

"Kentucky."

"Where you all headed?"

"Myanmar."

"Myanmar? What for?"

"Don't know, got an inkling about it."

Eyes swing.

"You sure that's where you headed?"

Willie nods his head.

They'd heard stories about Myanmar. Niggers being whipped in the street, strung from trees, burned alive. The devil and his disciples lived in Myanmar.

"Niggers ain't welcome there," the woman says, and has to untwine his fingers from the glass in order to take it.

"You ain't got no business there," the man says.

Young, soft, black eyes peer at him from behind the big man. Willie strains his neck and the eyes disappear behind the back of the old woman whose eyes swing and then slant.

"Here, neither," she says. And then, "Go in the bedroom, chile."

A soundless agreement, shuffling feet. Willie catches sight of the swinging material of a skirt before it disappears around the corner.

"You running?" The question is sudden.

Willie ponders this. He is, in some respect. Running from his past, from death, running toward his future.

"I guess."

Eyes blink.

"You made it all the way from Kentucky and ain't run into no paddy rollers?"

Willie's mouth twitches. "Ain't no need for them no more," he says slowly.

"What you saying, boy?"

Willie cocks his head and stares hard at the faces that look down on him before he speaks again. "War over, slavery done."

Faces go blank with confusion.

"What's that?"

"Lincoln freed all of us niggers."

Faces unfold and then the lips smile unbelievingly. The old woman waves a hand at him. "You must got fever, boy," she mutters.

"No ma'am; feeling weak, but not feverish."

Fire burning in the hearth, crackling, sending off flaming bits of ash that curl and fade on the floor.

"Foolish, then," the big man whispers, but leans in closer. "You crazy, right?" he says, but Willie can hear in his voice that he hopes he's not.

"Nah, sir," Willie says, shaking his head. "I got all my senses." He uses his index finger to press against his temple.

The big man glances at the old woman. There's shuffling of feet, muttering, and soft sighs.

"You sure?"

"Ay-yuh," Willie says, astonished at their ignorance. "You didn't know?"

"How long?" the big man barks at him.

Willie flinches. "Since June."

An hour passes, maybe two, and the grilling continues. Willie's throat goes dry as he recounts his story, but the old woman refuses to give him more water, or can't; she seems frozen by his words.

The big man removes his hat and fans his face with the brim. "My Lord," he utters, and looks down at his feet.

When the old woman finally gives him another cup of water, her hand trembles as she passes it off to him and most of it ends up on Willie's chest.

Then she turns questioning eyes to the big man, who seems to be void of answers.

The silence is long and stiff. They all remain in their places, pondering something that they can't just yet share with Willie. He remains silent, empty tin cup in hand, eyes floating over everything and everyone.

A grunt from the man Willie would learn was called Brother ends it all, and time suddenly starts up again. "Take 'im out to the barn," he says, and the old woman called Laney shows him the way.

It had none of the comforts of the saltbox, but there was a cot, and while the cold made itself known, the extra socks and coat kept it bearable. The horse and its mare didn't seem to mind, and Willie would make sure to let them both know that nothing like what happened to the goat would happen to them.

The big house that sat on the hill seemed empty. Slaves and no slave owners? Niggers living on all of this land and no white folk to be seen? Willie shook his head. Maybe things in Georgia went different from Kentucky.

Willie's eyes were growing heavy, but his stomach turned over. The plate of food they'd given him had burned away as quickly as it had dropped down inside of him, and now he felt ravenous.

He crept outside of the barn and stood in the center of the enclosed pen and stared up at the moon. Moving left, his eyes fell on the big house again and caught hold of a flicker of light traveling between the windows before blooming and then disappearing.

"Haints," he muttered before helping himself to what was left in the mare's trough.

"He telling a tale, been running too long, mind all mixed up and confused," Laney says.

Brother nods his head. "Could be, could be not," he says thoughtfully.

"You believe him?" Laney says in shock.

"He ain't got no reason to lie to us."

"Crazy is reason enough," Laney says, slapping her palm down on the table and then turning her head toward the window that looks out on the barn.

"Maybe." Brother's words are soft. "But that might 'splain why we ain't seen hide nor hair of a white man in months."

"What you think, they all dead?" Laney's tone is mocking.

"Not all but maybe most."

"You just as crazy as he is!" Laney shouts, and folds her arms across her breasts. "White men everywhere, take the hand of God to wipe the earth clean of 'em."

Brother turns somber eyes on Laney. "Maybe that's just what has happened."

Laney shakes her head in amazement. "That ain't what has happened; the boy done told you he seen 'em everywhere from Kentucky to Georgia."

Brother smirks.

"Sooner or later, one gonna show up right here," Laney says, and taps the wooden table for emphasis.

Willie makes five.

New moons come and go before Willie gets the whole story and the viewing.

Days stretch, and warm and wild crocuses lay a purple blanket across the land. Birds are singing and the sun is smiling down on them, warming even Laney's chilly disposition toward him.

Willie helps with the chores, does whatever he's told to do, says little and asks even less, but he's sure to keep his eyes peeled for a white man coming by to collect, show up and stare, ride up and point out what gotta be done next. But none ever come and the chores go on day in and day out like someone's watching. Maybe, Willie thinks, they doing it for God.

"So Laney your mama?" he chances and asks one day. He's been wondering all along, wanting to know who's kin and who's not.

"Godsend mother," Brother says and looks real hard at a knothole in the wood. "My real mama died some time back."

"Indian?" Willie ventures, having seen the curl and straight of the man's head whenever he thinks to remove his hat.

"Yeah."

"And the girl?" Willie hopes he doesn't sound too eager.

"My sister."

"Godsend?"

"Nah, blood."

Nothing for some time, then Brother giving him a wry smile and asking, "Ain't you gonna ask about Spin?"

And what of the big house on the hill?

He wanted to ask. He found himself staring at it for long periods of time. It was hard to ignore, but the rest of them managed to do it. As far as he could tell, their eyes hardly wandered up that hill and to the mansion that stood there.

He'd never been warned to stay away from the house, but the manner in which they pretended it wasn't there made Willie feel that he should act accordingly.

By June they had torn down and rebuilt the pigpen more times than Willie could count. Well, he'd stopped counting when he ran out of fingers and toes. That frustrated him—that and the sun beating down on his neck.

Winter had kept him humble, spring made him grateful, but this early summer heat just made him feel mad for some reason, so when Brother told Willie to pull down the east side of the pen again, Willie had to loose his tongue and ask, "What for?"

Brother didn't say a word, just used his hammer to point to the east side as he strolled past Willie and out toward the field.

Willie watched him for a while and then he thought about the hot meals and not-too-cold barn. He thought about Suce's soft eyes. He could do a lot worse than building, tearing down, and rebuilding a pigpen.

He moved to the east section and began extracting the nails.

"I think we can trust him." Brother spoke slow.

"Why?"

"'Cause he been here all this time and ain't asked but one or two questions."

"So?"

"So? You think he don't know something is wrong here?"

"And?"

"Look, Laney, he here, he helping out, he got a right to know."

"He want Suce. Did you know that?"

Silence.

Spin fumbled with his fingers, but kept his face calm.

"I see the way they look at each other," she pressed.

Brother's face was serene, his voice low. "Can't expect nothing less. She at that age and he far beyond it and alone, what you 'spect them to look at, the trees and the dirt?"

"Humph."

"Suce gonna need a husband. You want her to walk off down the road in search of one and not come back, like Tenk?"

"We don't know that's what happened! Tenk had a wife right here. I was his wife and I was right here, always right here!"

"Ain't nothing against you, Laney. I'm just saying, what you 'spect?"

Laney rubbed at her chin. "You talkin' foolish talk anyhow; Suce just a child."

"Won't be a child forever."

"By then someone else closer to her age might come along."

"Or might not."

They told him.

Well, Brother did most of the talking, while Suce kept quiet and Laney paced, and Spin just stared out the window into the night.

"Sure 'nuff?" Willie was astonished; he had been called a dumb nigger so many times that he thought it was true of him and the rest of his race. He slapped his thigh and laughed. "Well I'll be," he said, shaking his head in amazement.

Brother folded his hands across his chest and waited, while Laney just made a face.

It all made sense now. And he kind of smiled at Suce. It wasn't no haint, just Suce, he thought to himself. "Well I'll be," he said again.

"So now you know."

"Yes, yes I do," Willie said, still unable to wipe the look of amusement off his face.

"C'mon," Brother said, and jumped up from his chair. The move was so sudden, Willie's body jerked and he had to fight the urge to bring his hands up to his face in defense.

Brother threw him a baffled look, snatched his hat off the nail on the wall, and started through the door.

Willie hustled behind him, not daring to ask where it was they were going in the darkness. He realized he didn't need to when Brother turned left and started up the path that led to the big house on the hill.

It was a climb, and the farther they went, the darker it seemed to get. Willie felt his chest constrict and suddenly found himself gasping for air. Fear?

"Keep up," Brother muttered, and his stride quickened.

Willie sucked air and walked faster.

When they got to the door, Brother looked around cautiously before grabbing hold of the knob and pushing it open.

Willie hesitated. The main hall was dark.

"Well?" Brother said, and Willie looked up to see Brother's yellow-tinged eyes glaring down at him.

Willie stepped in.

There was a smell. Something he couldn't name. Willie sniffed at the air and then covered his nose with the palm of his hand and moved closer to Brother.

They climb the stairs, Brother surefooted and swift, Willie stumbling. Once at the top, they turn left and start down the narrow hallway. The light is better there; the moon is framed in the small window at the end of the hall. Willie's heart slows a bit, and he's able to straighten his back some.

They move toward the only doorway, located at the end of the hall. When Brother pushes it open, the hinges scream and that horrid feeling Willie was just able to shake off leaps back on him again.

"Who's there?" a small voice asks through the darkness.

Willie remains in the hallway while Brother steps inside and disappears into the gloomy darkness of the bedroom. There's some fumbling and the distinctive sound of a match being struck.

An orange-blue flame momentarily illuminates the darkness before it catches hold of the wick of the oil lamp.

Brother holds the lamp low over what—or who—it is he's brought Willie to see.

In the dim yellow glow, Willie's gaze slowly slides down the mahogany headboard, falling first on gray hair, then blue eyes lodged in a face that is as white as the bedsheets.

The mouth is the worst—thin lips, turned in, but still managing a ludicrous grin that barely contains the toothless pink gums.

"Who you?" the horrible mouth asks as the blue eyes roll frantically in their sockets.

Willie's tongue fumbles for his name, but is rescued from the task when Brother quickly extinguishes the flame and throws them all back into darkness.

Back down at the house, right in front of the door, Brother turned to Willie and asked, "You in or out?"

Willie looked up into Brother's eyes. "Well" was the first word that came to mind, because this here was a dangerous game they were playing. White folks were hopping mad at what Lincoln had done, and as much as things had changed, Willie felt sure that the old ways remained the same. He himself had seen smoking bodies swinging from tree limbs. And he was sure it was for some meager offense or maybe just the offense of having been born black. He didn't know.

If he had never been sure of any one thing in his life, looking into Brother's eyes made him sure of the fact that if his answer wasn't the right one, he would be dead before daybreak.

"In."

Now that he knew, he didn't know how to sleep at night.

"How you do it?" he asked.

"Do what?" Brother said as he examined the dull edge of his knife.

"Sleep. How you sleep at night?"

Brother looked at him with bewilderment. "What?"

"I can't sleep now." Willie's voice shook a bit and there was a small film of perspiration above his lip.

Brother stared hard at him and he saw that Willie's eyes were bloodshot. "You forgot how to do it?" Brother laughed and shook his head.

Willie let out a frustrated sigh. "You ain't worried you'll be found out?"

It was Brother's turn to sigh. "Think about it every day, but I ain't got it in me to worry," he said.

"What?" Willie questioned eagerly. "What's that?"

Brother turned the knife over in his hands. "What can they do to me that ain't already done?"

"They can kill you," Willie snapped back at him.

"Shoot." Brother laughed, turned away from Willie, and aimed the knife at the bark of the ash tree. He narrowed his eyes, pulled his arm back, and then brought it forward with a quick jerk, sending the knife sailing through the air. "I was born dead," he said as the point of the knife stuck in the bark of the tree with a thump.

Willie gave him a blank look.

"What, you sayin' you call slavery living?" Brother said, and started toward the tree to retrieve his knife. "Well lookee there," Brother chuckled as he pulled the knife from the tree. "Wasn't as dull as I thought it was."

Months pass and Suce becomes comfortable in her twelfth year and her place at the supper table, right next to Willie.

Brother sees that her eyes are moist with womanhood, even though Laney remains tight-lipped about the blood that had stained Suce's bloomers a month earlier.

Willie seems barely able to contain himself. Brother has spotted Willie rubbing himself up against the hard bark of the spruce, sometimes hears his shuddering cry from his place in the barn, and Brother was relieved to slaughter the cow, especially after he caught Willie eyeing it a little too closely.

Brother tried to push his own thoughts of lust and the want of a woman out of his mind. But sometimes they just seemed to rush at him, and he would have to go out into the woods and touch himself to beat back the heat that boiled inside of him.

Not only did Spin have half a mind and no words, he also had no shame. So when the feeling hit him, he whipped out his penis right where he stood and began to stroke it.

Laney had beat Spin near senseless with her broom the first time he'd done it in her presence, but now when she saw his hands fiddling with the rope that kept his pants up, she just waved a tired hand at him and said, "Go on away from here with that nastiness now."

Suce, stepping away from childhood with every footfall she took. Womanhood clinging to her hips and pushing out her chest. Barely five feet tall, still childlike in height, but anybody could see if he looked hard enough that no child's face could carry such an intense look of determination.

Brother supposed that living the way they were living growed her up a mite faster than if there wasn't so much to look out for and worry about. He himself was only twenty-seven and had a head full of gray hair. Laney was bent over so far, it was a wonder her lips didn't kiss the ground, and what was she? Forty-five, fifty?

Spin was the only one who didn't seem affected by their circumstances. Just about twenty, if Brother was counting right. Broad-shouldered and barrel-chested, arms too long and feet too big. Tiny head, small mind, dead tongue. Simple.

Brother wouldn't label the luck they'd had over the past year and a half. Wouldn't call it good or bad, but he would give it a sex: female.

Female because it could be fickle and could turn on you on a moment's notice. But the luck they had was still in its infancy, crawling. Brother supposed that when luck gained its footing, it would either pitter-patter around and cause some confusion or just stroll straight away.

They were living on borrowed time for sure, and so when Brother gave the word, Laney made Suce a wedding gown by stitching two of Lessing's fine linen tablecloths together. Spin made a crown for her out of the honeysuckle vines and daisies. Brother gave her a pouch of seeds that Lou had saved from the apples Buena had brought to her during their courting. Willie, embarrassed that he had no grand gifts to offer, blushed and presented her with the tiny slip of paper that said MYANMAR.

Suce frowned, embarrassed that she hadn't thought of anything to present him with. "You giving me you," Willie reminded her, and took her by the hand.

Down in the clearing, just in earshot of the stream, Brother shared some words.

He thanked the ancestors for blessing them and thanked the earth for providing. "Go on now," Brother whispered to the couple when he'd run out of things to say. "Go on and jump that broom."

Willie and Suce exchanged looks, peered down at the broom that rested at their feet, and leapt into marriage.

Laney uttered some words, sprinkled dried herbs at their feet, smiled when they looked at her, then sneered when her face was to their backs.

No children would bless that union for twelve years.

By 1867 the town is like a maggot, gobbling up whole tracts of land. Laney look at Brother and her look says, *See, we are not alone.*

Their middle of nowhere now seems to be the center of everywhere.

Wagons inch up and down the road, heavy with lumber. Curious faces, white and black, stare up at the house on the hill and then fall to the saltbox down below that has now grown into five rooms.

Some venture past the posts, walk right up to whoever is available. They ask questions, point, smile, nod, and in the end are sent away with a story that is worn thin with time and layered with dust.

Willie, Spin, and Brother wait until a December winter night to walk the few miles it takes to get to where the white clapboard of the new houses shines like lamplight from between barren branches.

They tilt their heads and inhale the old familiar scents—fried chicken, cabbage, stewed beef, pig's tail—that seem to be sprinkled in the air all around them, and they recall the aromas at each and every meal when Laney placed plates of boiled potatoes down before them.

There was nothing left. The winter had taken away the collard greens, peanuts, peaches, figs, and watermelons. Wild game was even more scarce, but they had a stable full of potatoes.

Brother supposed they had planned wrong or hadn't planned at all when it came to the food. It wasn't until Laney snapped the neck of the last fowl that they even thought about where the eggs would come from now.

And then they had to deal with the accusing looks from the rooster for two months before despair and dejection engulfed him and he flapped his wings and rushed the side of the house hard enough to shatter his beak and fracture one of his wings.

When the others heard the thump, they came running and were witness to the sad sight of the rooster running in circles, its face bleeding, one wing dragging in the dirt, before throwing itself headfirst against the house. The impact crushed its skull, and it collapsed. Dead.

Laney thought, as she collected the body to prepare it for dinner, that the rooster had the right idea.

Now Laney's eyes traveled across the bland faces around the table and she spit defensively, "There ain't nothing else I can do with a potato that I ain't already done."

Brother gave Laney a comforting look, but it was too late; feelings were hurt, the damage was done, and she just threw herself down into her chair and huffed.

"Someone's got to go," Willie muttered as Suce pushed her dinner plate away, thinking she cannot eat another potato, sweet or Irish.

"Someone's gotta go," he said again, nudging the plate back toward Suce and whispering, "You gotta eat."

Brother nodded.

He'd been fighting the reality for months, but now that every tin had been scraped clean, every flour sack emptied, Brother figured the fight was over; reality had won.

And there was still Lessing to think about, up in that room wheezing his way through the remaining days of his life, calling Laney "Mother" and Brother "Pa." He'd reached out for Suce one day and touched the swell of her breast and sputtered, "Nice."

After that, the sheet rose up from between his legs and Suce came down the hill and said she thought it best if Laney or one of the others tended to Lessing.

Willie thought they should just let him starve to death or, he'd whispered to Brother, "If you like, I can take care of it for you."

Brother hadn't answered him. He *wanted* Lessing dead more

than anything, but something in him told him that he *needed* him alive.

So yes, somebody would have to go.

It couldn't be either of the women.

Spin was just too slow in mind and, besides, he didn't talk. So it was down to Brother and Willie.

Brother had never ventured more than five miles away from the Lessing plantation. Willie, on the other hand, had walked clear cross two states. Brother lifted his fork, jabbed at a chunk of potato, and said, "You go."

Two days later, just before daybreak, Lessing's small velvet sack filled with coins in his pocket and Brother's straw hat pulled low over his forehead, Willie left after midnight to begin the twenty-mile trek east toward town.

The woods where he once found safety and shelter now held fear. Willie moved unsure through the thick of trees, twigs breaking away beneath his shoes, him looking over his shoulder every three paces. Shadows danced in moonlight-drenched places, and even though the night was still with no sound except the crunch of cold earth and twigs beneath his feet, Willie's mind was filled with the rolling sound of carriage wheels and he was sure he could smell the foul stench of death's breath wafting around him.

When the sky faded from black to purple and finally the pale blue of dawn, Willie caught sight of a white blouse, gray skirt, and black-buttoned boots.

He stopped, crouched, and waited. One swelled into five, five into ten, ten into twenty and more, until the road was teeming with people. Black folks walking, some on wagons.

He stepped out just as two young black women were approaching. They walked along smiling, baskets hanging from their wrists, whispering and giggling. All that stopped, though, when Willie emerged from behind a tree.

"Mornin'," he muttered, and tipped the tattered hat.

They nodded, but did not offer him anything beyond that. He fell into step behind them.

He was nervous, that was a fact, but no one seemed to notice. He checked himself, brushing away burrs from his jacket sleeves, making himself look presentable even though Suce had put him together quite nicely—she'd even been able to sew his old dust-lapping shoes closed again.

Closer to town, the road narrowed and went thin as a line and then spread out again. Shops made out of clapboard and pressed close together leaned on either side of the street.

Willie couldn't read, but there was a feed store, a bank, a post office, a tannery, a blacksmith, and a millinery shop. He moved through slowly, not knowing where to stop, but the saloon seemed the best place, as there was a black woman dressed in bright colors, leaned up against a post and smoking a cigarette.

"Afternoon," Willie said, and tried to keep his eyes even with hers. Trying hard not to let them drop down to the rounded mounds of her bosom that pushed up out of her corset.

Her eyes rolled over him and she smiled. "You a sight, ain't you?" She laughed and took a long drag on her cigarette.

Willie straightened his back and fumbled with the tattered material of his lapels.

"Uhm, I'm new in town, needing to know the ins and the outs 'bout here," he said, and chanced a glance inside the saloon.

"Uh-huh," she said, and took another long drag of her cigarette.

"Wanna know where I can buy some feed, maybe get some cheese, flour, and whatnot."

"What's the whatnot?" she purred, and rested her free hand on the curve of her hip.

Willie could do nothing else but laugh. Not a hard laugh, more like a snicker. "I dunno." He coughed and stepped out of the way of a white man who was exiting the saloon.

"General store right 'cross there," the woman said, and nodded her head to the left.

Willie's eyes swung in that direction, but the letters on the windows meant nothing to him.

"Where y'all staying?" she asked.

"Yonder," he said, but didn't nod his head in any particular direction. The woman tossed her head and humphed, then blew smoke over his head.

Willie's feet did a small shuffle like he was going to walk off, but then he stilled them and moved his eyes toward the battered saloon door.

"Niggers welcome in there?"

"There?" The woman threw a look over her shoulder. "Nah," she said, and snubbed out the butt of the cigarette on the bottom of her shoe. "But you all can buy a taste 'round back."

"That right?" Willie said, and fingered the velvet sack of silver coins in his pocket.

"You all got money?" she asked, coylike, but Willie saw the eagerness in her eyes.

"Some."

"You all sharecropping?"

"Yeah."

Another sound in her throat and her eyes just stretched into saucers while her hand reached out and fingered the torn buttonholes of his jacket.

He could smell her. Lord, he couldn't remember the last time he smelled something so good. Suce was clean-smelling, like the stream behind the house and the honeysuckle flowers she pressed between her fingers and rubbed around her neck. But this nigger woman smelled like what he remembered sex reeked of the first time he stole some from a woman twice his age down in the Kentucky bluegrass.

Willie rocked on the balls of his feet.

Suce fading and what he'd come to accomplish gone with one inhale of that harlot's perfume.

Willie's eyes fluttered closed and he rocked closer.

The shotgun blast tore through the spell, and his eyes flew open and fell on the woman's grinning, painted lips. He took two steps backward and shook away the cobwebs in his head.

"Fool," she muttered just as the moment slipped completely away and Willie's eyes cleared.

"You say the general store that a-way?" Willie's voice stalled and started again.

A laugh, a fling of her head, and then, "Yeah, nigger, right o'er there."

Willie double-stepped getting across the road, but he chanced a quick look over his shoulder to see the sashay of the woman's behind before she stepped between the swinging doors and the piano music swallowed her whole.

No, he didn't know what anything cost. He'd never handled money a day in his life, and so when the white man handed him the packages of flour, cheese, slab bacon, sugar, and meal, Willie just pushed a silver coin across the counter and started to walk away.

"Hey, nigga!" the white shopkeeper shouted after him.

Willie stalled, thought about running, but his feet didn't obey.

"Boy, you gotta give me *two* silver pieces!" The man slammed his palm down on the counter and muttered, "Stupid niggas."

Willie blew air out from his nose, turned around, careful to keep his eyes lowered as he approached the counter, and set another silver piece down on the flat surface before making a quick departure.

Twelve hours and no sleep. Suce pacing the floor and worried to death. Laney holed up in her bed and muttering to the ceiling. Spin walking the cold air in and out of the house until Brother gave him a threatening look and Spin stepped in and pulled the door shut behind him.

A soft rapping came at the door just when the moon was at its fullest. Spin and Brother looked at each other and then back at

the door. Before they could move, Suce had crossed the hard-
wood floor and swung it open.

Willie stepped in, his arms full of packages and a wide,
bright smile looming above them.

It seemed to take forever to get that cast-iron stove hot. In between stirring the kindling, mixing the flour, and rolling the
dough for biscuits, Laney and Suce tried to get all of what Willie was saying.

His words showered out in a rush of excitement. He did his
best to describe everything and everyone.

"Were you scared, Willie?" Suce asked.

"Sure 'nuff scared that one of them white men was just going to snatch me up and haul me away!"

In the end, they all sat gathered around the table at the
midnight hour and ate like it was the first time they'd ever
tasted food.

After they'd feasted, Laney went off to bed and Suce gathered herself on Willie's lap and fell asleep while Brother sat at
the table studying his fingers.

"What's on your mind, Brother?" Willie yawned as he
stroked Suce's hair.

"I'm thinking next time, I'm coming with you."

Next time came a week later, and Suce wanted to go too. But
Laney didn't. "And neither should you!" she said with a cough,
spitting a wad of mucous into the dirt. "I ain't trying to test
fate," she added, and shook her head.

Brother and Willie hitched the mule to the wagon and
made the trip by themselves.

The following week, Suce went along.

And after that, Laney couldn't stand it anymore and decided
that fate was what it was, and she and Spin went to go see.

There they were, five niggers living high on the hog, walking through town, careful where their eyes fell, not forgetting

how to address the white folk, and having to walk just a little stooped over.

They got some hard looks, just like Willie had said, but nothing really beyond that, except for the man at the general store who looked at Brother and said, "Are you Jennie's man, Thomas?"

"No sir."

"Damndest thing, you look just like him. Quarter-pound of lard, you said?"

"Yes sir."

They all came back laughing. Joyous, arms loaded down with packages of everything, including a new pair of shoes for Willie and new frocks for Laney and Suce. Medicine for Laney's cough, a ball for Spin to play fetch with the dogs.

Luck, Brother decided as he snapped the reins against the horses' backs, had earned a first name, and so he christened her "Good."

They came home with so many things, but the joy carried the most weight and so it hit the ground the hardest when the wagon turned the bend and there were two white men standing and smoking on the porch of the big house.

Willie had taken to calling her Suce-Suce. Enjoying the whistle of breath on his tongue that came along with the "Ssssss" that began her name.

It was her name he was calling, her fingers he was fiddling with, when Brother pulled the reins left and the horses turned down the path toward home.

Suce was laughing softly and shaking her head at her husband's foolishness when Laney muttered, "Help me, Jesus," and clutched her heart.

Suce's head jerked around, and her hands followed just as quickly, urgently grabbing hold of Laney's arm as she asked, "What is it, what's wrong?"

Laney's eyes were focused straight ahead. Not noticing, Suce shook Laney's arm and asked again, "What is it, Laney?"

And Suce's eyes never would have left the struck expression on Laney's face if it hadn't been for the nudge in her side from Willie. Suce's head swiveled toward her husband's face, where she found the same startled expression.

Her eyes followed his, and she almost jumped up out of her seat when they landed on what Willie and Laney were seeing, but Willie's hand came down hard on her thigh, crushing her urge to bolt.

Spin, who was sitting alongside Brother, looked at the white men who were standing on the porch of the big house, then down at the rough skin of his own knuckles. He felt a strange quivering in his chest and felt his eyes begin to fill up with water.

Brother snapped the reins, and the horses remained steady in their advance.

The white men, who were standing close to the front door, turned when they heard the wagon, and started across the porch and down the steps.

Willie looked down at his new shoes and thought how nice it had been to wear something that hadn't been passed down, tore up, and mended. He thought about the neck of the goat and the fatback crackling in the pan and his mother's soft lap beneath his young legs and how these last two years hadn't been bad at all—tense, but not bad at all compared to the first thirty. This whole experience had been a breath of fresh air where before there had been no air at all.

Spin's mind whirled and caught on something in his memory that had sparkled and given him great joy as a child. And there he remained.

Brother had no thoughts other than keeping the horses at a steady pace and meeting the eyes of the white men who looked back at them.

"Whoa!" he ordered, and the horses came to a stop. By then, the white men had made their way down the path.

"Afternoon," Brother said as he began to climb down from his perch on the wagon.

The first white man had familiar eyes and a face that was cratered and red. His hair was blondish-brown and he wore a fine suit that looked out of place on that backwoods property. The other one was thin, dressed just as fine, with a tall black hat and a nose so thin it was a wonder he didn't grab air with his mouth. He stood, lips pinched, eyes glaring.

The man with familiar eyes spoke first, but not until he'd tucked his thumbs into the slits of his jacket. "Is this Charlie Lessing's property?" he asked as he made a sweeping gesture with his hand.

"Yassir."

"Is he home?" the thin one said, pointing up toward the house.

"No sir."

The men exchanged glances.

"Well, what time are you expecting him back?"

"A day or so." And then, "May we ask who's inquiring?"

"Obery Lessing. His brother," the thin man said.

"And Fenton Lessing, his son," Familiar Eyes said, and waited.

Brother faltered a bit; his words started and then stopped when he realized that he had nothing more to say.

"Gone to Ohio to buy pigs," Laney said, and then dismissed the men as quickly as she would have a bothersome child. "Help me down, Brother," she said, and stuck a fragile hand out toward him.

"Pigs?" Fenton's voice betrayed his bewilderment as he watched the old woman carefully climb down from the wagon.

"Yassir," Brother said, and turned and nodded toward the pen.

"Oh."

"Well," Obery said, starting toward the horses that were tied to the fence, "tell him we called and we'll be back in a day or so."

They stood silent while they watched the two men ride off.

"The two boys he had gone off to fight and died. I saw Lessing cry the tears myself," Laney said as she shook her balled fists in the air.

"Got killed," Brother sighed.

"No matter how you say it, gone is gone."

"Where this 'son' come from then?"

"And a brother too?"

"Maybe they lying?"

"Nah, the boy got his eyes."

"Sure do."

"What us gonna do?"

"Cut and run."

"Yeah, cut, but running ain't necessary. We free, we can walk right out of town," Willie said.

"Yeah, and got money to do it with."

"This land is ours. We worked it. Brother, you got a mother

and brother buried here. I got three of my girls and a son dug in deep here, and a heck of a lotta others. I ain't leaving. You better find a way to make it right, 'cause I ain't going," Laney said.

Two days at most, that's all they had, and Brother had used up most of those hours standing over Lessing. Standing and just staring and thinking, he was sure of what it was they would have to do.

Yes, they could cut and—no matter what the hell Willie said, walking would not be an option—they would have to run as far away as possible. But town had been a journey to a place so foreign that they had found themselves feeling out of place amongst their own people. So what would the rest of the world be like? They would stick out like sore thumbs. Hard looks would be welcomed then, because the alternative would be questions, Brother was sure—questions that he wouldn't have answers to.

So what to do?

Suce came to him early in the morning; by then his legs wouldn't hold his weight much longer, even though his mind was still alert and racing over everything and anything he had seen and heard in his lifetime. So when Suce came creeping in, he got angry immediately because he didn't have the solution he was sure she was coming there to hear.

"What?!" Brother's tone shocked her. He'd never spoken harshly to her, not even when she was small and was fond of biting him, not even then, but now he addressed her as if she alone had put him in this predicament.

"We in deep," she said like this was news. Brother said nothing. "Laney right in one way, Willie right in another."

Brother fingered the drapes.

"I say we come this far, but I don't think we gone all the way."

Brother turned and looked at her.

"I figure we got a right to this land like Laney say."

Of course they did, but God didn't have niggers on his mind, so what she was saying were just words.

"I knows where the will is at."

Suce didn't have a child growing inside of her belly, but she did have want and desire blooming there. Not just in her belly, but stretching through her veins and spreading throughout her being.

No part of her was willing to give it up—that feeling, that freedom—and so all the want and desire clamped down and sprouted and she felt hate rush through her for the first time in her life. It curled her hands into fists and sprung something wild within her when she looked up and saw those white men waiting on the porch. It was all she could do to keep herself from leaping down from the wagon, rushing them, and scratching them blind and biting out their throats.

And so there she stood, having pondered just as long as Brother had, but unlike Brother she had pondered and fell on a possibility where there seemed no possibility had existed.

"And?" Brother said and waited.

"We can change it and make the land ours."

Brother didn't know anything about wills and such things; his mother had taught him that slavery was wrong, that owning the land was wrong, that taking more than was needed was wrong, and since slaves owned nothing, not even the flesh on their bones or the bones of themselves, wills weren't anything that had ever been needed or considered or brought up in conversation until now.

Suce turned away from him and moved to the small writing desk. Opening the middle drawer, she rummaged awhile and then pulled out a piece of rolled parchment tied with a red bow.

She turned back to face him and held it up like a scepter. That move alone made her look regal, and Brother lowered his eyes in honor.

"What's that?"

"Massa—" she started and then corrected herself. "*Lessing's* last will and testament."

Brother waited as she gently removed the ribbon and unfurled the document.

"It says here," she began,

"*I bequeath to my wife Isabel, ten tracts of land and plantation wheron we now live. One cow called Bell.*

120 acres purchased from Vicey to be divided equally between my sons, Jacob and Joseph.

I bestow the white mare called Snow to my wife and the mare called Ink to my son Jacob.

The Negroes: Laney, Tenk, Hop, Jim, and Suce and her increase are to be given to my wife.

Lynx, Lee, and Soap are to be given to my son Joseph.

Jeruey, Ida, Axel, and Smyrna and her increase are to be given to my son Jacob.

I appoint my son Joseph to be my executor."

Brother listened again as Suce read the words on the page to the group. Some sentences came as smooth as water, others contained words that came out jagged, but all made him think of being divided as easily as eggs and that made him angry.

"I don't know," Willie said, exhaling and sending the candlelight dancing.

"I do," Laney muttered and drummed her fingers on the table.

Brother said nothing. Suce was on her fifth piece of parchment, trying hard to imitate the swirling letters that split them up as easily as dough.

By morning, Suce's fingers were swollen and Willie's head was on the table. Laney had long since gone off to her room. Spin was curled in a ball on the floor in the sitting room, but Brother remained awake, his eyes red and puffed but his mind alert.

The final imitation looked as good as the original:

I bequeath to my wife Isabel, the home wherein we now live.

I bestow the Negroes: Lynx, Tenk, Ida, Exel, and Smyrna and her increase to be divided equally between my sons Joseph and Jacob.

Upon my death, the Negroes known as Brother, Laney, Hop, Spin, Willie, and Suce and her increase are to be released from the bondage of slavery and gifted forty acres of land for their good service.

I appoint my son Joseph to be my executor.

It didn't sound real, but the past two years had seemed like a dream, so Brother guessed it fit. The seal would be a problem—already it mocked them, thornlike and as red as the bloodiest of roses. Brother was sure if he touched it, it would prick him.

"The seal is somewhere in the house; it has to be," Suce said.

But after hours of searching and Laney calling them for the fourth time to come and sit down for lunch, still they'd found nothing.

Ham on the table, like a last supper. Corn bread and sweet potato, mashed and dripping with butter. Kale seasoned with salt pork, and peach pie set out and still bubbling hot when they arrived.

Last supper, for sure, and the sun already setting, hurrying up tomorrow and their deaths, for sure.

"That look real 'ficial like," Willie had said between bites of food.

"Well, it ain't. It ain't got no seal," Brother threw back at him, and scratched his head in frustration.

Willie stared at the document and blinked. "That there?" he said, using his greasy finger to point at the red smudge of wax on the original will.

Ignorant nigger, Brother thought, and cut a hefty slice of pie.

Suce nodded.

"Oh."

They all stared down at the paper, the signature, and the wax seal that made it all official.

"How'd they do that?" Willie asked as he leaned in to get a better look at it. Brother slowly slid the document away from him.

"What?"

"You got food hanging out of all sides of your mouth, you wanna ruin it?"

Willie used the back of his hand to wipe away the debris.

"It's candle wax, is all," Suce said.

"Well, we got plenty of that," Laney said, but Suce's and Brother's faces still looked troubled. "What's wrong?" Laney ventured.

"The letters in the wax," Suce said.

Laney peered at it. "Well, you could write those in too, can't you?"

Suce shook her head no.

"Why not?" Willie muttered.

"See here"—Suce used her delicate pinky finger to point at the seal—"there's little tiny hats all around the letters."

"Crowns," Brother corrected her.

"Crowns," Suce said exasperatedly.

"Shit," Laney said.

The seal had to be somewhere in that house. They dug through every dresser drawer, looked in places a seal wouldn't have had any business being. Laney asked Lessing point-blank, "Where the seal at, Lessing?" But all she got was a toothless grin that let on that he might not be as mad as they thought he was.

That grin of his sent something hot and crawling through Brother's body. He had to steel his arm at his side so as not to slap the old man. Jim's swinging and then burning, Lou pregnant with grief . . . the memories rolled into him, and he centered his hand at his side.

The sun was coming up. It was usually a slow rise, one that Suce had loved to admire, but that morning she decided the moon belonged to niggers and the sun to white folk, 'cause on that day the sun climbed into the sky faster than she'd ever known it could and shone brighter than she'd ever seen it shine.

Nowhere.

They hadn't missed a spot, a crook, or cranny, but still they turned up nothing. They mulled it over now, each in a plush parlor chair. Thinking, thinking.

"Hop probably got to it," Laney mumbled as she twirled a long gold thread around and around her finger.

"What you say?" Brother half inquired. His eyes were set on his shoes and the fine carpet beneath it.

"I said that Hop probably got to it."

Brother just snuffed, and a small grin broke through where there had only been placid resolve. Hop had light fingers, yes he did—could steal a tail feather from a blackbird and the bird wouldn't have noticed the loss.

Brother leaned back into the chair. His shoulders were aching, the lower part of his back tight and throbbing. "You might be right on that one," he said.

Suce nodded in agreement. "Well, anyone for coffee?" she said as if this new day was like every other day before it.

Brother just looked at her.

Willie said, "Ay-yuh, I s'pose I could go for a cup."

Laney's head shook no and then yes.

"You want it sweet?" Suce asked Brother.

Brother's head cocked a bit, like he was considering changing the way he'd been living since he was fifteen.

"You usually like it sweet," Suce said, hurrying up his sluggish memory.

"I think you're right," Brother said, and slowly raised himself up and out of his chair.

"Well, that's the way you always take it—"

"Not you," he said, pointing a finger in Suce's direction. "*You!*" he bellowed, and the finger swung to Laney.

Laney jumped. "What?"

"I bet you Hop got that seal," Brother said, his eyes glimmering.

"Hop dead," Suce reminded him.

"Get the shovel, Willie," Laney said, and started toward the front door.

"Ma'am?"

Behind the house, just paces from the stream, Willie worked at unearthing Hop's coffin. Plain and simple and mostly eaten away by wood worms.

Hop's body was wrapped in a quilt that was covered in maggots.

Willie covered his nose while Brother reached in and pulled out the small sack that Hop had kept his treasures in.

A silver coin, a button, a piece of blue granite in the shape of a bird, a jagged bit of looking glass, a red river rock, and, just like Laney said, the seal.

They couldn't go back; there wasn't anything to go back to. Slavery was done and over with, friends and family were either dead or in places none of them had ever heard of.

Nothing to go back to, but plenty ahead, and so all eyes turned to the window and the land beyond it after Suce pressed the seal into the cooling blotch of wax Laney had made red with gooseberries.

Nothing to do after that day but wait.

When the men do return, Brother is the one to walk out and meet them, the scroll of parchment clutched tight in his hands. He doesn't know what words he'll use, but he figures by the time he reaches the stern faces looking back at him, he'll know.

Laney reaches for her broom and begins to sweep the kitchen floor, the steady sounds the straw makes against the wood calming and rhythmical, and Suce, who is seated nearby, begins to hum.

"Mornin'," Brother spouts while he is still a good twelve feet away from them. His eyes are steady, careful not to linger too long on the soft-colored wood butts of the rifles they carry. Instead, he concentrates on the long metal part of the rifles, wonders if the steel is cool against the crooks of their necks.

"Hold it right there, nigga," Obery Lessing says as he lifts the rifle into the air and slowly lowers it so that the dark, round eye of the weapon is pointing directly at Brother's heart.

Brother stalls.

The son, Fenton, trains his eyes on the house.

"We been asking around town, and the story we got there is different from the one you gave me," Obery says, and brings his other hand up to help with the weight of the gun.

"Sir?" Brother says, giving Familiar Eyes a blank look.

Obery coughs, shuffles his feet, and the rifle sways. "They

talk about my brother like he ain't here no more!" he barks.

Fenton's head bobs up and down in agreement, but his eyes never leave the saltbox; his ears are trained hard on the musical sweeping, the humming that rises and falls like the cresting waves of the ocean.

"Ay-yuh," Brother mumbles, and clutches the parchment tighter. "Been gone some time now."

Fenton's eyes let go of the house and fall on Brother. "What's that?"

Brother, careful not to move too fast or too freely, slowly twists his head around so that his eyes can meet those of Fenton. "A year or more by now."

Fenton's face does something Brother is not expecting. The young man's face lights up and then he smiles.

Brother turns back to Obery, and he's smiling too. Gushing.

The rifle is forgotten, its mouth kissing the ground now as the two men gaze and grin at each other.

Inside, Laney pauses, cocks her head, and listens.

Laughter?

Suce's humming comes to a halt too.

They were laughing, bent over, clutching their sides. Laughing so hard, the corner of Brother's mouth began to twitch, but he cleared his throat and forced the smile back down inside of him.

"Well, well, well," Fenton said as he pushed on his knees and brought himself upright again.

Obery turned a glowing red face to Brother and asked, "Did you send that son of a bitch off grand?" He chuckled sarcastically, and Fenton let off another string of guffaws.

Brother didn't know what to say, so he said nothing.

"Umph," Obery said, and turned his back on Brother so he could take in the big house on the hill. "That sure is a fine house," he muttered as he pulled a cigar out of the breast pocket of his jacket.

"He would put it out here in the middle of no-man's-land, where nobody could find it," Fenton commented.

"But we did." Obery snickered happily before biting off the tip of the cigar and spitting it down to the ground. Then, almost as an afterthought, he pulled another cigar out of his pocket and handed it over to his nephew.

"And now it's ours," Fenton said as he took the cigar from his uncle and twirled it between his fingers and beamed.

They were going on like he wasn't even there.

Like he was a tree, a rock, something less than the silvery dust the crushed bodies of gnats left behind on Spin's pinching fingers.

Brother looked down at his hand, at the tube of parchment, at his shoes, at the ground, and at the inchworm that quickly made its way across it, and reminded himself that there was nothing to go back to. So he stepped forward and pressed the open end of the rolled parchment against the lower part of Obery's back and pushed so that the blade of the knife that was hidden inside of it slid as smooth as butter through Obery's jacket, the shirt beneath it, the undergarment beyond that, and straight into his right kidney.

The laughter had stopped and then the shouting started, so Laney began sweeping again and Suce pressed the palms of her hands to her ears and found a new tune to hum.

Brother was glad not to have to see his eyes, even though there was no pleasure in witnessing the blood that was pumping out of the hole in Obery's back and spewing all over his hand.

He pushed harder and Obery fell to his knees, his hands frantically reaching behind him, one hand swatting at Brother's face while the other worked at trying to remove the knife from his back.

By the time Fenton realized what was happening, Willie

had pounced from the tree and they both went rolling, coming to a stop right in from of Spin, who had eased out from his hiding place from behind the house, pitchfork in hand.

Brother removed the knife, raised his booted foot, and kicked Obery in his neck, sending him toppling over and into the dirt.

Fenton didn't have much of a fight in him. The ambush had knocked the air clean out of him and he lay on the ground, dazed. When Willie finally jumped off of him, there was little to do but turn his head as Spin brought the sharp teeth of the pitchfork down into Fenton's astonished face and then sauntered over to the squirming Obery and repeated the act.

Suce watched them drag the bodies away, out back into the woods. Seeing those bodies didn't do much to her, although it seemed to upset Laney, 'cause she held her mouth, squeezed her eyes shut, and turned her head away. Suce, she licked her lips, tasted salt there, felt the new feeling in her grow, thought about the brother she never knew, the father she never knew, the mother who was never well enough to care for her proper and then birthed an ocean and died . . . She thought about it all, hitched her skirt high enough that Willie took a second look at her ankle—hitched it high enough so that when she stepped over the dragging legs of the white man her husband was pulling, the material didn't even brush his cuff—held her skirt there, and started to hum a tune again as she made her way up the hill toward the big house, through the door, up the stairs, and to the bedroom where Lessing lay wheezing.

Cataracts covered his left eye, so he watched her with his right. He smiled at her when she approached his bedside and looked down on him. She didn't even move when his free hand reached up to touch the swell of her breast. She let him stroke her there where her husband's hands fondled and caressed; she let him stroke her there until the disgust ran from her and she became the hate and gently lay that part of herself across his face, pressing hard enough to rupture the bad eye, hard enough to cut the air from flowing, hard enough so that in his last seconds of life, Lessing would feel her heart and know it.

US 78

We stare hard at the sign that says, BIRMINGHAM 243 MILES.

I think about the four little girls who died there.

I think about the way the world was before today and how much of it has still remained the same.

I wonder if Sherry thinking the same thing.

The radio is on now.

We quiet.

Birmingham, Alabama

We arrive late. Almost midnight.

Streets are dark, wet, and shiny. Seem like we the only ones in the world up.

Sky black, a few rain clouds—moon bright, though.

One blinking yellow light, a parked police cruiser.

Sherry move slow. Looking hard.

She make a left on a street called Cullom.

My breath catch in my throat. The houses are beautiful. Large, spread out. Wow.

We stop in front of a three-story house painted white from top to bottom, blue door, healthy ferns in hanging pots all around the porch.

I look for a sign that say somebody's bed and breakfast, but I don't see none.

Sherry pick up her phone, press a few numbers, hold it against her ear, and wait. I hear the phone ringing in that big house—it's loud—I look around for the police cruiser.

Sherry say, I'm outside.

The house light up. First upstairs and then downstairs.

Whose house is this?

You'll see, she says.

She climb out of the SUV, I follow.

The door swing open and a small old lady standing there. She pale as snow, hair white like cotton, but she stand straight as a ruler.

Ms. Meadow, Sherry says, starting toward her.

I rack my brain. I don't know no Ms. Meadow. Don't know too many white women at all.

They embrace. Sherry hug her tight, I wait to hear the woman's bone crack—she look fragile like china.

Evenin', ma'am, I say, and extend my hand. I look closely: her skin white, but her features black.

The woman's eyes look on me; they gray and watery.

She say, Dumpling! And her whole body jump. She ball her fists up and pump the air, her feet do a little shuffle, and then she fly into me, hug me tight.

I hug her back, look over at Sherry, and mouth, Who is this?

Ms. Meadow step back, look me up and down, grab my hand, pull me inside, tell Sherry, We worry 'bout the bags later. Come on in and have some pie!

First slice and she just watch me eat. I try not to watch back, but I do, looking for something familiar in her face. But nothing come.

She older than me, maybe by twenty years—Lawd, put her near a hundred years old!

More tea? she ask me, just a-beaming.

Yes ma'am, thank you.

We sitting in her dining room. Biggest one I ever been in. Beautiful. Walls seem to be papered with flowers. Roses, red.

Furniture heavy and dark. But everything else look delicate like Ms. Meadow. Doilies, china, knickknacks.

You still don't remember me?

No ma'am.

Sherry smile like a cat with a secret.

Ms. Meadow lean back in her chair. Her hands shake a bit.

Well, I remember you when you were just a little girl.

I say, Really? but think, All the stories start that way.

Short and fat, she laugh and point. Not much change, huh?

No ma'am.

She laugh some more. Laugh till she cough and wave Sherry away when she jump up.

I lived right down the road from you in Sandersville.

I nod my head.

Me and your Aunt Helen was best friends.

Is that right, I say.

She nod her head, wipe her eyes, say, I sure do miss her.

Yes ma'am, she was a good woman. But how you know my Sherry?

Ms. Meadow turn and look at Sherry and say, Ain't you told her nothing?

Not a thing. I wanted to surprise her.

Ms. Meadow smile.

Sherry know my great-grandson, Arthur Lawrence. They went to college together, she say, and point across the room at the framed pictures on the wall. He the one in the military uniform.

I look across. Handsome boy.

That my heart, she say with a sigh, then say out of the side of her mouth, I think them two were sweet on each other way back when. She swing a crooked finger between Sherry and Arthur's picture.

Sherry shake her head and say, We were never more than friends.

That's what all them young people say. Ms. Meadow wave her hand. Everybody afraid to commit themselves these days. Oh well.

One day Arthur and I were talking and it came out that his grandmother was from Sandersville, Sherry say.

Small world, I mumble and yawn.

And great-grandmother too, Sherry add.

Uh-huh.

My eyes burn. I sneak a peek at my watch and it say after one.

Ms. Meadow and I have been talking for a long time, Sherry say.

That's nice.

She's told me a lot of stuff about the family.

Well, she would know, I say, and I feel another yawn climbing up my throat.

Even about Vonnie.

The yawn gets caught and I gag.

The Sin

1867 is like sandpaper rubbing up against her memory and chafing it to silt. With a blink of Suce's eyes, the powder-fine grains of yesteryear disperse and float in the air around her like the early-morning mist of a late spring before finally clearing and leaving the glaring luster of the here and now.

The here and now is 1915, and Suce's belly is scarred with the stretch marks of fifteen pregnancies between 1873 and 1900.

It was the scars she was thinking about in the generous kitchen of that saltbox as she looked up from her potatoes and out the window, spotting her last son, Vonnie, embroiled in a discussion with a white man whose face was unfamiliar to Suce. He stood with his hands pushed deep down into the pockets of his overalls while he nodded his head to what Vonnie was saying.

Suce laughed to herself. It was such a common scene now. Black and white folks talking. Some even visited one another— not past the porch, you understand, and not too long, but visits just the same.

Suce sighed.

Time changes everything; it wasn't too long ago she was eating and drinking fear for breakfast, lunch, and dinner, waiting for more white people to show up, accuse, claim, or at least ask questions. But none came, not for months. By then, the rains had washed away the blood and Willie had assured her that all that was left of the bodies were bones.

"The animals take care of the skin," he said after her face told him that she was still unsure.

By the time another white man came strolling onto their land, Suce was pregnant with her second child and she and the rest of them had found the taste of food again; she was able to sleep heavy, even if not straight through the night—the outright fear had dissipated to just a skipping heartbeat.

Big and pregnant and unable even to see her toes in 1875, the middle of August squatting down on them, pissing heat all day and night, and the white man was standing on her front porch with a white handkerchief tied around his neck as he melted away in his dusty black suit.

They were somebodys by then. Citizens, neighbors, landholding blacks who traded cotton for cash, raised pigs for slaughter, had cows and hounds and chickens and a story that backed it up all the way to 1866. They had a last name too, and kind words about an even kinder master who'd left them everything after he dropped dead from the fever, the pox, pneumonia—not uncommon—someone else had a similar story, not unbelievable, just unforgettable.

Brown shoes caked red with Georgia earth, the man smiled while he waited for Suce to undo the latch on the screen door, and that's when she saw the battered black leather attaché case he carried.

"Mornin', ma'am," he said, pushing a business card at her.

"Mornin'," Suce said, looking down at the card but not taking it.

"Is the man of the house available?" he asked with a wide grin.

Suce shook her head no.

There was an awkward moment of silence while the man swatted at a fly and mopped his forehead with the handkerchief. Suce took that time to look out across the field to make sure Brother and Willie were close enough to hear her scream, if she had to.

"I'm from the Metropolitan Life Insurance Company, and the reason for my visit today is to ask you if you and your family members are prepared for what may happen—God forbid—if you were to lose one of your loved ones."

The baby was in the back room sleeping; there were green beans in a bowl waiting to be snapped, some sheets that needed washing. Suce rolled her head on her neck and waited.

"Well," the man began again after there was no answer from Suce, "I am an agent for the Metropolitan Life Insurance Company, and I am here to offer you an Industrial Burial Policy. This policy, which today and only today I can offer to you for the very low price of fifteen dollars a year."

Suce gave him a blank stare.

The man cleared his throat. "Fifteen dollars a year will cover the expensive costs of funeral and burial expenses," he said, and then threw a longing look over Suce's shoulder into the coolness of the house.

He mopped his brow again and waited.

Suce considered him for a moment, scratched at her stomach, and said, "Come back tomorrow." Then she stepped back into the house, indicating the conversation was over, and let the screen door go and returned to her green beans.

"Will your husband be home then?" the man yelled through the screen.

"Yeah," Suce said, and settled herself back down into the chair.

The white man came back, not the next day, but the following month, enough time for Suce to mull it over and discuss it with Brother and Willie.

They could only safely afford to purchase one policy, so Brother said that Willie should be the one insured, since he was the one with a wife and family.

Fifteen dollars a year, one dollar and twenty-five cents a month. Lord knew there were months when they had to scrape it together, but it seemed the right thing to do—the white thing to do—and so Suce made sure they did it.

But when Willie died, Suce sent her eldest boy into town to send word via telegram to where the policy said to send it, and they never heard a word back.

Suce waited for the following month to come around, waited for the white man to come and collect his premium. Then she would show him the death certificate and the policy and collect her money, but no white man from that insurance company ever came back.

Other white men came from other companies, but none ever came back from Metropolitan Life.

Suce found a way and buried her husband, even though she had to promise a quarter of the cotton crop plus interest in order to do it. She would have put him down by the stream with the others, but another white man had come along one day and told her that it was a health risk and against the law to bury a body on any land other than a cemetery.

Brother passed a few years after Willie, leaving her alone with the children, but by then the boys were old enough and big enough to handle things.

Spin, well, he'd walked off a few months after the killing. Suce never did see any fear in his eyes after that day, just blood. She'd catch him smacking his lips when there wasn't a meal being prepared or a plate of food anywhere in sight.

She found out about the dead animals from Brother. She supposed Willie didn't want to upset her, but he'd taught himself how to shoot the rifles they'd inherited after the white men's deaths and started watching Spin closely, insisting on putting a bolt on the bedroom door.

After a while Spin graduated from slaughtering small animals and went on to the larger ones that could put up a fight. But the satisfaction he derived from it was minute, so he strolled off one afternoon and never came back.

Suce heard say from folks some years later, when she was comfortable enough to feel a part of the community that sprouted up around her, that "a big ole tree of a nigga came running through the main square with a pitchfork and sent it straight through the first white man he came upon."

It couldn't have been anyone else but Spin, though she'd second-guessed herself for a moment when the people went on to say, "When the white folks got hold of him, wrenched that pitchfork from him, slung the noose around his neck, and then asked if he had anything to say before they hung him, he looked at them and just laughed."

Suce had never heard Spin utter a single word, nor had she heard him laugh—not even a chuckle—but she knew he had a tongue and so she thought that his language was buried down deep inside of him. She supposed there was some happiness down there too and so, she thought, that's where the laughter came from.

Suce tore her eyes away from the window, her mind away from the memories, and looked down to see water rolling down her bodice. She didn't even think of her eyes and instead looked up at the ceiling to see if it was leaking again, even though the sun sat high and bright in the sky and not a cloud lingered.

The space above her head was bone dry, so she touched her face and her fingers came back wet.

It puzzled her and she set the small knife down on the table and checked herself for grief and there was none.

Suce wore as a bracelet the blue granite eagle necklace that had belonged to Lou and now she reached for the stone and fumbled with it.

Could be just thinking back over the years, she told herself. Sometimes the memories did that to her—made her sad.

Her mind rolled over them again, but nothing resembling grief stung her heart.

She set the paring knife down.

Could be one of the children.

She whispered each of their names: "Moss, Frederick, Ezekiel, Sara, Lou-Ann, Fleming, Vera-Bell, Vonnie, Sonny Boy, Lillie, Beka, Helen." A slight pause before calling the next group.

Now the dead ones: "Martini, Willie Junior, Sally."

Still nothing.

Suce twisted in her chair and probed deeper into the dark spaces inside of herself, looking for the sadness, but nothing jumped out at her. There were no shifting shadows, but still the tears rolled.

"Mama?" she whispered, and dragged the back of her hands across her wet eyes.

Lou had come to her every now and again. A branch pulled across the window, a cup left in the center of the table, upside down. Suce had seen her as clear as day the evening she herself spread her legs and pushed out her third child. Lou walked right out of the wall and looked down at the bloody baby and whispered, "Ezekiel."

Suce waited for the feeling, and still none came.

She balled her fist, becoming frustrated now. "Martini!" she yelled into the air.

Had to be . . . Maybe.

Willie Junior and Sawyer came out warm and dead. In the ground within an hour. Small wooden cross, names scrawled on it. Date.

Martini was almost grown. Had seen the sky, liked to laugh. Dead three years now, and angry for it. Hiding things, loosening bolts, dropping rusty nails where she knew a bare foot would tread.

Suce sighed.

Martini just gone. Helen in the bedroom trying to shake her awake, then getting scared and running to Suce and saying, "She cold, Mama. Like ice."

The hollering came after Doctor Dentist made it official. Checking Martini's face and feeling for a pulse on her wrist and neck and then looking directly at Suce, his mouth not moving, his eyes telling it all: gone.

Martini's eyes open and staring, lips parted and blue. No breath, but Suce could have sworn that a tear slid down her face just before Doctor Dentist pulled her eyelids down with his index and middle fingers.

Doctor Dentist said that Martini's heart had just stopped beating.

"A heart attack? She wasn't no old woman!"

"Happen to young ones too sometimes," Doctor Dentist

said, then snapped his black bag shut.

Suce watched his dusty shoes walk across her clean floors. Her child was dead.

The hollering went on for days, through the preparation, the wake, the church service, the digging of the grave, and the final *pat pat* sound the back of the shovel made across the dark mound of dirt that reminded Suce of the shape her belly took on when she was pregnant.

Now Suce just sat there, half-peeled potato in one hand and mouth whispering, "What, what is it?"

When Vonnie walked in, he just looked at the table littered with the curled brown skin and the naked taters already turning in the coarse air.

"Mama?"

She'd fall into these dazes every now and again, talking to nothing, answering ghosts. Now he wondered if her mind was leaving her seventy-four-year-old body.

Suce's eyes fluttered and she looked at Vonnie. "You forget your manners out in the field?"

Vonnie—tall and dark, the handsome part of him camouflaged by his ruined mouth. The midwife had almost dropped him at the sight of it. Later, Doctor Dentist would tell Suce and Willie that it was called a cleft palate. "Nothing you can do. Just one of them things."

"Evenin', ma'am," Vonnie said, and removed the straw hat from his head. Suce just nodded, retrieved the small knife, and began again what the sudden sadness had interrupted.

"What that Schiffer boy want?" Suce inquired without missing a stroke.

"Said he got some work down by him if I want it."

"Hmmm," Suce said, and tossed the potato into the bowl. "Got some collard greens on the stove. Neck bones and beans already done, but I was feeling for some boiled potatoes."

"Uh-huh," Vonnie said, and lifted the lid off the pot of greens.

"Nobody here, so I sent that boy Adam down to Miss Ellie for one of her apple pies," Suce said as she worked at skinning the potato. "Feeling for pie too."

"Where the baby at?"

"The mama come for her early today. Good. I was tired anyway."

"Beka?"

"Gone down to Eloise for a spell."

"Helen?"

"In the outhouse."

"Lillie?"

"Ain't seen her yet."

The sadness swelled, and Suce dropped the potato and slapped at her chest.

"Mama?" Vonnie didn't move, but his heart raced.

"I'm all right, just some gas."

So it was Lillie, she thought.

Couldn't keep her from town. Men and drink and music. Lillie was loose. Had just unfurled one day and liberated the tight, neat bun she'd worn since she could, swapping it in favor of the cascading mane that made the menfolk smile so broad, they looked foolish.

Wild, and Suce didn't know what had turned her that way. Bitten by something rabid. Some lying man who had promised her something for the something down between her legs. Love, probably, Suce thought. Women were always ready to give themselves over for love, when all the men really had to offer them was the word and not the meaning behind it.

"Shoot," Suce said, and plucked up another potato. "She go o'er to Mr. James today?" Suce tried hard to hold her words steady.

"Seen her heading that way; can't say that's where she ended up, though," Vonnie said as he stared down into the simmering pot of beans.

"You wash your hands?" Suce asked, her eyebrows lifting.

Vonnie set the top back down on the pot.

"Seen Mr. James, though, and he ain't ask for her, so I suppose—"

"Hmmmmm," Suce's murmur cut away the rest of Vonnie's statement. She rubbed at her chest again.

"Mama, you—"

"I want you to find out for sure if she went there today," Suce said, and gently put the knife back down on the table before folding her hands and sharing a worried look with the tablecloth.

Vonnie stood for a moment, watching her, before placing his hat back on his head and heading out the door.

It was Lillie, she was sure of it.

Night came and Vonnie followed, coming through the door, dragging a red handkerchief across his brow.

Suce was in her rocking chair, a small child across her lap whimpering and squirming.

"That the Poole boy?" Vonnie asked.

"Uh-huh. Robert."

"Where his mama at?"

"Headache. She come to me, I give her the headache powder, she hand him to me." Suce gently rubbed the baby's back. "He colicky, I think."

"That baby with you more than he with his mama." Vonnie removed his hat and hung it on the nail beside the door.

"Where Lillie?"

Vonnie glanced toward the kitchen. "Mr. James said she come and leave early."

"Left and went where?"

"He said she had to go and see Doctor Dentist."

Suce cocked her head, and the rocking chair came to a halt. "For what?"

"I didn't ask, but I don't suspect she would've shared her

reason with Mr. James," Vonnie said, and bent to untie his boots.

Standing clouds bearded the moon. Crickets sang for water and now Lillie had gone off and done something to herself.

Suce lifted the baby to her shoulder and began to rock again.

Three days later an older man stood before Suce. Tall, thin, one leg two inches shorter than the other. Suce couldn't stop staring at the shoe and how the sole was built up to hide his defect. Everything else on him looked okay, she guessed. Not a man she would have wasted a second look on—long face, creased in the cheeks and across the forehead. Eyes too close, nose spread too wide. Suit dusty around the cuffs and tattered around the collar.

Helen and Beka sat quietly and waited. Vonnie was in the kitchen pacing the floor between the window and the door.

Lillie, waterfall hair hiding her small shoulders, slipped her arm around the man's waist, pulling his hip in to her side. He wobbled a bit and then steadied himself and blushed.

"What they call you again?"

"Corinthians, ma'am."

Suce eyed him closely and rubbed one bare foot over the other.

"Where your people hail from?" she asked, and reached over and touched the bare wood of a small table that sat beside her rocker.

"Oklahoma," he said as he watched her fingers stroke the wood.

"How you all end up here?"

"White folks run us out, burn down the town, kill off good right many Negroes too."

"Sad."

"Yes ma'am."

"Most men comes and asks the family for the woman's hand in marriage," Suce said, and folded her arms across her chest. "They don't just show up and proclaim it's done already."

"Yessum, I was—" Corinthians started.

"I told him all that wasn't necessary. I told him I was

grown and didn't need nobody's permission for nothing."

Suce looked at Lillie, a little bitty thing with too much mouth.

"Still," Suce continued, "t'aint right."

Silence.

"So where y'all been?"

Corinthian's mouth opened, but Lillie's words flew past him: "We been on our honeymoon."

Suce smirked. "Honeymoon?"

Vonnie grunted from the kitchen, the girls pulled at the hems of their skirts.

"That's right."

"You ain't got no job no more, you know that?"

"Don't care, moving anyway."

"What?"

"Where?" Vonnie said from the kitchen, a glass of ice water clutched in his hand.

"Phila-del-phia," Lillie sang.

Suce looked confused.

"That's in Pennsylvania, ma'am." Corinthians spoke slow and loud.

"I know where it's at." And then, "My daughter tell you I was stupid and deaf?"

Eyes blinked and his skin turned scarlet. "N-no ma'am."

"Why Phila-del-phia?"

"Got a house there."

"Really?"

"And a congregation."

"You don't say? You a minister?"

"Yessum."

"Hmmmm, and didn't have the good sense to ask for her hand proper?"

Corinthians dropped his eyes in shame. "It all happened so quick," he mumbled.

"Uh-huh, things always go quick with Lillie." Suce snuffed.

Vonnie spat up his drink of water, caught most of it in the palm of his hand. The girls hid their smiles.

"Fool," Lillie muttered at Vonnie, and then threw a sharp look at her sisters.

"Y'all going to Phila-del-phia by train?" Suce asked.

"No ma'am. By car."

"You all got an auto-mo-bile?"

"Brand new."

"Is that right?" Suce breathed and looked down at her hands. She was lost for a moment, trapped in an earlier time when her eldest son, Moss, came back from town in a coughing, hacking piece of junk on four wheels. It'd taken him a good two hours to get it home, him not knowing how to drive an automobile, and the road not willing to have it on its back driven by someone with no experience.

Suce laughed at the memory.

"Ma'am?" Corinthians said, leaning in.

"It's nothing," Suce replied, and dabbed at the corners of her eyes.

Lillie searched her mother's face for some glimmer that would tell her that Suce was impressed, but Suce's expression remained bland.

"How long you know'd our Lillie?"

"He know me long enough to know that he love me and want to take me the hell away from here!" Lillie screeched.

Suce's cheek twitched, and she threw a look at Corinthians's strange shoe again.

"You know what you doing?"

The question was so heavy that Corinthians pulled at the collar of his shirt and looked toward the open window and wondered where the air went off to.

"Yes ma'am," he said with as much force as his unsure voice would allow.

"Uh-huh." Suce moaned and then turned her attention to Lillie. "Y'all gonna come back and visit?"

Lillie, as if she had been waiting for that very question, flicked her waterfall hair over her shoulders, threw her head back, and laughed. "The only way I'll ever come back here will be in a pine box!"

The girls held their breath and reached for each other's hands.

"What so bad 'bout here?"

"Ask them," Lillie flung at her sisters, and then turned on Vonnie. "Ask *him*. He know."

Suce turned an inquisitive eye on Vonnie, but her mouth didn't utter a word.

In Philadelphia the neighbors welcomed Lillie with open arms.

They pretended to mind their own business even though they eavesdropped from behind lace curtains, watched out in the open, right on the porch while seated in wooden rockers and pretending to read the paper or enjoy the day.

By the time Corinthians was dead, they *tsk-tsk*ed loud enough for Lillie to hear and made sure she saw the arch in their backs and the upward tilt of their noses whenever she was near.

Back then, Germantown, Philadelphia, was divided into pockets of Southerners. Alabamians to the west; South Carolinians to the south; North Carolinians with a sprinkle of Virginia people to the east; Georgians, Floridians, and Kentuckians on the north side, the rest settling in the middle. So there were some who knew the Sandersville Lessings personally, and the first words that got back to Suce said:

Lillie come to Phila-del-phia, to Germantown. Married woman. Minister husband. She sitting up in the front pew of the Church of the Black Virgin, white gloved, proper dress, singing the Lord's prayers, smiling at her minister husband, bringing cookies to bake sales, buying furniture on credit, belly swelling, first baby come, a girl, she the sweetest thing you ever did want to see. Light skin-ded, head full of black hair, pretty l'il thing—they name her Love.

Second set of words say:

She bought two life insurance policies, a new car, more kids come, a boy named Bernard Moses and a girl named Clementine Marie.

Her hands full, one walking, one teething, one crawling. House nice, new porch, hanging flower baskets. They doing all right for themselves.

A credit to the community. A credit to her race.

Third set of words come:

She a good wife. Visiting her husband in the hospital twice a day, finding another minister to stand in for him at the church. The children clean, look sad for their ailing papa, though.

Fourth set say:

He went hard. Lillie bawl like thunder, fell out at the coffin. Cash in the policies, sold off the church and the building beside it. Men coming and going, she wearing red gloves, red lipstick, red beads around her neck, drinking, the devil's music playing in the parlor, another baby come (even though her husband dead), a girl, Lillie name her Wella. What foolish kind of name is that?

Fifth set say:

Well, any one of us could have told Corinthians as soon as we laid eyes on Lillie Lessing that she would be the spade to dig his grave. But he couldn't see it. Blinded by her fair skin and long hair and whatever it was she did to him in bed at night that kept him grinning like a idiot.

She was too young for him anyway and not even a virgin!

Now Lillie barely minding her own children, leaving them for days at a time while she whore around Phila-del-phia, around Germantown, like she done lost her goddamn mind!

The eldest girl too grown for her own good. Grown and passionate about red. Red scarf tied around her neck and we've even seen her clomping up and down the streets in her mama's red high-heel shoes, sitting on the porch, legs crossed like a harlot, face painted up to match.

Now is that any way for an eleven-year-old girl to act?

Somebody better get up here and see about these chirren!

Suce had never been on a train in her life and wasn't about to get on one now, but Vonnie had to tend the land and the others were off making a way in Detroit, Chicago, St. Louis, Kansas City. Raising families, crammed into two-by-four places called tenements. Working hard at putting some distance between slave and sir, mammy and miss.

So Beka and Helen would have to go.

Sunday dresses, money pinned to the inside of their brassieres, polished shoes, purses dangling from wrists, hands clutching brown paper bags with shiny, greasy bottoms.

Trees streak by outside of their window, army men laughing loud around them. Women clutching babies, old people nodding off before the first whistle blows.

Helen and Beka try to hide their excitement, try to look like this is just one of many train rides, but they give themselves away when they point and giggle like schoolgirls at everything and anything.

They don't have money for a compartment with beds, and even if they did, colored folk aren't allowed that luxury, so when their eyes begin to burn from staring too long, they finally sleep; Beka's head resting on the glass window and Helen's on Beka's soft shoulder.

They arrive in Philadelphia in the middle of a rainstorm, their dresses soaked through, water running down the vinyl seats of the taxi. Wrong way, right street. "What's the house number again?"

Beka and Helen standing on the porch, sure every eye that peeks out from behind eyelet drapes knows Beka has a rip in her hand-me-down slip.

Press and curl done for and grease dripping in globs from their ruined hair, Beka bangs on the white front door while Helen presses her face against the window, trying to spot some movement in the lamplit parlor.

"You sure this the right house?" Beka screams over the thunder.

Helen digs down into the front of her dress and pulls out a slip of paper. She eyes it for a while and then says, "Yeah, this it."

"Let's try 'round the back!" Helen yells over the downpour, and they take off down the stairs and round the house toward the rear.

Helen sees them first, and stops dead in her tracks. Beka, blinded by the torrential rain, runs smack into Helen's back. "Oh, shoot I'm—" Beka starts, but then sees too and gasps.

Half-naked children, wallowing in the mud like pigs.

They stand in amazement and then a slither of amusement snakes through them and Helen yells out, "What y'all think you're doing?" Her voice is light and laughter pushes out her words.

Three of them stop. The smallest one keeps wallowing.

"Who you?" Beanie Moe asks, and takes a step toward them.

Baby Wella finally stops rolling, and her small hands smack at the mud that's clinging to her face. She looks at him and then follows his eyes to the women before popping her fat thumb in her mouth.

"Oh, baby, don't!" Beka shrieks, and moves past Helen, scooping up Wella and starting up the back porch stairs.

Helen wipes at the rain on her face and leans in to one leg. He has a right to ask, she thinks as she rests her hands on her hips. They are family, even though she has never laid eyes on him, or any of the others.

"Get offa my sista!" Beanie Moe screams at Beka, and the skin covering his scrawny build tightens and Helen can see every bone in his body.

"We your aunties," Helen barks. And then, "Ya'll get on in the house." A wave of her hand toward the back door and serious eyes follow.

Beanie Moe watches her, chest rising and falling, but no feet start walking. Clementine, who they call Dumpling, throws a cautious look, takes a step, and then stalls. Another look, a blast of thunder, and her feet start up again and she scurries past her siblings, up the stairs, into the house, and waits, dripping and watching from the doorway.

"C'mon, now," Helen urges.

Beanie Moe is still blowing air like a bull and his hands are balled into the most pitiful fists Helen has ever seen.

She raises her hand quickly to her mouth to hide the smile with a cough. "We all gonna get pneumonia out here. Now, get on in the house."

"C'mon, now," Beka pleads weakly from the doorway.

Thunder rolls across the sky and a jagged fork of lightning cuts through the darkness.

Beanie Moe looks up at the sky and then back at Helen.

"Beanie Moe, now, I ain't playing with you!" Helen yells. "Don't make me come over there and drag you into that house!"

Another shuddering boom of thunder and then the sound of a heavy limb breaking away from an elm across the street.

It's the sound of his name and not the thunder or lightning that rattles him. *Beanie Moe*, the letters rolled and came together on that stranger's tongue, spinning out and sounding as sweet as it did when his mother called it.

He squints at her. There is a resemblance, but she is taller, darker.

The standoff lasts a few more seconds, and just as Helen makes her mind up to tackle Beanie Moe, he suddenly turns and calmly climbs the stairs and walks into the house.

Now standing there, all of them shivering and soaking wet. Helen eyed the children, while it was all Beka could do to keep her mouth shut.

The house was a mansion compared to their Georgia saltbox. Fine parquet floors twinkled beneath the gaslights. Rose-colored carpet climbed the staircase. A large, oval, mahogany table graced the spacious dining room, and the parlor held, from what Beka could see, two sofas and at least three sitting chairs.

"Ain't there four of y'all?" Helen asked the crowd of young faces that looked back at her.

The children said nothing.

Helen sighed. "Where's your mama at?" She threw the question out into the air and waited. Still no one offered a breath or a word. "Y'all don't speak?" Helen asked, her hands gripping her hips.

"Sure they do." The words floated to them from the top of the staircase. Beka's and Helen's heads snapped toward the sound and they found themselves blinking wildly and then thought to laugh, but just smirked.

"Oh my," Beka started. "If you don't look just like your mama."

"If you ain't your mama's child!" Helen said, and stepped forward to get a closer look.

Lovey's face was placid as she started down the stairs. She held the women's eyes with her own until she reached the landing and then shot her siblings a quick, slicing look.

Lovey examined the soiled throw rug they stood on for a moment and shook her head pitifully before looking back at her aunts.

The posture her body fell into was years beyond her age: hip stuck out, arms crossed and floating at her waist, neck straight, head steady—that stance should have been out of her reach, but she had it anyway, gripped tight and perfect.

"Who are you, and why you in my house?"

Beka's and Helen's heads pulled back a bit before they looked at each other to make sure all that they were hearing and seeing was real.

"*Your* house?" Helen laughed and pressed her palm against her chest.

"I'm your Aunt Beka, and this here is your Aunt Helen. We

your mama's sisters," Beka said, and offered Lovey the smile she used on the sweet-faced children that attended her Bible-study class.

"My mama ain't got no sisters," Lovey replied matter-of-factly, and then had the nerve to examine her fingernails.

Helen's eyes rolled and she felt her head get hot.

"Where you get that from?" Beka asked, astonished.

Right then they became air, invisible, because Lovey didn't say another word to either of them, just raised her right hand and pointed a finger toward the stairs. "Beanie Moe, Dumpling, y'all take the baby and get on upstairs and get yourselves under some water. Now."

Eleven years old and more woman than Helen and Beka had ever come across in someone that young. They tried to keep the astonishment off of their faces, but it stuck out—stunned and as plain as day.

The children filed past Helen and Beka quietly, moving obediently up the stairs.

They were visible again, because Lovey moved to the front door, swung it open, narrowed her eyes in their direction, and said, "Get out."

Outside, the rain beat down on the sisters' forgotten suitcases and whipped the fragile stems of the white and pink that blossomed in the planters lining the stone steps.

Beka was more than ready to get going. She hadn't wanted to come in the first place. Lillie was her sister, but they had never been friends.

When Lillie had left, the bad talk about her followed—and so did the tension between them. So when Lovey's lips pressed tight again, Beka started forward but Helen's hand caught hold of her wrist and jerked her back into place.

"We ain't going no goddamn place," Helen spat.

Lovey wavered.

They'd seen it, a quick flutter of lashes, a twitch of the mouth, and the whole top part of her body jerked. For a moment she was eleven again, but just for a moment; if they'd blinked they would have missed it.

"I'll call the law," Lovey said, and pushed the door farther back on its hinges, welcoming the rain in and soaking the floral piece of carpet that sat at the door.

"Call 'em," Helen said, and folded her arms across her chest. Puddles at their feet now and someone complaining up-stairs about the tub being too full. Lovey's attention snagged on that possibility and the yellow stain sitting on the ceiling above her head from the last time the tub ran over, Lillie cuss-ing and the switch that left lines across her thighs, and now these women claiming to be kin when Lillie had made it per-fectly clear that "all them people in Sandersville are dead." Or was it "dead to me"?

Lovey couldn't remember which one it was.

"I will. I'll call the law," she said, and her voice squeaked.

Call the law, Helen wanted to say again. Shoot, she had things she might be able to tell a Phila-del-phia lawman that she couldn't tell Sheriff Oakland back home. Even though it had begun and ended so long ago, just living in that house and seeing Vonnie every day made it seem as if it was still going on.

Nobody had ever said it was wrong, but something about it had never felt right and she didn't think it had anything to do with it happening at night or without words or right alongside her sleeping sister.

And it was understood, without words, that what had gone on at night wasn't something to be discussed at breakfast the next morning or even taken out of the door to the little white schoolhouse the county had put up for coloreds or even into the AME church with its splintered pews and worn Bibles.

Call them, please! she wanted to holler, because even getting the news about coming to Phila-del-phia had come in the dark of night, like Lillie and Phila-del-phia was a dirty, nasty, for-bidden place that could only be discussed after sundown.

"Got the train tickets today for you and Beka," Vonnie had whispered to them from the doorway.

Helen hadn't even known where to place her eyes, so she just looked at the darkness above her head.

"Y'all leave day after 'morrow. I already got the time squared away with Mr. Paul."

How could his words feel like fingers? How did he do that, say a few words in the dark and shuttle her mind right back to the first time, the times in between, and the very last time too?

No sense in crying about it anymore. No sense in being angry about it anymore. The anger had desiccated into shame, and everybody knew that shame was soundless, so he was safe.

And that night, not just his words like fingers, not just the clink of the timepiece dropping into his pocket and against the loose change, not just his back and the wooden door closing softly behind him, but the sound of Suce saying something to him from her room. Where had her words been years ago when he was offending them? Where had her now wide-open eyes been then?

So Helen moved slowly toward Lovey, her eyes challenging her to do it, but her hand acting on its own and grabbing hold of the door, pulling it from Lovey's grasp and calling over her shoulder to Beka, "Get the bags." And then the slamming sound of the door and her mouth taking sides with her hand and saying, "Now, where my sista at?"

None of them children had the answer, and so Beka and Helen waited and tried not to get too used to the gaslights and inside plumbing.

Five days later Lillie came sauntering through her front door and wasn't at all surprised to smell peach cobbler bubbling in the stove, but the lilacs, vased and sitting at the center of the dining room table, caught her off guard, and she was fixing her mouth to call out to Lovey when she heard the flip of paper and turned to see the big crossed legs of her sister Helen and the half-drunk glass of sweet tea sitting and sweating on the small wooden table, uncoastered.

Twelve years had streaked by like twelve days, and besides the occasional letter, new Easter hat she sent for Suce every year, Christmas telegram, and the five-dollar bills she sent home when the mood hit her, Lillie didn't give Sandersville or her family a second thought.

Now here they were invading her home and ruining her furniture.

"You ain't never had nothing and so don't know how to treat nothing!" Lillie snatched up the glass. "Look at this shit here," she continued, shaking a finger at the wet circle already leaving a ghostly ring on the wood. "Country-ass Negroes," she spat, and stormed off to the kitchen.

Helen calmly closed the magazine she was reading, placed it down on her lap, and watched Lillie's sashaying hips move through the rooms and disappear into the kitchen.

After a while she returned empty-handed, stopping a foot from Helen's big legs, and stared.

Lillie had gained some weight, Helen thought to herself as they eyed each other. Glamorous, though—full-fledged and way past the practice part that had started back in Sandersville. False eyelashes, powdered face, blue-shadowed eyes. Red lipstick on her lips and red polish on her nails. Helen wondered if her toes were done too.

"Well howdy-do to you too!" Helen finally said, and offered Lillie a genuine smile.

Lillie just huffed and smirked at her. "I know you ain't come here alone," she said as she sauntered over to the chair across from Helen and sat down. "I can smell lavender all through the house." She threw her head back and crossed her legs. "That Beka probably done used up half of my bubbling salts."

Helen smiled, but said nothing. They had both used quite a bit of the bubbling salts, luxuriating in the bathtub morning and night since they'd arrived.

"I suppose you all have had a good time rifling through my shit," Lillie breathed, her eyes on the ceiling, one leg bouncing to some tune that went through her head.

They had.

Been all through her bureau drawers and the hatboxes that lined the shelves of her closets.

"Been sleeping in my bed too?" Lillie frowned.

Every night, and it had been like sleeping on a cloud.

"Where else you 'spect us to sleep?" Helen laughed.

"So what y'all want?" Lillie was looking at her now. The tune was gone and her leg was still.

Helen rubbed at the back of her neck and fingered the knot of the scarf she had tied around her kinky hair. "Ain't you got a hot comb 'round here?"

Lillie huffed with exasperation. "What I want with a hot comb?" she said and pointed to her silky mane. "Do it look like I need one?"

"You may not need one, but them two younger girls of yours certainly do."

Lillie smiled. "They got they daddy's hair," she said, and her leg began to bounce again.

They said nothing for a while and then Lillie softened, her whole body going to butter, melting into the chair, and her lips spreading into a sweet smile that was as close to a waving white flag as she was going to get. "Mama sent y'all up here to check on me, right?"

"And the children," Helen said, and folded her leg across her knee.

"Where they at?"

"Who?"

"My children."

"That should have been your first question," Helen said, and picked up the magazine again. "They gone down to the ice-cream parlor with Beka."

Lillie's face twisted. "Lovey too?"

Helen nodded. "She ain't have no choice," she said as she closed the magazine, took a long look at the model on the cover, and then finally tossed it onto the small table. "She a woman if there ever was one," Helen continued, folding her hands behind her head and giving her body a good stretch.

"She grown, that's for sure," Lillie responded with nothing but pride in her voice, and then she suddenly stood up. "Hot, ain't it?" Lillie pressed her palm against her forehead and then under her chin.

Helen smirked; they had the same ways about them, Lillie and Lovey—could dismiss and move on in a tick's heartbeat. But Helen pulled Lillie back in. "She what, ten now?"

Lillie pulled at the waist of her dress and then at the rounded collar. "Shoot, must be ninety degrees," she said as she hiked her dress up around her waist.

Laced garters. Helen tried to swallow her jealousy, but it was out and stomping all across her face. Lillie moved to the wall and rested her hand against it for balance as she slid first one garter off and then the other. The stockings followed; those she rolled into a ball and tossed onto the chair. She started off toward the kitchen. "That pie 'bout done?"

Helen rose and followed. "Should be."

"You say she how old?" Helen pushed when they met up again at the stove.

"I didn't say," Lillie spoke into the refrigerator as she pulled a pitcher of lemonade from its depths.

Helen pulled at the oven door handle and peeked inside.

"Can't you count?" Lillie said, and placed the pitcher of lemonade down onto the table.

"Sure I can, just ain't sure." Helen wrapped the dishcloth around the pie pan and gently lifted it from the rack.

Both sisters peered down at the pie and a look of satisfaction spread across their faces before Lillie moved to the upper cabinets and retrieved two glasses.

"Eleven."

"Going on forty," Helen laughed.

"Enough about Lovey," Lillie said as she filled one glass with lemonade and then the next. "What y'all want?"

"Ain't you gonna ask about Mama?" Helen eased herself down into the kitchen chair.

"How's Mama?"

"Fine."

"Good, now what y'all want?"

What they really wanted was to stay. Stay in that famed place that Lillie had made wicked in Suce's mind and outrageous and attractive in the heads of those women who called Sandersville home and still bathed in tin tubs out in the yard when the weather allowed.

They wanted to stay and call Phila-del-phia home and one day be able to say the name of that city without the sag and drag of their Georgia tongues.

As far as they were concerned, twelve years earlier Lillie had walked right out of hell and into heaven and all that she complained about—the blast of car horns and too-loud music during the weekdays, the husband and wife who lived next door and fought all weekend long, the white man across the street who spit at the colored children because he had woke up one day and found his neighborhood swarming with brown faces and stinking of salt meat—all of that was just angels and harp music to Beka and Helen.

What they wanted was not to have to hear the cocks crow at dawn or the cows moo or to step over the hound dogs that sprawled themselves out across the very paths they had to take to everywhere.

They didn't want to snap peas for dinner when they didn't even want peas for dinner or wash clothes that weren't theirs. They didn't want to light kerosene lamps for light or go to church every Sunday, 'cause shit, even the Lord rested on that day, so who was watching and listening while they sweat like pigs in the summer and froze like the ground in the winter all the while singing His praises?

They wanted to stay and forget about the first time, the first time the quilt was lifted from their bodies allowing the night chill to climb over them and the sound of their own sleepy voices, dreamlike and hushed in the room, asking, "What's the matter, Vonnie?"

They wanted to bury the flint and flame and his face lit and long in the darkness looking like nothing they had ever seen before, the hands pushing their nightgowns up to their chins and his eyes, wells of nothing and way past black, and them not saying a word, but bodies shivering, minds alert and spinning and trying to understand.

And could moving to Phila-del-phia stamp out the horror those prodding fingers pressed into them or the sight of the dancing light cast down between their legs so he could see good and clear just where it was he needed to be?

So what they really wanted was to never ever pack up and go back to relive that first night, the middle ones, or the very last.

What they really, truly wanted was to stay.

But Helen didn't say any of it. She didn't have to, Lillie knew it all, had lived it right alongside them, and so Helen just stretched her legs out before her, clasped her hands behind her head, and said, "We just want to know that you and the children are okay."

Lovey didn't want anything from her. Not even the double scoop of ice cream Beka held out to her.

"Suit yourself," Beka said with a shrug of her shoulders and passed the cone over to Dumpling, who expertly avoided Lovey's hateful gaze as she wrapped her fat fingers eagerly around it.

Beanie Moe's feet did some odd shuffle, and his eyes darted between Lovey and the remaining ice-cream cone that Beka held, and just when Beka thought he was going to refuse, he quickly grabbed it from her hand. "Thank you," he murmured between licks.

"Welcome," Beka said with a satisfied smile. "You sure you don't want one?" she said to Lovey, who just rolled her eyes and snorted. "O-kay," Beka sang. "Two more, please," she said to the young white girl behind the counter.

"Here you go, Wella. Be careful now, okay?"

Wella nodded her head cautiously as her small hands retrieved the cone. She stared at the melting scoops of ice cream, admired it as if it was an amazing gem.

"You better hurry up and start licking before it all melts away," Beka warned.

She pushed the door to the ice-cream parlor open and waited while the children filed out ahead of her. Beanie Moe in the lead, Dumpling waddling behind him, Wella at Beka's hip, and Lovey, scuffling along, bringing up the rear.

The day was hot, no doubt about that. The heat rose up from the pavement, burning through Beka's thin-soled shoes. But she didn't mind, and she distracted her mind from her baking soles by focusing on the trees, heavy and green, and the window boxes brimming with colorful flowers. If she concentrated hard enough, she could forget not only the burn of the sidewalk, but the fact that she looked out of place in her worn country dress.

Yet the eyes that passed over her made it difficult for her to pretend that she was dressed in anything else but that brown frock with the rounded white collar. Those eyes asked, *Girl, where you get that dress, Red Cross? And what's going on with your hair?*

Beka had done the best she could with her hair and no hot comb. *My—my sister don't got no hot comb*, is what she wanted to tell those questioning eyes. *I used the fancy pomade in the silver container, and it still don't lay down.*

But her mouth stayed clamped.

She thought the pink ribbon might make a difference.

"That's my mama's!" Lovey had screamed when she saw Helen tying it into Beka's hair. She'd run up on them and snatched it right from Helen's hands.

"Give it here, girl!" They had struggled with Lovey until Helen raised her hand and threatened to slap the girl into next week. Even then Lovey didn't just hand it over, but tossed it down to the floor and stomped on it before darting off to some other part of the house.

All that fight and the ribbon didn't even hold. It just slid right off Beka's little piece of ponytail as soon as she stepped out and onto the porch.

Beka laughed at the thought of it. And Wella, face sweet and sticky with ice cream, looked up at her and laughed too.

It hadn't been easy, the last couple of days. Sleeping with one eye open and jumping at sounds that seemed out of place in the night. Shoot, she and Helen had been lulled to sleep by loons and crickets, not the churning sound the wheels of motor cars made as they moved up and down the busy streets.

By the time they'd shown up, there was little food left in the house. Just some corn meal, grits, sausage, and a dried piece of pig tail in the refrigerator.

Dumpling heard Beka say, "This the last of the sausage," and, "Where you suppose you go and get groceries 'round here?"

"Don't know," Helen replied as she stared into the icebox.

"I suppose we can just make do until Lillie come back."

Dumpling panicked and rubbed her tublike stomach with worry. Who knew when Lillie was going to come home?

Although she hadn't uttered more than a "yessum" to her aunts since their arrival, the possibility of starving made her light on her toes. She eased out from under Lovey's ever-watchful eyes and found herself standing alongside Helen and whispering, "Market on Cantor Street," out of one side of her mouth.

That was three days ago. Now, walking back home (Lovey had corrected her good and swift when Beka had said "home," reminding her that it wasn't *her* home at all), Beka could appreciate the feel of the pavement beneath her feet (hot as it was) and how she wouldn't have to shake dirt out of her shoes once she arrived at Lillie's doorstep.

She liked the fearless way Phila-del-phia Negro women handled color. Dresses and hats in turquoise and pale pinks— even the dark-skinned ones donned yellows and baby blues, not seeming to mind at all the attention it called to their skin.

And the men sure did take on a different shine in the slick suits they wore every day of the week. Not like back home, she thought, when a man could only be caught in a suit on a Sunday, unless of course someone got married or there was a funeral to attend.

Rounding the corner they stumbled into a flock of imperial butterflies feeding on a wall of white clematis. The children cried out with joy and leapt at the beautiful flying insects, trying without success to capture them in their small hands.

Even Lovey forgot her grown-up composure and allowed a smile to slide across her face.

At the porch now, then up and through the door, the house quiet, the black patent-leather clutch resting on the table beside the vase of flowers, and Lovey already calling out, "Mama!"

The rest of the children tearing off—up the stairs, into the parlor, and then through the kitchen and out the back door.

Baby Wella struggling to get free of Beka's hand and then off like a shot behind Beanie Moe.

"Here she is!" Lovey's voice was flecked with excitement and sounding like the big-band music Helen had taken to playing on the Victrola at night. Beka popped the last bit of cone into her mouth and followed the song out to the back porch.

"Beka." Lillie blew her name out along with the cigarette smoke she'd just inhaled.

"You smoking now, huh?" Beka said, and walked over to stand beside Helen, who was sitting and sipping something that was as clear as water, but the ruddiness of her cheeks and the droopy way her eyes looked told Beka it was something else.

"I'm grown," Lillie said, and took a long drag on her cigarette.

Wella was in Lillie's lap, happily fingering the long red beads that draped from her mother's neck. Lovey stood behind her, hands resting protectively on Lillie's shoulders. Beanie Moe and Dumpling settled themselves down on the top step.

"Mama, they come in here and—" Lovey began, but her tongue was working so hard and moving so fast that it tripped over her teeth and she had to keep starting over again. "Mama, they come in here and—"

"Hush now. Later, Love," Lillie said quietly, and kissed the top of baby Wella's head before lifting her up and handing her off to Lovey. "Take Wella on up and put her down for her nap." She flicked the long ash of her cigarette to the ground.

"But it's almost supper," Lovey boomed as she balanced Wella on her hip.

Lillie let out a small laugh and then smashed the butt of the cigarette down into the crystal ashtray. "Go on now," she said with a wave of her hand.

"But Mama—"

It was done so quickly and Lillie was already lighting up

another cigarette by the time Beka and Helen saw the large O that Lovey's mouth had taken on and then the angry red blotch of flesh on her arm where Lillie had pinched her. There was no more discussion, just Wella's cries of disapproval and the sound of the children's shoes against the white wood porch.

Two bottles of gin. Lillie seemed to have them hidden everywhere.

Short dogs, she called them—half pints that they sipped over ice. Suppertime came and went, but Lovey took care of it, and by the time the second pint was gone, the moon was up and both Beka and Helen had each had their very first cigarette.

The hot day had led to a hot night, and the burn of the liquor in their bellies just added to the boil. Dresses hiked up almost to their waists, leg spread open, hands fanning down between them and up around their necks. Lovey bringing ice cubes wrapped in washcloths, her hips swinging to Louis Armstrong's "Keepin' out of Mischief" that streamed from the Victrola. Whatever anger there was between them was pushed aside with every tip of the bottle and every new song that played.

Whatever unspoken, known thing that floated around them was blown away by their raucous laughter.

Was Sandersville really that bad?

Each one looked at the other.

Who had asked the question?

"Well," Helen moaned, "seems to me that there were some good times."

"More than some," Beka said. "Christmastime was always good."

"S'pose you right. Mama in the kitchen rolling pie crust."

"Papa up behind her, messing with her while she was trying to do it."

"She say, *Go on now, nigga, git on away from me!*"

"An' pop him with her dish rag."

"Ambrosia!"

"Oooh, that was my favorite."

"Can't nobody make it like Mama."

"Nobody."

"Corn pone the night before."

"Dipped in sweet milk. Lawd!"

"Fire in the hearth just a-blazing and—"

"All we kids 'round it, singing!"

Was Sandersville really all that bad?

"Only at night," Lillie said.

And the truth took on more weight than the heat.

They would have cried, but they weren't crying drunks no matter how heavy the hurt. So they laughed it all away because they were in Phila-del-phia and there was nothing lurking through that darkness with flint, flame, and a silver timepiece.

"Just another week," Helen whispered in Beka's ear when she hugged her tight on the platform.

Beka knew that was a lie. And her lip trembled beneath the tears that filled her eyes. "Stop it now," Helen said, giving her a pat on the shoulder and then turning away.

"You could stay, you know," Lillie said between puffs on her cigarette.

No, she couldn't. "Mama needs me," Beka reminded her for the umpteenth time.

"You sure it's Mama you concerned with?" Lillie said, and threw her a sidelong glance.

Beka stiffened. What was she suggesting? Was she suggesting that she liked it? Beka dropped her eyes.

"All aboard!" the conductor called out, and the train's whistle let off a long piercing shriek.

Beka grabbed hold of the railing and hoisted herself up onto the step. Lillie caught her by the elbow. "We could bring Mama here," she whispered, her eyes pleading.

"Mama ain't never gonna leave Sandersville," Beka mumbled in resignation.

The train's wheels began to slowly churn and Helen trailed

alongside the car. "That's her fate, not yours!" she yelled as the train picked up speed.

Yes, it was, Beka thought sadly while she watched Helen fade to a speck.

When she arrived in Augusta, Vonnie took the suitcase and started off ahead of her.

Only four people had gotten off in Augusta, and from what she could see, six got on. It would be at least a two-hour ride to Sandersville and with none of the excitement she and Helen had bubbled with a week earlier.

Vonnie dropped the suitcase into the back of the pickup and then opened his door and climbed into the cab. Beka just stood there, staring at the dirt and thinking of how much she missed the feel of the Phila-del-phia pavement beneath her feet and how much trouble it would be to shake the red Georgia earth from her shoes again.

"You comin'?"

His hat low over his eyes, a piece of straw dangling from the corner of his mouth, one hand gripping the black knob of the gear shift, the other resting slightly on the curve of the steering wheel, jaw flexing, and in all that heat not a drop of sweat on his brow.

Beka opened the door and climbed in.

Two hours and Vonnie doesn't say a word. His eyes never waver from the road, not even when they're close to home and Bark Patterson waves hello from the shadow of his porch. Vonnie acknowledges the old man with a flick of his wrist just before taking a hard right.

"Where she at?" Suce asked, looking down at Beka's suitcase and then behind her, like Helen was small enough to remain hidden from her view.

"She decided to stay," Beka responded, and moved past Suce and toward her bedroom.

"Stay?" Suce said the word like it was new in her mouth, like Helen was the first of her children to walk out of Sandersville on the pretense of visiting or marrying.

"For what?" Suce inquired as she followed Beka.

"Uhm"—the lie churned in Beka's throat—"Lillie wasn't feeling too well." She hoisted the suitcase up onto her bed and flicked the locks open.

"Not feeling well?" Suce rounded the bed and planted herself directly across from Beka. "What's wrong with her?"

Vonnie remained in the hallway outside of the bedroom and casually leaned his shoulder against the wall as he watched and listened.

"Headaches."

Suce considered this. "She always had a problem with that," she said thoughtfully and then placed her hands on her wide hips. "How the chirren?" she asked, as she studied the things Helen removed from the suitcase.

"Fine."

Suce looked down at her hands and then at the slant of sunlight along the floor. "I hear that husband of hers left her a fine house. Is that so?"

"Yes ma'am. Right fine house." Beka dug into the suitcase and removed two tattered bras, three pairs of bloomers, a girdle, and then her hand hesitated as she reached for the brown dress.

"Inside plumbing, just like she say?"

"Uh-huh."

Suce watched Beka's hand hover over the brown dress and so she reached in and snatched it up, revealing the bottle of bath salts and silk stockings beneath it.

"Humph," Suce said, and tossed the dress down to the bed.

Vonnie strained to see from his place in the hallway and made a disapproving sound.

If she was light-skinned enough, Beka would have turned beet red. But she wasn't, so the flesh of her neck burned beneath the collar of her dress.

"When she coming back?"

She ain't, Beka wanted to say, *not ever.*

"Next week, I guess."

"You guess?"

"She say on Tuesday. Maybe."

"Maybe?"

Beka breathed. She was a coward, wasn't she? The eldest and the weakest. Cursed for sure. Grown and still cowering like she was five.

"That's what she say, Mama." Beka's voice climbed a level too high for a child, grown or not, and she felt more than saw Suce go rigid.

"Sass? Where you pick that up at? The train, Lillie, Phila-del-phia?"

Beka said nothing. Suce turned and walked away.

As she went, Vonnie followed, pulling the silver timepiece from his pocket and staring down at its face as if the answer to Suce's questions lay in the Roman numerals and the reach of the black long hand.

That was a year ago and now Beka was back in Phila-del-phia trying to help Helen pack away thirteen years of Lillie's life.

Dead, just like that.

A cough.

A rattle, but no sneezing.

Too weak to stand and dizzy when she tried.

"Maybe you pregnant," Helen had whispered.

"Nah, been pregnant four times and ain't none of them felt like this," Lillie wheezed.

"Each one is different," Helen said.

"How would you know?"

Helen put her to bed, went to work, came back, and found Lillie as white as a sheet.

"I'm gonna get you a doctor," Helen said, her voice worried, her face dark. "Lovey, you go next door and ask Mrs. Casey if you can use her phone."

"I ain't leaving my mama," Lovey said venomously, and moved to Lillie's bedside.

Helen glared at her and then turned to Beanie Moe. "You go. And don't give me no mouth."

Helen held one hand and Lovey held the other while Dumpling held Wella and watched from the corner of the room.

Helen jumped up when she heard Beanie Moe burst through the front door and bound up the stairs. "Doctor say he can't come before six," he said, out of breath.

Helen looked at her watch; it was four o'clock.

By six, Lillie was breathing heavy, gasping for air, pushing away the glass of water Helen tried to get her to drink, snatching off the wet washcloth Lovey had placed on her head, and still no doctor.

Her skin was raging by then, fever eating her up from the inside out and Lillie mumbling about home and babies and Vonnie.

At the sound of her brother's name Helen's hands began to flutter about nervously and she leaned in close to Lillie and whispered, "Shhh, now, sister."

At seven, Lillie's eyes flew open and fixed on the ceiling. Her lips were chapped, with angry red seams running through them. "Damn him, damn him," Lillie sputtered, and Helen knew just who her sister was cussing. She patted Lillie's hand and threw an expectant glance at Lovey and then toward the doorway of the room. "He gonna suffer too. He gonna suffer worse!" Lillie yelped, and then gulped in a great amount of air.

Lovey's body jerked in surprise and Helen braced herself. She could see that Lillie was trying to hang on to the air, and she helped her along by holding her own breath until Lillie's eyes rolled in her head and she squeezed the hands that held hers. Before Helen could utter a word, a cry, or a sound, Lovey leaned over, pressed her open mouth over her mother's, and took Lillie's last breath.

The children mourned the loss of their mother in different ways.

Beanie Moe went around punching walls, Dumpling ate until she puked and then ate some more, while Lovey just walked around pretending that her mother being dead didn't matter at all. Wella, too young to understand most of what was happening, began asking for her mama less and less as the days went by.

Beka had told them about life in Sandersville: outhouses, hauling spring water, feeding hogs and chickens, milking cows, and picking cotton.

"Picking cotton?" Lovey's eyes narrowed. "I ain't no slave."

"Got to watch out for snakes," Beka said in a quaking voice. "*Sssssssssss*," she said as she leaned in to Wella's ear.

All the children laughed—except Lovey, who made a face.

"And the white folk. Gots to be careful 'bout the white folk," Helen added matter-of-factly as she scanned the room for more breakables.

"What about them?" Beanie Moe asked.

"Nothing," Beka said curtly, snatching a vase up and handing it to her sister. "You ain't got no more to worry 'bout white folk in Sandersville than you do with white folk here in Philadel-phia."

"White folk and Vonnie," Helen muttered under her breath.

"Who?" Dumpling asked, eyes bulging.

Beka's head snapped around. "Have you forgot yourself, sister?"

Helen looked down at the vase, concentrating on the small red flowers that dotted its surface. Yes, yes, she had forgot herself. Had done it purposely, left herself right there on that train that brought her to Philadelphia and stepped down onto that gray platform a determined woman. She'd forgot herself is right, forgot who she was in Sandersville and threw herself into who she could be in Phila-del-phia. Forgot herself in the pots she scrubbed and the shirts she pressed. Forgot herself at the Friday-night dances and the Sunday picnics. Forgot all of herself when she let Irving Matthers press himself up against her and kiss her full on the lips.

And even as she packed and wrapped, she was still forgetting herself, because she had pinky sworn with Lillie that she would do everything in her power to keep her kids in Phila-del-phia and away from that place, should something ever happen to her.

And here she was, so well forgotten that she couldn't even remember how to say four simple words: *No, they ain't going.*

"I guess so." Helen breathed and grabbed at a piece of newspaper and began wrapping it around the vase.

The way Lovey explained it, out there on the front porch the day before they left Philadelphia forever, Dumpling's ugliness started at the bottom, on the soles of her feet, fanning out into ten horribly deformed toes and then the acorn-sized growths that sprouted from the sides of her big toes like cabbage heads. Not only that, she was fat.

Beanie Moe was string-bean thin with buckteeth and bulging eyes that forever graced his face with a look of utter stupidity or eternal surprise. And he was black—pitch, in fact.

Baby Wella, just three years old and still shitting herself, bowlegged, with a horrible habit of sucking her thumb.

Lovey was the only beautiful one. The only one with any sense; she told them so as she lined them up single file on the front porch, inspecting their ears for wax and the corners of their eyes for cold while she reminded them of their ugliness and why they'd better learn to mind or Grandma Suce would send them off to one of those homes for children who had no parents.

Lillie, dead for nearly eight days and the smell of carnations still lingering everywhere, and the children were not able to close their eyes without seeing the soft beige of the coffin, the brass handles, or the red laced gloves on the hands that lay crossed and still on Lillie's silent chest.

Eight days and sounds all around them and still their ears rang with the heavy notes that came from the organ, the solemn words the pastor spoke to the few faces that looked back at him.

No one had out and out wept except them, the children. Although the men looked pained and the aunts' eyes ran water and their hankies came back damp and dirty with face powder after they'd dabbed at their faces. But their bodies did not shudder with sorrow, not once, and that made Lovey angry.

Eight days and Lovey and the rest of the children were still biding their time at the wide picture window, boxes all around them—some packed, others empty, nothing taped closed, the lids flipping open like limp wings.

How do you pack away thirteen years of living?

Helen and Beka aren't sure, but they try their best and claim Lillie's dresses for themselves. Those, along with the china and pieces of jewelry that neither one of them can tell if they are real or not. There wasn't enough money to ship the furniture back home, and it hurt Helen's heart to see that fine sofa and dining room set sold away to strangers.

Eight days and the children only have words for one another, except for Wella who is too young to understand death. But she understands *gone* and asks, "When Mama coming home?"

The rest, though, mill around the picture window and whisper to one another and themselves as they stare through the daylight hours and moonlit nights willing Lillie back amongst the living and strolling down Bangor Street gay and laughing, high-heeled and hair just a-bouncing or swaying, depending on which walk she felt like using. Some new beau at her side, grinning as he carted a bag of groceries or some new boxed hat or bagged dress. And them waiting on the porch for her, happy to know that she'd come home from wherever she'd been and not minding at all that there was a man with her, because they knew how to share.

There would be kisses and introductions and the man, whoever he was that week, would press pennies into their palms without barely looking at them and would never ever remember all of their names, his mind stuck on and mesmerized by Lillie's legs and that gorgeous "follow me" ass that cocked out behind her like a black ant's.

Later, while the man waited in the parlor, twirling his hat in his hands and checking the crease in his pants, the children—if they were clean—would sit on the settee and watch him until the perspiration trickled down the sides of his face and his questions about schoolwork and other stupid things adults say to children waned to just small noises in his throat. Lillie would reappear in whatever new dress he had bought her, with Evening in Paris dabbed on her wrists and behind her ears, saving him from the steady stares of the children, and off they would go. Lillie brushing kisses against their cheeks and reminding them to be good and to listen to their big sister Lovey and then, "Mama be back soon," "Mama be back late," or just "Goodbye."

Sometimes *soon* or *late* was the following Monday or Tuesday or a whole week later. Those times, Lovey thought that the goodbye was for real, but she never let on to the smaller ones and held it all together just like Lillie had taught her.

And she would do the same again, even in a place as godforsaken as Sandersville, Georgia.

Suce rolled the child's name over in her mind: *Love*.

Love, Suce had decided, was everything but.

Unkind to everything, it seemed, that walked and breathed: the chickens, the hog, and the runt of a mutt called Vim.

Boastful about her beauty, long-haired and bright in color, and those eyes—gray most days, green in dim light—and proud as hell of her height, her figure, and the delicateness of her hands.

Rude enough for five of her kind and self-seeking in the worst way; nothing was happening if it didn't benefit her, and if it happened anyway and she wasn't included, the anger would come on like a storm.

Good at recording the wrongs of others and slack when called on to remember her own.

Just downright evil, and a liar to boot. When Vonnie went to fetch Beka, Helen, Lovey, and the rest of the children from the train, Lovey took one look at her uncle, lifted her hand, pointed a long delicate finger at him, and declared, "Eeeeeeeeew, what ran over your mouth?" while the other children just stared.

Bernard Moses—"Just call me Beanie Moe," he'd said, and stuck out his hand in greeting when he was presented to Suce—was a sight: long and lanky, bucktoothed, and not easy on the eyes at all. Just seven years old and looking everything like that short-legged man who'd come and took Lillie away in his fancy automobile. Dark-eyed and kinky-haired. No doubt Corinthians had planted *that* seed.

Dumpling—Clementine Marie on the birth certificate and scrawled in ink on the back page of Suce's Bible. Short and round, with eyes like moons and a belly to match. Hair thick, yet short and a mess to get into on Saturdays. But a joy to be around, always smiling, and mouth always working at something—a peach, a slice of watermelon, a chicken leg. Happy as long as she was full, ecstatic if she was near busting.

Now Wella—odd name, and Suce was just calling her baby girl, but neighbors steady on finding a nickname for her. A cute little thing. Pudgy but particular about what she ate, and rough too, keeping up with Beanie Moe and not wanting to kiss Suce or any of her aunties and preferring instead to share that sweetness with the thin lips of the dog.

In Suce's old age and after birthing fifteen children and raising twelve to adulthood, she had become a mother again, to four.

The morning was the best time of the day, Vonnie mused, as he stepped through the doorway and inhaled deeply. The air was freshest just before dawn and sweet, even in the wintertime when the flowers were dead.

He took a few steps, and the hounds that slept close to the house peeked over their paws at him and their tails began to thump the ground.

Surveying the land, Vonnie felt his chest swell with pride. This was his, every inch of it. Every blade of grass, every weed and blooming wild rose.

He grinned.

His father had told him it would be this way. "You know," Willie had said when Vonnie was just six years old, "this here will all be yours when I'm gone."

Vonnie had eyed Willie as he swung the saddle onto the horse's back. There were other sons, but Vonnie had an eye for things. A way with the pigs, knew how to handle the earth. He was the one who should get it; the others had fire in their eyes and North on their minds.

"All of it?" Vonnie had asked.

Willie nodded his head as he expertly pulled the strap tightly through the buckle of the saddle. "Everything that lives, breathes, and grows on this land will be yours," he said as he checked the saddle's sturdiness and then stood back and waited for Vonnie to hoist himself up. "And don't you ever let no white man try and take it away from you, ya hear?"

He'd heard.

Heard it more than once. Heard it whispered, bellowed. It came as a demand, a threat. The story had always been scattered and confusing. Not one person wanting to tell it all or tell it straight.

But from what Vonnie and his siblings were able to put together over time, it was a story so unbelievable that they'd had to dismiss it as fable.

Slaves taking over a whole plantation, right in the middle of one of the most racist slave-holding states in the Union? "Puleeeeeeze," Lou-Ann would always say whenever the story came up.

Vonnie scratched at his neck and walked on, the voices of his siblings ringing in his head.

"And what was that mess about the last will and testament? The white men?"

"Shot them dead on the front porch."

"Nuh-uh, sliced their throats."

"You a liar!"

"Not."

"Mama never said that."

Willie had told Vonnie.

Vonnie knew: stabbed and punctured. He looked up at the sky.

"Mama don't say much. Brother told it one night from the bottom of a jar. I was real little, but I remember."

Mama speaks to me. She trusts me. She tells me lots of things.

"Jar?"

"Filled with corn liquor."

"Oh."

"Anyway, bloodstains still there."

Wasn't no bloodstains, those washed away with the first rain, Vonnie mused.

"I ain't going up to that house."

"Haunted."

"Evil."

"And the will?"

"Never seen it."

"I don't believe it."

"I do."

Vonnie moved out to the edge of the rows of cotton, plucked a blossom, and examined it.

Their childhoods would have been lonely if there hadn't

been so many of them. Only faces they saw for many years were one another's and those that stared back at them from looking glasses and the stream.

Papa, Spin, and Brother were the ones to go to town to buy provisions and sell the bales of cotton. Mama and Brother taught them their numbers and letters.

No one else came looking, asking questions?

Not that I ever heard.

When Mama had just five of us and was pregnant with the sixth, she looked up and a house was going up right across the road.

Our first neighbors.

Our first.

Then Brother got down.

Yeah, something started eating away at his toes.

And clear up his leg.

And clear down the other.

Died in his sleep.

Best way to go.

Spin got into some mess in town, didn't he?

Something about a white woman.

I think it was a white man.

Ain't it always?

Sure 'nuff.

Papa wouldn't go and stand up for him.

Couldn't. There would be questions.

That's true.

What happened to him again?

Hung.

Lynched.

Gone.

Then things changed, right?

Yep.

We had neighbors.

More than one by then.

People stopping by to call.

I remember the first little girl I saw that wasn't kin!

And then Papa died.

Saw the whip marks on his back when Mama washed his body down for burial

Me too.

Broke my heart.

Broke all of our hearts.

Papa was gone.

That part I know is true.

Good man.

Kind man.

Papa was gone.

And then things began to change again.

Mama said nowhere to go but forward.

Sure 'nuff.

Marriages and moving on.

Marriages and moving on.

One by one.

Sometimes in twos.

Mama said, Go on and spread that seed, I'll be all right.

And she was.

And she is.

"Don't you ever let no white man take this land from you!"

Vonnie had heard, and the words became part of him.

Everything that lives, breathes, and grows . . .

"You treat the land and what's on it the right way, and God will reward you twofold," Willie had said, holding up two long dark fingers.

Now, the sun just breaking the horizon, Vonnie moved slowly up and down the rows of cotton, carefully examining the stalks and the white puffed blooms they held and smiled, his mind clinging more to the new blossoms that slept comfortably inside of the house than the ones he fingered.

Willie had been right: God would reward him twofold.

It was the same every morning.

Suce walking through the house, swinging open bedroom doors, snatching at shutters, and tugging off blankets.

"Mornin', time to get up now."

Most times Dumpling was already awake, the smell of frying bacon and boiling grits getting her stomach going before her mind even stirred.

Beanie Moe was a hard one to rouse. It took Suce two or three visits and a swat on his behind before he would even open his eyes.

Lovey was the worst. She would suck her teeth and snatch the covers back over her head and mumble something Suce was sure was foul. "You ain't too big for the switch," Suce reminded her.

At the breakfast table, Lovey would sit with her arms folded across her chest and her face screwed up so tightly her eyes almost vanished, while Dumpling's right hand gripped her fork and she watched like a starving pup as Beka or Helen moved from one child to the next, spooning grits, scrambled eggs, and smoked sausage onto their waiting plates.

Beanie Moe, forgetful of the rules, would shove a forkful of food into his mouth before the morning blessing had been said and now had a tender spot on the back of his head where Suce, Beka, or Helen had taken to popping him.

Lovey would take a few bites, push her plate away, and asked to be excused. "I'll eat it," Dumpling would sputter through a mouth already crammed tight with food.

"Pig!" Lovey would spit at her and storm from the room.

"I told you about that trash talk in this house," Suce said.

It was hard for her, for all of them. Suce knew it; she'd lost her own mother young and still wept for missing her so much. She knew the children had had a different life in Phila-del-phia, but this was their life now, and they'd better try and get used to it.

"I'm done warning you; next time it'll be me, that filthy mouth of yours, and the lye soap!"

Lovey had found a hiding place far up the hill alongside the skeletal remains of the big house. In that place, where wild honeysuckle clamored for space on the rotting beams and a young sap pushed its way through the decaying floorboards of what used to be the center hall. Birds made their nests on windowsills that stuck out like lips, and black squirrels scurried up and down the corroding stairway.

Lovey was not afraid of that place, dark and looming as it was. However, Dumpling and Beanie Moe found it to be spooky, and anyway, they warned Lovey as they started back down the hill, "Granny said we're not to come up here."

"I don't care what she said," Lovey slung back at them, and settled herself down on a tree stump.

She'd seen Lillie up there. She wouldn't tell them that, though. If she told them, then she would have to share her, and she didn't want to do that.

She'd seen Lillie sitting cross-legged on the hill, bathed in the blue full moonlight, dressed in red, smiling, throwing kisses down at her, beckoning her to come. And she did, stealing out of the house and running barefoot but sure through the late-night cool.

When Lovey reached the top of the hill, breathless, eager, Lillie was gone, but the scent of Evening in Paris was everywhere and so Lovey knew that she had not been dreaming.

Every night after that, Lovey went to the place, singing the bedtime lullabies Lillie had once sung to her, humming tunes that her mother had once swayed to in their Philadelphia parlor. Every night she went in search of her, peeking behind trees, lifting loose stones, calling out, "Lillie, Lillie girl!"

It wasn't until the night she carried the red gloves along as an offering and laid them across the spot on the ground she'd first seen her mother resting on that Lillie finally came.

First as a glow of ruby and then a full woman, peeking around the sycamore tree like a small child.

Lillie, done up in a red silk dress with a blooming skirt that made rustling sounds like dried leaves. "Oooh," she moaned as she stepped from behind the tree and looked lovingly down at the gloves.

"I know you miss them, Mama." Lovey spoke in a quiet voice that was laced with excitement. She folded her hands and held them at her middle, unsure if she should step closer.

Lillie nodded her head yes.

Lovey saw that her mother was as beautiful as ever—hair gleaming and curled at the ends, pulled to one side and cascading over her right shoulder. Lovey quickly used her hands to smooth down her own hair. She rubbed at the cold in the corner of her eyes, licked at her parched lips. She wanted to look good for her mother. She wanted to look just like her mother.

"Go on, Mama. Pick 'em up," Lovey urged, so eager to please, not caring one bit that Lillie hadn't said how much she'd missed her.

Lillie just stared and then her eyes fluttered and set on Lovey. They were sad, brimming with tears.

"Can't you, Mama?"

Lillie sadly shook her head no.

Lovey bent down and retrieved the gloves; she stroked the material and Lillie moaned softly. Lovey slipped one glove on and Lillie's tears disappeared. The other now and Lillie flung her head back in ecstasy

Lovey understood. "I can wear them for you, Mama, huh?"

Lillie smiled.

Lovey was elated. "Anything else I can do for you, Mama?"

Lillie's smile became menacing as she slowly turned her head, moving her gaze from Lovey and planting it squarely down on the saltbox.

So there, in that place wrapped in shadows, away from Wella's babbling and Dumpling and Beanie Moe's endless battles over food, away from Suce's spite and threats, away from Beka's and Helen's comforting hugs and Vonnie's cruel mouth, Lovey could have her mother again, could rock to the lullabies she sang to her, could feel her completely, could be her.

"Be careful with her, Vonnie," Helen warned as she watched from the doorway. Vonnie had Wella by her hands, swinging her through the air. The child's face would twist with terror and then glee with each round they took.

"What he doing?" Beka came up behind her. "Oh," she gasped when she saw what was happening. "He's certainly taken a liking to her."

Helen wasn't sure, but she thought she heard some malice in Beka's voice and she turned to look her full in the face.

"What?" Beka said, her eyes innocent.

Nothing.

They stood watching until Wella hollered, "Stop!" and Vonnie reluctantly set the girl on the ground. The whole top part of Wella's round body swayed and she raised her pudgy hands and pressed them against her head.

"See, now she's dizzy," Helen called, and started toward them.

Vonnie stood stiffly aside as Helen gathered Wella into her arms and took her back to the house. He seemed not to know what to do next and stood staring at the spot where Wella had been until Beka made a sound in her throat.

"You seen Lovey?" she said, needing to fill the emptiness between them.

Vonnie didn't answer, but he turned his gaze up toward the house. Beka's eyes followed, and she shook her head in dismay.

Vonnie looked back down at the ground and then suddenly said, "Tell Mama I went to town."

He strode off, back straight, hat pulled low over his eyes, and climbed into his pickup truck and drove off.

No one would suspect him to be a middle-of-the-day type of man. Him—black-skinned, wide-brimmed hat, and heavy black boots. Everything about him screamed after sundown and before dawn. But there he was, climbing out of his pickup, just before noon.

Sawyer smiled as she watched him through the lace curtains of the window. Below her, the barbershop buzzed with conversation and the clicking sounds of scissors. In the next room, a man moaned loudly and the thumping sounds that had gone on for less than three minutes came to an abrupt end.

Sawyer fingered the cross around her neck and then her fingers absently searched the thin gold chain for the clasp, unhooked it, and tucked it safely away into the top drawer of her bureau.

Vonnie didn't like religion.

He moved slowly and with no great conviction down the four streets that made up the District. Familiar faces turned away or lowered, and hands came up to conceal, but Vonnie knew them all. The hard ones—the sanctified, single, married, and lost.

The District, a shotgun of a place that was never supposed to be anything more than a pit stop between Augusta and Myanmar but somehow grew into a cluster of rag-tag buildings that leaned in high winds and seemed almost imaginary during the long hazy, heated days of summer.

Sawyer meets him at the doorway, the scent of lavender water sailing from her bare elbows. She wants to kiss him on his mouth that is so unkissable, dying to know what those ruined lips will feel like against her own, but he won't allow it and so she just smiles and steps back, letting him through.

The room is less than appealing: stained and peeling wallpaper, cracks stretching along the ceiling like cobwebs. Sawyer has tried to make it beautiful, soft. Sheer curtains, a colorful gypsy's wrap thrown across a cluster of oil lamps. A mauve-colored cushioned stool sits in one corner of the room, a standing mirror crowned with stalks of heather in the other.

Vonnie sits down heavily on the foot of the bed. He does not remove his hat but waits for Sawyer to do so, and she does, placing it on her head as she hums a foreign tune and begins a slow dance of seduction.

Vonnie watches nothing but her feet, and she knows it will be awhile before his eyes break loose and crawl up her calves. He likes her knees and so will spend some time there before gathering his courage again and scaling her thighs, rounding her hips, up her stomach before stopping at her breasts, which poke out at him from her cupless brassiere.

By the time his eyes fall on those succulent, jutting nipples, he will be more than ready for her. He will feel like perfection itself and will have no problem tilting his head skyward without the broad brim of his hat casting shadows and hiding his cruel mouth.

There in the District in the middle of the day, curtains pulled back and dazzling sunlight spilling in and igniting every inch of Sawyer's body, there he could take his time and push away the nasty comments his cleft palate brought. Could toss out the adult faces that stared in horror and then whispered behind cupped hands. There he could erase the pointing children that mocked him for the two years he went to school.

In that place he could forget the angry tears he'd cried because he wanted what all boys his ages wanted, but no girl would give him because of his mouth, which drove him to take it from his own gene pool.

There he could twist his father's words to make it all seem okay and right.

There in the District and in the middle of the day, he could caress and sink into that wet place that was so yielding, so warm that he imagined heaven itself was lodged there and he did not have to swallow his moans. His timepiece was of no consequence, and the ownership was brief and paid for. And when it was over, he could lie there in the crook of her arm and smell the stink and sweet of them both and listen to what the world sounded like beneath the beating heart of a body that was spent and glistening, while she stroked his cheek and told him that he was beautiful.

The days sizzle on and after nearly a year, Lovey still does not understand how one can tell the difference between spring and summer in that part of the world. She is as miserable in June as she was in April. Dumpling has started to drag her words and Beanie Moe is always walking around with a stalk of hay dangling from the corner of his mouth, like some cowboy.

Wella is all but lost, because when Lovey points to the framed picture of Lillie, Wella looks back at her, blinks, and asks, "Who you say dat is again?"

Down here with the heat that didn't seem to let up until January, and everything the young teacher Mrs. Pace was teaching, Lovey had learned two years earlier. Now she sat, twirling her pencil in her hand and staring out at the open road and the field beyond.

Some part of her still half expected to see Lillie come strolling out of the blue, or at least down from the big house, handbag swinging from her wrist, the heels of her pumps leaving tiny half moons in the dirt. A year earlier Lovey had thought that if she wished it hard enough, it would happen. But it never did, even though there were times when the room was suddenly overwhelmed with the scent of Evening in Paris and Lovey would look around for a jutting hip, curling cigarette smoke, and a splash of red.

And to make things worse, the prized red pumps were missing and all she had left to dote on were the crimson-colored silk gloves and the red plastic beaded necklace.

"Women in the District got a passion for red too," Suce told her after she'd bitten off a piece of snuff and tucked it into the corner of her jaw.

Lovey shrugged her shoulders and continued clearing the table of the dinner dishes.

"Don't you like no other color?" Suce probed.

Lovey shrugged her shoulders.

"Yellow is nice." Suce breathed. "Green too."

"I guess."

"Blue, how about blue? Do you like blue?"

"Not as much as I do red."

"Blue like the sky. Big. Everywhere you look, can't miss it. Always on display, always noticed. Not like red, most times you gotta search for red, gotta dig it out of something living."

Lovey had never thought of it that way. "Hmmm," she said, and started to walk away, but Suce caught her by the wrist and held tight.

"What you say we exchange?"

Lovey twisted her lips. "Exchange?"

"Yeah. You give me them red beads and I'll give you something blue in return."

Lovey snatched her hand away from Suce. "Them beads belonged to my mama!"

Suce kept her voice steady. "I know, and your mama belonged to me."

Lovey just stared.

"I ain't got nothing of hers to hold on to," Suce added.

"You got plenty."

"Well, nothing as special as them beads." Suce rolled the tobacco across her tongue and tucked it into the other cheek. "It ain't like they leaving the house; you can come see 'em anytime you want."

Lovey smirked. "What you going to give me?"

"Got a blue ceramic pig your Uncle Ezekiel sent me from Chicago."

"I don't want no pig."

"Uhm . . . I know, I got a blue ribbon—ain't never been worn," Suce said hopefully.

"I got blue ribbons."

Suce racked her brain. "Well, I don't know, child. What you think you want?"

Lovey knew, had spotted it the first time she set foot in that house and Suce reached out for her. "That," she said, pointing to the blue granite eagle hanging from the leather strip around Suce's wrist.

Suce felt her breath catch in her throat and her hand went immediately and protectively to the charm. "This?"

"Yeah, I'll trade you the beads for that," Lovey said emphatically.

Suce slowly rubbed her thumb and forefinger over the stone. "What you want it for?"

Lovey smirked again and leaned heavily on one leg, jutting out her slim hip. "Don't worry. You can see it every day and I'll let you visit with it whenever you want," she said sarcastically, and then grinned slyly.

Suce's eyes snagged on the child's hip before breaking free and finding her face. She had to blink; it was the first time she realized how much Lovey resembled her own Lillie.

"Well?" Lovey said, pushing her open palm closer to Suce's face.

Suce shook her head clear and even managed a stiff laugh as she slipped the charm from her wrist. It was just a piece of stone. It wasn't like she was passing it along to a stranger, this was her grandchild, she thought, and then aloud she said, "This belonged to my mother."

"Uh-huh," Lovey said, still pushing her eager open palm out toward Suce.

"Uh-uh. Even exchange," Suce said, and pointed a finger at the red beads around Lovey's neck.

Lovey smiled and then carefully lifted the necklace of beads from her neck and held them out to Suce. "Okay, on the count of three." She laughed, and on three Suce grabbed hold of the beads and dropped the blue eagle into Lovey's hand.

Maybe it was the weather that day—not too hot, a hint of November cool in the air, even though it was just early September.

Maybe the silence, the blue sky, and the paintbrush streaks of white that were too thin to be clouds.

Maybe it was the sun, so pale it was almost white.

He could look back on a number of those things and think: *Maybe . . . ?*

But it was just her, just Lovey.

Walking slowly up the hill and toward the big house, that birthmark that looked like a G on the back of her thigh, visible beneath the flouncing hem of her skirt. She was twirling a dandelion in her hand and humming something—what, he didn't know, but she could have been the pied piper from the storybooks Suce had read to him as a child, because he found himself helpless and stumbling up the slope behind her.

She had to have heard him coming—the soles of his boots crunching the earth, the clink of the timepiece bouncing against the ignition key in his pocket—but she never turned around, slowed, or quickened her pace. The humming got louder, though, and the dandelion began to twirl so fast, its thin petals became a blur of yellow and the G on her leg was as clear as if he'd written it on his eyeball.

Up at the house, the day seemed to go from morning to evening with one step. His heartbeat slowed a little; he was most comfortable in darkness.

"I sure do like it up here," she threw over her shoulder.

Lovey, now seated on a tree trunk, legs crossed, dandelion stuck behind one ear, lips wet, said, "Nice and cool, don't you think?" Hands rubbing her knees, down between her legs, up where breasts were just starting to bloom.

Vonnie's mouth went dry.

"Don't you think?" she said again.

"You were told not to come up here," he whispered, legs weak.

"But," Lovey said, and undid the first button of her gray blouse, "it's so much cooler here." Second button now. "And quiet." Third button. "And private."

No T-shirt, just skin and brown freckles that looked like eyes. And the blue eagle dangling from the leather strap on her wrist. He raised his hand, pointed a steady finger, and opened his mouth to ask, "How you get ahold of that?" But what came out was:

"What you trying to do to me?"

"What you want me to do?"

By the time Lovey smirked and slung, "You mean *gorgeous* ass," at them and then sauntered out of the room, leaving behind gaping mouths and climbing eyebrows, Helen knew that Vonnie had gotten to her.

Who knew *gorgeous* could be made to sound so foul. But Lovey had a way with words, she could take *sweet* and make it sound like *shit* with the flick of her tongue.

And now her reply to Suce's, "Get your ass on outta here wit dem red whore gloves on," was bouncing between them and off the walls and ringing louder than the town hall bell.

"What she say?" Suce asked, her head cocked to one side, hand floating in midair, the pinch of chewing tobacco forgotten between her index finger and thumb.

"She said *gorgeous ass*," Wella repeated, and tossed a pecan shell into the crackling flames of the fireplace.

The night shifted outside the window, then the front door pushed open and Vonnie stepped through, bringing the cool evening air with him. His face was drawn, looked ragged beneath the flaxen light that came off the kerosene lamps. He'd lost some weight too—his clothes hung on him—and he shuffled instead of walked.

"Evenin'," he muttered as he removed his hat from his head and hung it on the nail by the door.

The women just stared back at him.

"What?" Vonnie said as he started toward them.

"Did you tell Lovey she had a gorgeous ass?" Beka snapped suddenly.

Surprised at Beka's forcefulness, Helen found herself quickly ingesting air and wincing at the bite in her sister's words.

Suce's face was still working at recovering from Lovey's slur, and now she turned her astonished gaze on Beka. "What you say, gal?"

Had she actually said it out loud?

"She must have heard it from somewhere." Beka's recovery was weak; Helen's expression told her so.

"And that *somewhere* is Vonnie?" Suce blinked and finally stuffed the tobacco into the corner of her mouth. "Why in the world would your brother, my son, say something like that to his niece?" she sputtered, and her lips glistened brown. "His own flesh and blood?" Her head shook in disbelief.

He wouldn't say something like that. Wouldn't say anything at all, Helen thought to herself, not unless the game had changed.

Vonnie pressed the tip of his tongue against the bottom row of his teeth, but his face remained stagnant.

The game had changed indeed. There was no flint and flame, no shameful eyes that looked away from him in moonlit bedrooms.

Lovey had changed the game. She had become the stalker and he had become the prey.

Enticing him, teasing him, sprawled out on that swinging porch chair with one leg thrown up over the wooden back, the other leg dangling over the edge, dress hiked damn near up to her waist.

And those fucking red gloves.

He would try to pretend not to see her, but she wanted him to. Well, she practically handed herself over to him the day he tried to walk past her and she snatched at his pants leg and sang, "Hey, Vonnie," sounding everything like her mama.

He had turned to her and said, "You forgetting something, ain't you?" And his voice, the one that never rose or dipped, stalled and then cracked when he said it.

Lovey in that chair just a-swinging and the air lifting the light material of her dress so that he could see the insides of her thighs, and Lovey smiling at how easily she'd unnerved him. Her eyes laughing at the power she had over him.

"*Uncle* Vonnie." The words slithered from her mouth and something cold wrapped itself around his spine.

He hadn't touched her the first time he followed her up to the big house. He'd only stared at the brown dots on her chest, watched the spinning dandelion. And when she'd stopped talking and opened her legs wide and started humming, he'd listened, but he didn't touch her.

Two days later, same thing: brown dots, spinning dandelion, humming that now sounded like flapping wings, her laughter like a roar.

Lions roar, don't they?

He'd read it someplace, read about roaring lions, but had never heard it until then.

How could that be? How could the sound of a lion be coming out of Lovey's mouth?

Didn't matter; she stripped down naked and extended her hand to him.

He asked again, "What you trying to do to me?"

And her response had been a hard kiss, her hands everywhere on him, ripping at his shirt, cutting through his skin. Her fingers like claws, like talons . . .

And she'd sprouted wings, yes she did! They popped right out of her back. Broad, black wings that flapped and then curled and enclosed them both.

Yes, he'd said it, Lord help him, God save him—even though the devil had already laid claim to him—he'd said it over and over again while his bare ass rubbed against the top of that stump, Lovey up on his lap, his hands gripping her small round behind and her riding him until his eyes rolled back into his head.

He didn't get any pleasure from it. If he could tell them that, he would.

Not one bit.

In fact, he'd hated every hellified moment of it.

She felt like fire up inside of her, hot boiling lava. It was like sticking his dick into a boiling pot of beans, and he'd screamed—hadn't they heard him?

Screamed and tried to throw her off of him, but she'd held fast and those wings pressed tight and she told him to say it. She said, "Say I've got a gorgeous ass!"

All he could do was cry and beg and pray and tell her how much it hurt.

"Say it! Say it!" she ordered, and dug those talons into his neck.

And finally he did.

"What's this you saying?" Vonnie finally asked, feigning ignorance.

Suce waved her hand and dismissed the whole sordid situation. "That child just acting the fool as usual," she said as she leaned back into her rocking chair and began working the tobacco in her mouth. "Go on, baby girl, and get my can from off the back porch," Suce called to Wella.

What Beka had said sounded ridiculous to Suce, and she'd turned a crooked eye on Beka, but Vonnie hadn't missed it swinging back his way.

Like taking a wife could fix any of it.

Like it could change what he'd done to them, bring Lillie back, and erase the crooked look Suce had slung his way three months earlier.

Well, he had to do something. Suce's eyes had swung his way and asked, *Well, did you?* even though her mouth hadn't said a word.

So he had to do something, because Lovey was fucking him dry. Killing him slowly from the inside out.

It was all he could do to get up in the morning. Legs weak, eyes swollen, back hurting, and his dick refusing to stiffen for anything—not even his morning piss. Nothing except Lovey-Lillie-Lovey—he didn't know who or what or which.

So he had to do something.

Black feathers stuck in his hair, tucked in his pockets, and Suce watching him sideways, asking, "Where these feathers coming from all of a sudden?"

He wanted to say, *Lovey got wings, got claws, and roar like a lion. The horses get skittish and run when she around; ain't you seen that, haven't you noticed? She ain't human, she something from hell. I want to kill her, but it look like she gonna kill me first. Help.*

But he didn't, so he just said, "Blackbirds."

"Blackbirds?" Suce didn't say any more than that.

The nylon-clad leg stepped out of the passenger side of the pickup.

District trash, Beka mused as she watched Sawyer's heel sink into the damp Georgia soil.

"Won't need those 'cept on Sunday." Suce snuffed, and pointed down at Sawyer's black pumps.

"Can't offer you much, but I got a house and you won't have to lay up under anyone but me."

That was his proposal.

Sawyer considered his words as she watched him pull up his pants, sit, and then bend over to put on his boots. He was getting thin and the whites of his eyes had taken on a yellowish-brown tint.

Not eating right, not sleeping well, working too hard, she thought.

But she could find no justification for the angry welts on his back, no matter how hard she searched.

"Okay," she said, and packed up the few things that she owned.

No fanfare. He didn't want any of that. Just the minister in the sitting room, Beka, Suce, Helen, and the children looking on. There was a moment when he thought Lovey was going to shout out some obscenity or sprout wings and roar, but she'd just sneezed and then yawned loudly.

He'd agreed to a honeymoon—one night in the back room of a friend's house, on the outskirts of Myanmar.

Now back home, his new wife smiling sweetly as she hobbled her way across the moist earth. Vonnie thought by taking a wife, he could make everything that had been wrong, right again. But no wife or the children that would follow could ever fix what he'd broken.

Things changed outside of that saltbox, but few things changed within it until Helen came home one evening from a day of scrubbing toilets and tile, chastising white children, and preparing and stewing meat, and announced, "I'm headed north in two weeks."

Suce, bent now, shuffling and completely gray, talking out loud to the spirits that haunted her and laughing at inappropriate times, blinked at her girl child and said, "Sure 'nuff?"

"Yes, Mama," Helen said and pulled the quilt up a bit so she could tuck it beneath Suce's fat chin.

"Well, I s'pose it was coming. Mama told me so."

"Uh-huh."

"Didn't you, Mama?" Suce said, and looked off to the empty space to her left. "Sure did."

The house was crowded, even with the three new rooms Vonnie had built on to accommodate the babies that Sawyer pushed out one year after another.

"Seeds need to scatter." Suce laughed and scratched hard at her scalp.

"They sure do," Helen said, and reached for the comb on the bureau. "Let me get that for you, Mama."

Beka cried buckets and begged Helen to stay.

"Can't," Helen said matter-of-factly, "but you can come along."

"I'm scared to leave," Beka sputtered through her tears.

"You should be scared to stay," Helen said, and folded a skirt in half and set it gently down into her suitcase.

"He ain't touched me—us—in years," Beka countered, and wiped at her wet face.

"Maybe not, but that don't change what he done. And what about Lovey?"

Beka went quiet.

Lovey—at school selling pussy look-sees for a penny. A touch cost five cents. She had the poor sharecropper boys stealing dimes to push into it. In a minute, she'd either be pregnant or working full-time in the District.

"That ain't true." Beka sniffled. "What they sayin' 'bout her ain't true."

"Uh-huh," Helen said as she examined a worn black skirt and then tossed it to the side. "Too crowded here," she went on in a dreamy voice. "Harlem calling me."

"Harlem ain't never called a soul in its life!"

"Calling me, though." Helen laughed. "Calling you too, but you just too stubborn to hear it."

By the time Sawyer looked up and saw Vonnie gawking at the neighbor's daughter, she was big with her fourth child and had none of the beauty that came with it. All that glamour had been replaced with Sandersville dust and the hard lines of disappointment that came along with being black and Southern in America.

Her body flinched, and her heart flickered with jealousy inside her chest as she eyed the pretty young girl with the begging eyes and large ass.

"Why you eyeballing her like that?" Sawyer asked one day when she couldn't hold her tongue anymore.

What made it nasty was the fact that he was cradling their young son in his arms.

"Ain't nobody eyeballing that little girl." Vonnie's eyes didn't break away immediately, but they slid down Cora's ass, traveled along the dirt ground some, and then climbed up to his son's sleeping face.

"I ain't blind. I know what I saw."

"Woman, don't get up under my skin today, hear?"

Sawyer watched him for a moment. Thought about what she could have and what she did have. Both sides held nothing, and so she sucked her teeth, held her tongue, and wobbled back into the house.

Then Suce died.

In her sleep.

Smiling.

Buried her 'longside Papa.

'Longside the babies who didn't make it.

And the one who didn't make it all the way.

Not too far from her mother.

And brothers.

After Mama died, we felt all alone in the world.

Crying for them every now and again, even though we were mamas and papas ourselves.

Don't matter; we was their children first.

And last.

Always.

Amen.

Dumpling sat in the front pew, hands folded neatly in her lap. New dress straight from Harlem, straight from Aunt Helen with a note that just said, *Soon*.

"What that mean, Aunt Beka?" Dumpling had inquired.

"Don't know," Beka said, folding the paper into quarters and tucking it deep into the cup of her brassiere.

Soon didn't mean much to Beka. Getting older by the minute. Gray hair crowding her head like weeds. The only man in her life was the memory of a long-ago Phila-del-phia man who had held her hand and patiently guided her across a ballroom floor.

Soon? What the hell could she connect that to? Nothing more than an answer to myriad questions:

When dinner gonna be done?

When the kids coming home?

When this lye gonna come outta my hair?

Soon didn't mean shit. But she kept the notes anyway, just in case one day it could.

Now Dumpling was sitting there in her new blue dress with the crinoline slip that she couldn't keep her fingers from fiddling with, even though Beka kept nudging her with her elbow and then using her chin to indicate that it was the Bible Dumpling should be focused on.

Twelve years old and short. The baby fat finally slipping away from some places but still hanging on to others. Breasts coming in, behind too, but her face is all baby and she's still a tomboy, even though her interest in the crinoline is a sign that all of that is about to change.

Many things are about to change.

Vonnie is white-haired with sullen red eyes and has fathered six children by the time he decides to swap planting cotton for peanuts. He spends more and more time away from home, afraid to be around Lovey, even around his own daughters—hard on the boys though, 'specially after a jar of corn liquor and a cheap cigar.

Sawyer doesn't know how it is she keeps coming up pregnant. He barely touches her anymore, except maybe to knock her down or up against a wall.

Easter Sunday.

Eggs dyed every color of the rainbow and hidden everywhere—rabbit holes, beneath the porch steps, up in abandoned robins' nests. The children rip, run, search, and squeal while the adults sit quietly on the porch, fanning themselves, sipping sweet tea, and cradling the one who is too young to walk.

A ham baking in the oven. Sweet-potato pies cooling on windowsills, and the slow build of the crickets' serenade all around them as the sun beams down hot and searing.

First Beka rises to go in to check on the ham. Sawyer follows, the sleeping small one in her arm.

Just Vonnie is left, corn liquor jar in one hand, stinking cheap cigar in the other.

"Uncle Vonnie, Uncle Vonnie!" Dumpling bounds up the steps from the yard. She stands before him, hem of her dress turned up and gathered in her hands, something cradled in the material.

"What you got there?" he asks, and leans forward.

"Eggs," Dumpling spouts proudly and moves closer so that he can see.

"Sure 'nuff. A hell of a lot too." He laughs.

"More than the rest of them!" Dumpling proclaims.

"Ay-yuh. Seems so." Vonnie sucks on his cigar while Dumpling positions herself on the edge of the porch and begins to carefully set her eggs down into a crooked line.

"Look here," Dumpling says, pointing to an exceptionally brilliant blue egg. "This one here is the prettiest."

"Looks that way," Vonnie says, squinting.

Dumpling plucks it from the line, lifts herself to her feet, and brings it closer for Vonnie to see. "I made this one myself."

"You did?"

"Uh-huh."

"All right now."

A cry rises up from the children, and Vonnie lazily cocks his head to see what the commotion is about.

"Don't you think this is the prettiest one?" She's climbing into his lap now. Pushing the brilliant blue egg into his face. Wrapping one hand around his neck.

"Yeah, yeah," he says, careful not to burn her as he uses his arm to help her get comfortable in his lap.

Another swig from the jar and a puff on the cigar.

"Make circles, Uncle Vonnie!" Dumpling squeals, and tilts her head back.

"Okay."

Circles, over and over again. Sailing over her head, around the finger she holds up. Another swig and more smoky circles and his lap is getting hot beneath her bottom.

More circles and he thinks the cigar is making his head spin and so outs it on the leg of the chair and lays it to rest on the table beside him.

Dumpling's eyes are growing heavy, and her shoulder is pushing into his chest, her head resting in the crook of his neck while his hand lays still and innocent on her knee.

Vonnie's eyes flutter and close.

He was dreaming about Lillie or maybe Lovey—he didn't know which. They were one and the same. Teasing him, tossing stones at his face, calling him ugly, shaking their asses and baring their breasts.

He got hold of her or them, hands around their necks, squeezing, squeezing until they cried out, "Stop, stop, please!"

But he wouldn't, and he just kept squeezing and then the blood started to eke from their skin and that's when Vonnie woke up and found Dumpling looking at him, her eyes crying, her mouth uttering the words from his dream: "Stop, stop, please!"

He shook his head, started to ask: *Stop what?*

And then felt the wetness on his hand and remembered

the blood from the dream and looked down, his eyes falling on his forearm and wrist but his hand is missing, hidden beneath the blue dress material and white crinoline; beneath that, his fingers are clinging to virgin flesh, wet with urine.

Birmingham, Alabama

The sun is up now.

We all holding hands. Ms. Meadow's arms stretched out across the table, blue veins long and telling.

My eyes wet. All of our eyes wet.

I thought it was the blue dress, I say. That and me.

Yes, Sherry say, and squeeze my hand.

Or the crinoline beneath it.

Oh, Dumpling, Ms. Meadow cry.

I never put you in blue. Did you ever realize that? I say to Sherry.

Yes.

It's such a beautiful color. But I hated to have to see it after that day. Do you know what it's like to look at the sky and want to cry? To see the ocean and feel afraid? He made blue ugly for me after that.

He was the ugly one. Ugly on the inside. Sick, Ms. Meadow say.

He took blue away from me and made me feel dirty. Helen saved us, you know.

Yes. Ms. Meadow bows her head.

She came down to visit not too long after that.

Yes, yes.

I think she saw the look in my eyes and knew.

Hmmmm.

And I took the blue dress off the white doll she brought down for me.

I remember that story.

I ripped it to shreds and burned it in the fireplace.

Yes, yes.

Then Lovey came up pregnant.

Viola.

Yes, her first one. His.

Yes.

Helen sent for all of us after that.

Your first trip on a plane, right?

I was so afraid!

Of flying.

No, the seats. I was afraid of the seats; the seats were blue.

Oh.

Too afraid to move, even after the plane had landed. We just sat there.

Ahh.

Helen had to come on the plane and get us. She saved us. Raised us like we were her own children.

I know.

But I still felt dirty. I would wash four or fives times a day. For years. I thinks I got it off most of my body. But it's still on my hands. You can't see it, but I know it's there.

Yes, yes.

Lovey was doing it too, washing herself, but she was just doing it different.

Sherry say, Uh-huh.

Laying down with all them men and telling them: My papa named me Love because he had love for God and creation. My papa named me Love because I was created with love in mind. My mama the one that put the "y" after the "e," when I was just five months old, Lovey told the mens and they just a-grin and touch her face and then get to swaying. Something in her made them sway.

She'd bring them home and run all them children she had out of the room.

Shoes come off, socks discarded, tie and pantyhose tossed aside. She'd bring them beer, dance for them. Smoke cigarettes and blow smoky circles in their faces.

Lovey would give herself over to them if they told her what she wanted them to hear.

What was that?

She told them: Tell me I got a gorgeous ass.

They said, Yeah, baby, you got some kind of ass.

She say, No, tell me it's gorgeous.
You got a gorgeous ass, they said.
She say then, Say my name.
They say, What is it again?
Love, nigger. Love.

Sandersville, Georgia

July 1995

Dumpling

Sandersville right down the road. Ms. Meadow, that house, and Birmingham like a dream behind us, floating in my mind, clinging to me.

I look at Sherry and she move into the right lane and slow down to a snail's pace. Here we are, I think. And then she say, Here we are.

Yeah, I say. Here we is.

You ready?

Ready as I'm ever going to be.

You nervous?

A little.

Yeah. Me too.

I'm sorry.

For what?

For everything, I say. And the slap. I touch her face then.

Oh, Mama, I understand now.

Mama? I like it when you call me that.

You do?

Mama. Mama. Mama. Mama. Mama.

She sing it all the way to Sandersville and I don't even think about my hands or if they clean. My heart is clean, that's all that matters, and anyway, my mind is wrapped all around Sherry's voice and the song she singing to me.

Mama, mama, mama, mama, mama, mama, mama, mama . . .

I can see the saltbox from where we stop, and my heart flutters. At least twenty cars and SUVs lined up on the road. Doors swung open, music streaming out of some of them, little children's legs dangling out of others. Faces look over at us, faces in all colors, shapes, and sizes. Hands come up and wave, beckon; lips break into smiles, shout out, and say, That there look like Dumpling!

My heart flutter again. Them my people, my folks, have mercy!

I turn to Sherry, say, Hurry up, let's get out!

She say, Wait a minute, Dumpling. I want you to talk to someone first. She pick up her phone, press some numbers, listen, smile, and say, Baby, we're here. Yes, safe and sound. Uh-huh, I got somebody special here that wants to meet you.

And she pass the phone over to me. I look at it, not sure what I should say, and then start the only way I know how: Hello?

He say, Mrs. Jackson, how are you? How was your trip?

I say, Fine, good, thank you for asking. How you?

He say, Well, missing my Sherry and looking forward to meeting you.

I say, Let me ask you something.

Anything, he say.

You know my baby's heart?

He say, Know it like I know my own.

I say, Good answer, look forward to meeting you. Now, I got family waiting on me. And I jump out the car, run toward the first familiar face I see, my arms spread wide like wings.

Sherry

Something like I thought it would be, but then like something else.

The big house is gone, but I feel it there.

Family faces look at me, hug me, kiss my cheek, offer me food, grab me by the hand, and drag me here and there. "This your cousin," they say. "This your kin. This your family!"

Some of them look like me or they tell me I look like someone else and take me to the person and say, "See, y'all two look just alike!"

Madeline, her husband, and the kids are there. Madeline can't even get a hello out before the questions come.

Sonny Boy is there with some pretty girl on his arm. He introduces us and she hugs me hello and it feels good. I look at her and think that they will make babies together who are beautiful inside and out.

Uncle Beanie Moe and his second wife are there with two of their sons and three of their grandchildren. Beanie Moe sputters through the spaces in his teeth and hugs me tight. He's getting older, I think. And thinner too.

Wella, baby-faced, stout, looking like Dumpling but younger and always smiling, shows me the latest picture of her Nellie. "She flying in from Paris this evening," she says proudly.

"And the children?"

"Oh, they daddy driving in from DC. Should be here soon. You look good, girl. Filling out in all the right places." She laughs.

"I feel good, Auntie, now that I'm here." Wella gives me another hug and a smile and then waves and walks away when she sees someone who hasn't been seen in years.

I move away from the crowd and down behind the house, where the first ones are buried.

I spot red. It's laid out and shocking against the dark green grass. A little closer, pale skin comes into view.

Old lady with a shock of silver hair stretched out on her back and draped in red from head to toe.

Sherry, the lips whisper.

Aunt Lovey, I say, and lay myself down beside her. Our hands lock.

Ain't that sky beautiful?

Sure is.

Your mama used to love blue as much as I love red.

She loves it again.

That's good. It's been too long.

You like being back here?

Yes. My people are here. The North was too hard on me.

You should have come out west with us.

Nah. Your daddy, God rest his soul, didn't like me.

I laugh at the truth.

You talking about God now?

Well, you gotta make peace, you know?

Yeah.

I suppose.

So how you doing?

Fine.

You in love?

Why you ask?

I see it all in your face. Something else too.

What?

You expectin'?

What?

Silence. Then: Don't try and deny it, I can see it.

Really?

You young people always thinking you putting something over on the old folks. I guess that mean you ain't tell your mama yet?

No.

Well, don't make her wait too long.

She roll over on her side and I roll over on mine so that we're facing each *other.*

Not a crease in her face. Her gray eyes are stormy, but the white around them is as bright as snow.

You look beautiful; pregnancy agrees with you, she says.

You look beautiful; life agrees with you, I say, and reach out and touch her face. We smile at each other and she reaches over and touches my shoulder. The blue eagle peeks out from beneath the cuff of her blouse.

There it is, I coo.

Her eyes follow mine. If you want it, it's yours, she says.

Really?

She slips it off her wrist and says, My baby-shower gift to you, and presses it into my palm before turning onto her back.

I do the same.

Who are we lying on?

Lou.

Hmmmmm.

Can you feel her?

Yes, I think I can.

—The End—

Are We Related?

Nowhere Is a Place was first published in 2006. The story was inspired by my own genealogical research, which I started back in 1995. I've had a lot of help along the way and so would like to take this opportunity to express my gratitude to Antoinette McFadden, Valerie Beaudrault, and the members of AfriGeneas.com—without their kind assistance, I would be years behind in my research.

I believe in "six degrees of separation"—so it's not unlikely that many of you out there may be familiar with some of the names listed below. Maybe still, you and I will discover that we are kin!

Great-great-grandpa: **Reverend Tenant M. Robinson** was pastor and founder of the First Baptist Church of Macon, Georgia (the cornerstone bears his name). Tenant Robinson was born on the Edisto River, near Charleston, South Carolina, in 1839. His mother was sold when he was five years old and carried to Aiken, South Carolina. She was again sold to a man by the name of Nat Black and carried to Graniteville, South Carolina. In Augusta, Georgia, Robinson embraced the religion of Christ, was baptized by Reverend Henry Johnson, and was united with the Thankful Baptist Church. Soon after becoming a member he was united in marriage with **Miss Louisa White** of Hamburg, South Carolina, in 1866. They had four children: **James, John, Emma,** and **Chappo.**

The reverend died in 1895, and his widow took the Metropolitan Life Insurance Company to court because they refused to pay the $2,500 death benefit. From what I've found in the newspapers, the case languished in the court system for a few years. I have not been able to ascertain what the final outcome was.

Great-great-grandpa: **Mingo McFadden**'s place of birth is unknown, but he married a woman named **Lizzie Bailey** (born in Texas) and resided in Texas. My great-grandfather **Isaac McFadden** was born to them in Texas on July 4, 1860. (Little is known about this line of the family.)

At some point Isaac McFadden married **Chappo Robinson**. Isaac was a cook and Chappo was a music teacher. They had a son **Isaac**, who died before 1917. Chappo and Isaac had another son while living in Louisville, Kentucky. They named him **Harold**. Isaac and Chappo lived in Lebanon, Pennsylvania, Washington, DC, and Louisville, Kentucky, where they had my grandfather, **Harold McFadden**, in August of 1917. Isaac died in October of 1917.

In 1922 in Grand Rapids, Michigan, Chappo married **Samuel Elliott**, and at some point they moved to Harlem, New York. Harold married **Gwendolyn Gill** of Brooklyn, New York, and the union produced two children: **Isaac Aubrey McFadden** and my father, **Robert Lewis McFadden**.

Harold was a musician. He abandoned the family in 1942 or 1943. He toured the country as a musician and was incarcerated in 1945 (Massachusetts) and then again in 1954 (New Jersey) for selling narcotics. He died in Newark, New Jersey, at the Martland Medical Center, in 1958. His mother preceded him in death in 1951 (Trenton, New Jersey).

I don't know if Harold produced more children—but I suspect he did. I don't know if his father (Isaac) had siblings or children from a previous marriage—but again, I suspect he did.

Do you have the pieces of my family tree that continue to elude me? Are we related??

We are?! You do?!

I look forward to hearing from you. I can be reached at: bernicemcfadden@hotmail.com.